The redhead Revealed

Also by Alice Clayton

Wallbanger
The Unidentified Redhead

The redhead Revealed

alice Clayton

GALLERY BOOKS
New York   London   Toronto   Sydney   New Delhi

G

Gallery Books

A Division of Simon & Schuster, Inc.

1230 Avenue of the Americas

New York, NY 10020

Originally published in 2010 by Omnific Publishing.

First Gallery Books paperback edition November 2013

For information about special discounts for bulk purchases, please contact Simon & Schuster Special Sales at 1-866-506-1949 or business@simonandschuster.com.

The Simon & Schuster Speakers Bureau can bring authors to your live event. For more information or to book an event contact the Simon & Schuster Speakers Bureau at 1-866-248-3049 or visit our website at www.simonspeakers.com.

Interior design by Aline C. Pace

Library of Congress Cataloging-in-Publication Data is available.

ISBN 978-1-4767-4123-9
ISBN 978-1-4767-4129-1 (ebook)

For my sister,
who never recommended that I "tone it down"
or "cool my jets" or "settle."
I thank you tremendously for this.

acknowledgments

To my new publishing family at Simon & Schuster—thank you for taking a chance on a crazy girl and letting her play with the big girls. Thank you especially to my editor, Micki Nuding, for helping me to trust my voice.

To my Omnific family—thank you for the encouragement and constant support. And especially to my dear friend and editor, Jessica, who has pushed and challenged me in all the right ways. To my parents, who have always been amazing. And to my very dear girlfriends, who I modeled the character of Holly after. Thank you for remaining silly with me. And, finally, to all the Nuts Girls out there . . . *schmaltz*.

The redhead Revealed

one

$\mathscr{I}$ pulled my orange scarf a little more snugly around my neck and knotted it again so it tucked right under my chin. The air was cool this morning, and the first leaves of autumn fell around me, blown about by a blustery breeze. Sheltered from most of the wind, I took the opportunity to gaze at the scene before me.

Brownstones. Concrete. Yellow cabs. A deli advertising both pastrami and falafel.

I sipped my coffee and marveled at my life, where it had taken me. I loved New York.

The last few weeks had been amazing—and difficult. It was now late September and fall was officially on its way. The air was growing crisp, the early birds had pumpkins on stoops, and I was having the time of my life. I was insanely happy.

Except, I was really missing my Brit.

Let's go back a bit.

When I first got to New York, I immediately went into re-

1

hearsals for a show in a small West Side studio space. After meeting the cast, I realized just how unique and special this show was and how grateful I was to be a part of it. The music was magical, and the character Michael had created in Mabel (enter me, Grace Sheridan!) was exhilarating to explore. She was in her thirties, a former beauty queen, and having an early midlife crisis as she struggled to define herself after a failed marriage. The show was witty, irreverent, and brilliant. We'd been workshopping for only a few weeks, but the investors and producers were already discussing the possibility of mounting a full production.

I was maybe about to be in my very first off-Broadway show! This was an ensemble piece, with a cast of fewer than ten, and we had grown exceedingly close. When a brand-new show is put together, everyone inhabits characters who have never been given life before. This lends itself to a lot of introspection and analysis.

Learning, working, growing . . . I was eating this shit up.

I spent my days in rehearsal and my nights exploring the streets of Manhattan. I was utterly enchanted with this city. Having spent time here on business throughout the years, I thought I knew it fairly well. No, ma'am. That's nothing like when you can call New York your home. And though I didn't know how long I'd be here, I was determined to get the most out of my time.

As soon as I arrived, I'd begun using my daily runs as self-guided tours. I ran through the Village (East and West), NoHo, SoHo, the Bowery, and made myself quite at home in Central Park. I felt freshly and more deeply acquainted with my new town, and I was keeping my butt in top form for the show.

I went to museums, shops, and parks, and I saw a show at least twice a week. I still had the same feelings when I went to see live theater that I had when my friends back home took me to see *Rent* all those months ago: I was emotional to the point of tears, my heart raced, and my palms got sweaty. But this time, when I saw the actors onstage and heard the music and applause, I was filled with pride. I'd made it back into the community I had never—in my true heart of hearts—really left.

Also, Michael O'Connell (the show's writer and creator and the friend who'd broken my heart in college) and I were spending a lot of time together. After not speaking for so many years—the result of an ill-timed one-night stand and the subsequent I-can't-be-friends-with-someone-I-slept-with game he played wholeheartedly—we were slowly but surely beginning to know each other again. He was still delightfully funny, and he made my transition to New York a seamless one.

When the rest of the cast found out we'd gone to college together, they were fascinated. We all spent evenings at least once or twice a week having cocktails at different bars around the theater district and telling stories about our wilder days. Michael and I never acknowledged our night together. Speaking about it in a group setting was obviously unthinkable, but we never spoke of it privately either—we just didn't go there. I simply relished having my good friend back, and he was one hell of a tour guide.

In addition to my self-guided tours, I had his suggestions, and I was experiencing the city as an insider. It was enthralling. Spending time with Michael made it easier to deal with being away from home, and he definitely helped me focus on the show and my part in it.

And Jack Hamilton, my much-missed Brit? Well, this was a bit of a pickle . . .

We spoke on the phone at least once a day, usually more. We sent buckets of texts back and forth, usually laced with enough smut to make us blush if we read them in the company of others.

He tried several times to come for a visit, but between MTV appearances, countless interviews, and meetings for the upcoming movie he was starring in, we just couldn't get it worked out. I tried to get back to L.A. a few times as well, but my rehearsal schedule was so intense, there was no way for me to leave. We both understood the demands our careers were making, but that didn't make it any easier.

Long-distance relationships typically work best (if at all) when the couple has been together a lot longer than we had. We went from a brief intense period of cuddle and sex and love to zero face-to-face contact—and it was proving more difficult than we'd thought it would be.

But we kept things spicy as best we could. The phone sex, the online sex, the pictures sent on the iPhone: hot. If anyone ever stole my phone . . . oh man. His fans would implode.

Nighttime was the hardest. I really missed having my Sweet Nuts in bed next to me, warming my skin with his sweet breath as he kissed on me, his hands around my breasts as we snuggled in for sleep. I missed that the most, and I was having trouble sleeping, even though I was usually exhausted after a day of rehearsal.

I had made some new friends, and I bonded instantly with Leslie, who played my nemesis in the show. Her character was everything I used to be: young, pretty, young, talented, young, and a bitch. Leslie was also hilarious in real life, and when we realized we were both entertainment-gossip junkies, we had something else to bond over. It killed me to not tell her who Jack was, but I knew it was best that he and I keep our relationship under wraps. As far as the cast knew, I was seeing an actor who lived in L.A. Only Michael knew the exact truth. And he was strangely silent about the whole thing.

But something was up with my Brit.

He was going out—a lot. Which was fine, because frankly, at twenty-four, that's what you do. He was playing a few open-mike nights, and I was sick over not getting to hear him. I really missed listening to him play, especially the action soundtrack he'd compose each morning as I got ready. With the three-hour time difference, I usually talked to him at night, before I went to bed and before he went out. I was also in occasional contact with Rebecca, his costar in the soon-to-be-released movie *Time*, which was guaranteed to make them both household names. We texted from time to time, and she informed me that while she remained on full Skank Patrol, the masses were definitely starting to covet the Hamilton with a frenzy.

Jack starred as Joshua, a time-traveling scientist whose cinematic escapades were based on a series of wildly popular erotic short stories. The stories' fans had begun to transfer their affections to Jack, and they were getting quite . . . hmm . . . *excitable*. Women were really into him, which I totally got. The fact that he shared my bed made my understanding that much more complete.

Heh-heh, you sleep with him.

Yes, yes, I do.

He was always dealing with fans, and from what he told me, they were generally polite and kind but the constant scrutiny was beginning to get to him. One night he called late, really late. Or I should say really early. It was after 4:00 a.m. East Coast time.

"Hello?" I mumbled.

"Hello, yourself," he whispered thickly.

I rolled over to look at the clock. "Are you okay? What's wrong?" I asked, sitting up in bed.

"Nothing's wrong. Does something need to be wrong to call my girlfriend in the middle of the night?" he asked, his voice a little rough.

"No, of course not, but it's crazy early here, Jack. Are you sure nothing's wrong?" I pressed as I lay back down.

"Wrong, no. Weird, yes, definitely," he said, his voice still sounding strange.

"What happened, love?" I asked, pushing back a yawn.

"Some girl grabbed my ass tonight! And then another girl— Oh hell, Grace. Are you sure you want to hear this?"

"Hmmm, I don't know, do I? Tell me—you didn't grab her ass back, did you?" I laughed, letting him know I was okay and he could share without judgment.

"I was walking out to the car after leaving this club, and there were cameras, of course," he muttered.

This was a fairly new development. Paparazzi were taking more and more pictures of him, and it wasn't uncommon for me to see him on E! or TMZ at least once a week. It was weird seeing your guy on *Entertainment Tonight*, but that's how we rolled.

"Okay, so there were cameras. Did you keep your ball cap pulled down low?" I asked, trying to get him to laugh. It was standard for him to wear the ball cap every freaking day now, and if the cameras caught him in it, I teased him mercilessly.

"Ha-ha. I *did* have it on, yes. Anyway, I was walking out to the car, and this girl came out of nowhere and tried to . . . well . . . she tried to . . ."

"Did she kiss you?" I asked.

"She tried to, yes. But she didn't. Grace, I swear I did *not* kiss her," he said firmly.

"Hey, it's cool, George." (His private nickname.) "I know how aggressive fans can get. You should have seen me the first time I saw New Kids on the Block, when I was in high school. My friends and I followed their bus halfway across town before we realized we were actually following a group of senior citizens on their way to Branson." I laughed. We were so sad when we pulled in behind them at the Flying J truck stop and saw the shuffleboard set disembark.

"You followed a tour bus? Why are girls like that?" he asked, laughing along with me. I could feel him calming down. Jack didn't like crowds, as a rule, and when he had a lot of people looking at him, it made him extremely self-conscious. Tonight he just seemed to need to hear my voice, and I loved that I could soothe him.

"I would explain it if I could," I said. "All I know is when Holly and I saw them perform earlier this year, we screamed like we were fourteen again. I felt exactly like I did when I saw them the first time, like no time had passed. I think that's why you're cornering both the teen and the cougar market, too." I giggled. "You remind us of when we were young enough that squealing was expected."

"Hmm, and the press has called *you* a cougar, Grace. Are you just using me for sex?" he teased, his voice silky.

"I'm not quite a cougar yet, but I'm for sure just using you for the sex," I teased back.

"I knew it," he said, laughing.

We were quiet for a moment, and then he sighed.

"What is it?" I asked, sliding deeper into the covers.

"I just miss you. I miss being in your bed," he said quietly, and I could hear the desperation in his voice. I felt it too. It wasn't just the physical lovemaking but the simple touches we took for granted when we saw each other all the time. I missed him washing my hair almost as much as the intense orgasms he'd given me daily.

"I do too, love. I miss the way you hold me—especially where your hands always end up." I giggled.

"You mean on your beautiful boobies?" he whispered. He teased, but I could hear his need building. It mimicked my own, which he could always bring quickly to the surface.

"Mmm, yes, please. I love how you know exactly how to touch me." I moaned a little into the phone, my other hand beginning to travel restlessly under the sheets.

"Oh, you do, do you?" he asked, his accent getting deeper and thicker.

"Oh, God, yes. You have the most perfect hands. I love your fingers especially. They're so strong," I whispered, propping the phone on my shoulder.

"Where do you like me to touch you, Grace?" His breath was coming faster now. I could imagine where his own hands were.

"I love when you peel my clothes off slowly and then graze my nipples with your fingertips. Mmm," I moaned, and I heard him moan in response. "And then when you touch me with your tongue, moving from one breast to the other— oh, God, that always feels amazing," I said, my own breath coming faster now. My hands dipped beneath my panties to

8

feel how wet I already was, just imagining his hands all over me.

"Grace, where's your hand now?" he asked, his sexy accent now off the charts.

"Where do you want it to be, love?" I asked wickedly.

"Mmm, if I were there, I'd be running my fingers through your hot, wet . . ." And he moaned the word that made me ache. He made the word absolutely drip from his tongue.

"That's exactly where my hand is, and as I'm touching myself, I'm imagining all the naughty, nasty things you do to make me scream," I purred.

"God, Grace, you get me so hard," he whispered, and I could hear him beginning to lose control. The thought of his elegant, strong hands gripping himself while talking dirty to me was almost too much to bear.

"I love making you hard. I love to see you get hard for me—just for me, Jack." I moaned, my fingers beginning to rub my sex furiously, imagining his face buried between my legs.

"Nothing gets me harder than seeing you come, love— making you come with my lips and my tongue. Nothing tastes as good as my sweet girl."

"Oh, God, Jack, you're getting me so wet. If you were here—oh, God, you fuck me so good," I panted, thrashing about on the bed as my orgasm began to build, strong and full.

"Grace, I think about you all day sometimes—the taste of you and the way you look when you lose all control. Oh, God, Grace, you're so beautiful when you come . . ." He moaned, barely able to speak, and I could tell he was getting close himself.

Sweet Jesus, he's good at this . . .

I needed to finish us both off.

"Mmm, I love when you come inside me, when I can hear you and feel you inside me . . . when . . . you are . . . deep . . . inside me . . . Oh, God . . . Jack . . . it's so good!" I lost it, my fingers finally pushing deep inside me, and I imagined it was him driving into me, filling me.

He groaned, staying with me as I screamed his name, my fingers and his voice bringing me to the release I needed. I could hear his breath get heavier, and then he came too. I could see him in my mind's eye: his eyes shut tight, his brow furrowed, his jaw clenched.

God, I missed him.

I trembled as I pushed the covers down. I was so worked up and hot, covered in sweat.

"Fuck, Grace, you're amazing," he whispered, still breathing heavily.

"Oh, love, I wish I was there. I'd scratch your head and let you fall asleep on me," I said, almost able to feel his weight.

"Would you let me hold your boobies?" He chuckled.

"You don't even have to ask, George. My boobies are your boobies," I teased, my heart starting to slow to a normal rhythm.

"Hell yes, they are! I'm going to make a little sign for you to wear that says THESE ARE SPOKEN FOR and then everyone will know your boobies are mine."

"Mmm, I love when you get all caveman on me. Will you throw me over your shoulder and carry me back to your cave?"

"Yep, and then I will ravage you before making you cook me up some T. rex." He laughed.

"That sounds heavenly, Sweet Nuts, just heavenly," I sassed, then yawned.

"Shit, Grace. I forgot how early it is there. I'll let you get back to sleep. I'm sorry I called you in the middle of the night."

"Do you feel better?" I asked.

"Well, yes. I do, actually," he said sheepishly.

"Then you call my ass whenever you want. That's what I'm here for—that and the blow-your-mind phone sex."

We laughed.

"I miss the shit out of you, Gracie," he said quietly.

"I know, George. I miss you too." I smiled into the phone.

"Okay, I'll let you get back to sleep. Love you."

"Love you too. 'Night."

I hung up the phone, sighing, and rolled onto my side. At this point in the program, had I been with my Brit, boobies would be held, sweet nothings would be whispered, and a *Golden Girls* episode or two might even be viewed.

A pang of loneliness washed over me, but I quickly pushed it aside and turned my thoughts to the scene I'd be working on the next day. Mabel was meeting with her ex-husband for the first time since the divorce, and my separation from Jack would help me create her feelings of isolation. I missed Jack, but I would use it.

☆ ☆ ☆

And so it went. Days turned into weeks. I rehearsed and sometimes went out with my new friends. Jack did interviews and photo shoots and went out with his friends. We talked all the time and continued the frequent phone sex. He asked me lots of questions about the show and wanted to know everything about my new friends, the cast, and how things were going. I told Jack about everything, although I may have glossed over exactly how much time Michael and I were spending together outside rehearsal.

Some nights we met up to work on scenes he was rewriting, but we usually ended up back at my apartment, talking, reminiscing, and laughing, more than anything else. He said it helped with his rewrites to spend time with me, and I found more and more of myself showing up in the new scenes. He admitted once that he'd modeled some of Mabel's character traits on me, especially the earlier scenes where Mabel is in college and falling in love with all the wrong guys.

One night we stayed late after rehearsal to work on a new scene, and when my tummy's growling began to rival our rather loud discussion, I suggested we head back to my place and order a late dinner. I'd recently moved from the W hotel to a small apartment on the Upper West Side. It was clean, close to the rehearsal space, and already furnished—everything I needed in a temporary home. Since I'd moved in, we'd fallen into a habit of ordering greasy Chinese, and the restaurant around the corner from my apartment was our number one choice.

Secretly, this sometimes made me a bit nervous. Since battling my way back from a good deal of extra weight several years ago, I'd been dedicated to making smart food choices. But the noodles . . . oh my goodness, the noodles. I let myself pig out on occasion, because I knew now I could control it. I ate really well most of the time, I exercised like a maniac, and I was truly proud of my new body. This was what I was meant to look like. Nevertheless, when the noodles called, I answered. I just had to run an extra mile or two to combat them. It was worth it. Seriously, the best garlic noodles ever.

We picked up the order and settled into our usual spots:

me on the couch and him on the floor next to me. He tended to make a mess, so I made him either wear a bib, or sit on the floor, where his mouth was closer to the noodle bowl. He chose the floor.

"Who was that guy you were dating sophomore year? The one who had the thing with no body hair?" he asked, shoveling in the noodles like someone was going to take them away from him.

"Um, Jason, I think? Ugh, I haven't thought about him in years! He was odd—not one of my better moments. But fantastic in the sack, I must say." I sighed, thinking of how happy he'd made me, but only when horizontal. He'd waxed his chest and legs, armpits, and even his bits and pieces. And this was back before anyone had ever heard of manscaping. He had zero body hair and, sadly, zero personality. He was equipped with nine inches of fantastic, though, which tended to make up for his little eccentricities.

"Yes, I remember you started taking yoga around that time . . . something about keeping yourself limber." Michael winked mischievously, and I hit him on the head.

"Michael! Jeez! I can't believe you remember all that. That was like, twelve years ago." I laughed, spearing a broccoli and nibbling as I thought about how long ago it really was. Hanging out with Michael now felt like we were back at my old college apartment. He'd bring over his laundry, and we'd watch movies until we both fell asleep on the couch.

"Grace, I remember everything," he said softly.

"Really? I bet you don't remember the first time we met," I challenged, pointing at him with my broccoli stalk.

"I'll bet you the last egg roll that I do and you don't," he countered, his face serious.

"It's a bet, sucker. So if you don't mind, I'm going to mix up my soy sauce–hot mustard concoction so it's ready for my victory egg roll." I reached over him for the bag of condiments.

He grabbed my hand. "Why don't we wait on that, since I'm totally going to win this bet," he said, moving my hand back to my side.

"Hmmph, whatever. Okay, when we first met: Freshman year, first day of class. We were in Professor Miller's Acting 1, lower level of the theater, room 301. We got paired up for scene work. I was wearing khaki shorts, Keds, and a Sigma Nu T-shirt. You were wearing a black ball cap, a Ministry T-shirt, jeans, and your Vans. I remember because at first I thought your shirt said 'Minister.' I thought, 'Well, that sucks. I can't very well bang a man of the cloth.'" I blushed, remembering that I really had been attracted to him from the start. "So there," I finished, sticking my tongue out and blowing a raspberry.

He smiled, and I reached across him again to take my egg roll. He stopped me once more, though. "That isn't the first time we met," he said, grinning big.

"What? The fuck it isn't. I remember it like it was yesterday, O'Connell." I fought him for the egg roll, but he continued to hold my hands back, laughing now.

"The first time we met was the week prior to classes starting. I was at registration, and you were in line in front of me. I heard you telling the registration clerk you wanted to switch your Acting 1 class to a different section so you could take some astronomy class. When you left the line, you tripped over the rope and fell down."

I felt my face grow red at the memory. "Shit, that's right! I totally fell flat on my face, and some guy helped me get all my shit together. I was so embarrassed because my birth control pills fell out of my purse, and he handed them back to me with a huge smirk." I'd hightailed it right out of there, convinced my entire college career would be marred by the incident. "And you saw that? How mortifying!" I laughed.

"I was the guy who handed you your pills, you dork! And then I made sure the clerk switched me into your acting class," he said with that same smirk I remembered from registration. "And you were not wearing a Sigma Nu T-shirt that first day in class, it was an SAE shirt. And they weren't khaki shorts, they were cutoff jean shorts," he finished quietly.

We looked at each other for a moment.

"Take the fucking egg roll," I finally said. "You totally won."

He grinned and took it, eating half with one bite. Then he offered the rest to me. "We can share it. I can't believe you remember the Ministry shirt."

"Ya know, Holly was in that class too but we didn't meet until later, when we all decided to grab a beer. I can't remember what she was wearing that day," I said thoughtfully, crunching down on my half of the egg roll.

"Neither can I, Grace," Michael said softly, eyes on me.

My eyes locked on his.

I chewed my egg roll.

He scratched his nose.

Mrs. Kobritz's yappy dog barked upstairs.

Our eyes stayed locked.

My cell rang. And rang. And rang.

Our eyes stayed locked.

Answer your phone, Grace.

My phone? Shit, my phone!

I broke away, grabbing my phone right before it went to voice mail.

"Hello? Hello?" I shouted unnecessarily into the phone. Michael chuckled and leaned back into the couch.

"Gracie? Hey, I was just about to leave you a raunchy message," my Brit said.

"Do you want me to hang up so you can leave it?" I asked, a little out of breath. I pushed myself off the couch and went into the bedroom, out of earshot.

"Nah, I'd rather tell you what I wish I was doing to you—that way I can hear you react." I could hear his voice change into Johnny Bite Down mode. I could never resist him when he nibbled on that lower lip—swoon-worthy for sure.

"You want me to react, huh?" I asked, wondering how I could get Michael out before Jack got me off. I was about to head back into the living room when Michael appeared in my doorway, leaning against the frame.

"I'm going to take off, Grace. I'll see you tomorrow," he mouthed, kindly keeping his voice down. I waved good-bye and followed him to the door, still listening to Jack.

"Yes, love, I'm dying for a reaction from you to my talented sexy ways, as I work my magic through your fingers," Jack continued in a low voice.

My body responded, as it always did when I heard his voice get like that. Fuck, he could get me hot in 2.3 seconds. Three thousand miles couldn't make a dent in his sex vibe. When he wanted a reaction from me, he got one—even across the Continental Divide.

"You're dying, are you?" I laughed as I opened the door for Michael.

He stopped and looked back at me as if he were going to say something but then lifted his hand in good-bye. I waved back, smiling, and he disappeared down the hall.

"But first, Crazy, I have some great news," Jack said as I locked the door, leaning back against it and sighing.

"You okay, sweet girl?" he asked.

"I'm good. I just miss you, is all," I whispered, feeling a lump in my throat. Suddenly, I missed him so much I literally ached.

"Then you'll be happy when I tell you my news, love."

"What is it, please?" I asked, not daring to hope for what I wanted.

"I'm coming to see you," he whispered.

I closed my eyes, leaned my head against the door, and said a silent thank-you.

"Gracie? Are you there?"

"I'm here, George," I whispered, my throat tight. "And I couldn't have gotten better news. I'm thrilled!" A grin broke across my face that rivaled Jack Nicholson's Joker. Then I broke out in a fit of giggles, unable to stop. I laughed so hard I began to cry, and I could only imagine what it must sound like on the other end of the line.

Jack laughed along with me, indulging my outburst with the patience of a saint. Truly, no other twenty-four-year-old man on the planet had his tolerance, especially when dealing with me.

When I finally calmed enough to form sentences again, I sighed deeply, crawling toward the couch from where I'd collapsed in front of the door. When I finally lifted myself back onto the coach, I groaned dramatically.

"What the hell was that, Sheridan?" he asked, laughing again.

"Just a little emotional breakdown, Hamilton. So when are you getting here? Don't tell me you're already in the hallway!"

I smiled, my heart leaping at the thought he might be that close.

"No, sorry. I'll be there this Friday night, though. Soon enough for you?"

"You'll be here in four days?" I squealed, arching off the couch as every muscle in my body clenched involuntarily.

"Yes, ma'am. Will you be ready for all that lovin'?" he teased, his voice getting lower.

"Oh, God, Sweet Nuts, I'm gonna work you over so good, you won't be able to get back on that plane. How long will you be here?" I asked, my voice getting husky as well.

"What if I said you get to keep me until Tuesday night?"

I closed my eyes and bit down on my knuckles to keep the shrieking inside. "Four days? Do you have any idea the kind of damage we can do to each other in four days?"

"I have some idea. What do you want me to do first?" he asked, indicating the beginning of phone sex.

I smiled contentedly, imagining all the ways I could answer that question. They were spectacular in their promise.

two

"So what do you two plan on doing this weekend—as if I don't already know?"

Holly's voice made me smile. "Believe it or not, we actually did make some plans that don't involve a bed," I said. "We're seeing a show Saturday night and a new exhibit at the MoMA on Sunday. Between my rehearsal schedule and his interviews, we'll barely have any quiet time at all." I sighed, stretching out across the old couch in the back of the rehearsal studio.

Holly had called from L.A. in between early-morning phone meetings. Being both my best friend and my manager—not to mention Jack's manager—was a multifaceted role she was handling really well so far. She was great at her job, especially with new talent like Jack. She was crafting his career with precision, keeping him visible but not overexposed.

And speaking of Jack, he was due in tonight! His flight got in around five, and I was meeting him at his hotel. We didn't want to waste any time, and I expected that our hellos would be quickly followed by my panties' removal.

"Why do I think quiet times aren't on the menu this weekend anyway? More like screaming times," she chuckled, no doubt remembering the caterwauling she'd had to endure all those weeks at her house in L.A.

I blushed. He did make me scream louder than any man before him, and then there were nights when he stunned me silent. Oh, God. *Is there a way to speed up time?*

"So how's the show going? You and Michael still getting along, or have you scratched his eyes out?"

"No, actually things are going surprisingly well. I forgot how damn funny he is, and we're really having a good time together. It's like we never stopped being friends." I was so glad we'd put the past behind us.

"Uh-huh," she said.

"What does that mean?" I asked.

"Nothing. Just saying 'uh-huh,'" she said, the smile back in her voice.

"Holly, you never say anything without meaning something. Now give it up, bitch."

"I'm just glad you guys are friends again. It isn't weird at all? No old chemistry knocking around, nothing coming up between you two?" she asked.

"No, none at all. Thanks for asking, though, you scandal whore." I laughed. There *was* nothing going on. But while Michael and I had spent plenty of time reminiscing, we hadn't addressed the feelings we'd had for each other back then, or any impact they might have on the present. I thought briefly of his eyes locked on mine during the egg roll standoff but brushed that aside.

"So when are you coming to visit, you dumb bitch?" I subject-changed smoothly.

"Nice talk. I'm trying to get out there before Thanksgiving. And by the way, where are you planning on spending the holiday? Can you get back here, or will you still be in rehearsal?"

"I don't know, but my guess is I'll be here. Hey, I'll get to see the Macy's parade up close and personal. That'll be kind of cool!" I hadn't really thought about the upcoming holidays.

"Maybe I'll wait and come out then. Can't have my best friend alone on Turkey Day," she said.

"Aw, that's sweet, babe. You know there's no one I'd rather share yams with than your badass self." I chuckled.

"So when's he getting in?" she asked.

I ignored the obvious double entendre. "Around five. I have to be here all day for rehearsal, but that's good. It's keeping my mind off things. I'm so freaking excited! I really didn't expect to miss him as much as I do."

I sighed, leaning back on the couch. It wasn't even lunchtime yet, and I knew this day would positively drag.

Six hours until boom-boom . . .

"I have to tell you, he's like a little lost puppy without you," she said.

"Really?"

"Yeah. He's doing a ton of promotion and going out with his friends at night a lot, but I can tell he'd rather be with you, watching your god-awful *Golden Girls.*"

"Yeah, I'm sure he'd rather be snuggled up watching Bea Arthur than out on the town," I sniped.

"Grace, you're an idiot. The boy is in love. Let him miss you," she said.

21

I chewed my lip thoughtfully. "I know he misses me. I miss him too. A lot."

Just then Michael came into the studio with the musical director.

"Hey, Holly, I gotta go. I'll call you later this weekend," I said, rolling off the couch and walking over to the piano.

"Don't you dare call me when you should be fucking the shit out of your hot British nasty! I love you, good-bye," she said, and hung up.

I smiled as I clicked off the phone.

"Was that Holly?" Michael asked with a grin.

"Yep, she was harassing me." I laughed as we began to page through the sheet music.

"About this weekend?" he asked, his smile tightening.

"Yeah, she's always trying to give me advice. You know how she is," I said, nodding to the accompanist to begin.

We worked together on the song, finding the emotional beats and drawing out the subtext. Once we finished, I sat back down on the couch and Michael packed up to leave just as Leslie came in from the studio next door.

"So I heard your boyfriend is coming in this weekend. Are you stoked?" she asked, bounding into the room and curling up on the couch next to me.

"He *is* coming in. How did you know that?" I asked.

"Michael told me," she said, digging into her bag and pulling out a few magazines.

"What are all these?" I asked as she spread them out on the couch.

"My favorite crush, Jack Hamilton, is supposed to be in them. I thought we could begin a little shrine for our dressing room!" She bounced like a schoolgirl.

I was beginning to wonder if I should tell her about me and Jack. I didn't mean to keep it a secret so long, but I was following Holly's directive that we keep our relationship private—out of the newspapers and off the Internet—even though I knew Jack was against it. He trusted Holly implicitly, though, and knew we were only looking out for his career.

It wasn't that it was a secret, we just weren't public. And my being on another coast solved a lot of problems with the press, especially now that Jack was doing so many interviews.

Holly had taught him the phrase "I'm not dating anyone right now," and he was sticking to it in the interviews. If those few pictures they got of us in L.A. stayed on the back burner, we'd be okay. Still, I knew Leslie would eventually find out, and I didn't want her to think I was keeping things from her.

"Wow . . . he is so hot," she sighed, finding the first picture in the teenybopper magazine and ripping it out.

I allowed myself a quick glance, which of course made my heart do a little double-time, and then I looked at her. "Hey, Leslie?" I started.

"My God, he's on fire, that boy! I might need to concentrate on booking more jobs in L.A. I wonder if he's single?" she continued, flipping through the pages of the next magazine.

"So listen," I tried again. "There's something I've been meaning to tell you. My boyfriend, the one who lives in L.A.—"

I was interrupted by another squeal. "Jesus! Look at those eyes! I mean, they just scream sex, don't they?" She tore out the picture and added it to the pile.

"Yes, yes, they do. Anyway, like I was saying—"

"Holy shit—Jack Fucking Hamilton," she said softly.

"Jesus, Leslie, enough already! I'm trying to tell you something about my boyfriend!"

Sitting there with a ripped picture in her hand, she looked dazed. It *was* a pretty hot picture.

"What about your boyfriend?" a sexy voice said behind me with a distinctly British accent. My eyes grew wide as I slowly turned, now realizing what Leslie meant by her *Holy shit—Jack Fucking Hamilton.*

He stood in the doorway, leaning against the door frame with a bag over his shoulder. His eyes were bloodshot, his clothes rumpled, and his hair needed its own zip code. He smiled at me, and I was struck stupid by the sight of him.

"You were saying something about your boyfriend, I think," he asked again. His eyes twinkled, the green getting dangerously dark. Then he bit down on that damn lip.

I was off the couch and across the room in seconds, and I jumped at him. He caught me in midair, dropping his bag, the force of my jump carrying us out into the hallway. I pressed myself into him, wrapping my legs around his waist and my arms around his neck. He stumbled backward, laughing at my exuberant welcome, and his back hit the wall.

I didn't see the other cast members in the hall. I didn't see the ballet students in their tutus on the way to a dress rehearsal on the main stage. I didn't see Leslie, still dumbfounded on the couch, mouth hanging open, surrounded by pictures of my very own Sweet Nuts. I didn't see Michael standing at the end of the hallway, watching.

I saw nothing but the front of Jack's T-shirt as I clung tightly to him, the colors beginning to swim as I blinked back sudden tears. I smelled nothing but the scent of warm pipe tobacco, cozy chimney smoke, chocolate, and Hamilton. I felt nothing but his strong arms enveloping me and his hands running up and down my back, soothing my shaking body. I heard nothing but his quiet laughter, and then his perfect voice whispered, "Aw, Gracie, I missed you too."

And then I tasted nothing but his sweet lips, pressed firmly to mine, as I kissed him *like it was my job.*

When things threatened to get out of control, I finally peeled myself off the Brit and brought him back into the studio, where Leslie was still sitting and waiting.

"I can't believe you took the red-eye and didn't tell me, you ass!" I yelled, pummeling him.

"I know. It was last-minute. But I finished up what I needed to in L.A. yesterday, and I couldn't wait any longer, Nuts Girl," he said, tucking me into his side like he always did.

I looked at Leslie, whose eyes were still as big as dinner plates. "So, Leslie, this is my boyfriend who I was trying to tell you about. This is Jack."

He extended a hand, and she took it wordlessly, beginning to realize she was meeting her celebrity crush.

"Leslie, it's nice to meet you. Grace has told me all about you. Sounds like the two of you are quite a handful together, yes?" He grinned wickedly at her.

He was doing that on purpose, the flirty fuck. Those fans didn't stand a chance.

"Hi—um—hi," she stammered, and then quickly got control. "Sorry, I'm not usually so ridiculous, but we were just cutting out pictures of you, and then you're standing there, and Grace is trying to mount you in the hall— It's a lot to take in. It's nice to meet you," she finished.

I heard someone else come in and turned to see Michael.

"Hey, I heard there was soft-core porn going on in the hallway," he said. I noticed his fists were clenched.

"Hey, Michael. Sorry about that. Jack kind of surprised

me. You remember Michael, right?" I asked, turning to Jack.

They looked at each other for a second, then Michael held out his hand. "Hey, man, good to see you again. That was quite a surprise. Grace wasn't expecting you until tonight," he said, pumping Jack's hand twice, then dropping it.

"Good to see you too. Yeah, I have to keep her on her toes. I'm good like that," Jack said, running his hand down my back and wrapping his arm around my hip.

We were all silent for a moment, then Michael cleared his throat. "So, obviously, Grace, why don't you skip rehearsal this afternoon? We can block around you. Why don't you take off?"

"Are you sure? I'm sure Jack has things he has to do—" I started.

"Nope, we're cool. Get out of here," he said, nodding toward the door.

"If you're sure, then I guess we'll take off," I said, thrilled at this sudden turn of events. Jack grinned down at me. I knew he was thrilled as well.

"That's cool, man. Thanks," Jack said, grabbing his bag and mine and throwing them over his shoulder.

I hugged Leslie good-bye; she was still slightly dazed. I gave Michael a hug as well. "Thanks, O'Connell, I appreciate it. See you tomorrow?"

"Yep, have fun." He nodded, eyes distant, as Jack clasped my hand and pulled me to the door.

We grinned at each other the whole way downstairs. Seeing him, being able to touch him and breathe him in— Wow. I had missed me some Hamilton.

When we got outside, Jack had a car waiting for us. It

wasn't quite a limo but longer than a town car, with a divider between the front and the back.

And I knew we were in trouble. We simply weren't going to make it to the hotel in time. When the driver opened the door for us, I asked him to take us to Grant's Tomb. He nodded, we both climbed in, and we were off.

I quickly found the button for the divider and raised it, sealing us in our own little leather-upholstered world.

"Grant's Tomb, Grace? What's that about?" Jack asked, his hands beginning to roam across my shoulders.

"Simple. It's all the way uptown. It'll take us a while to get up there." I swung one leg over and sat on his lap.

"Okay, but why are we going up there, love?" he asked again, sweeping my hair off my neck so he could kiss it.

I moaned as I felt his warm lips caress my skin. It had been too long.

"Well, I could've asked him to just drive around while you fuck me until I black out, but I wanted to uphold at least a modicum of decency," I purred in his ear, my hands digging into his silky curls.

He groaned. His eyes blazed liquid emerald. "Gracie, you bad girl . . ." He buried his face in my neck, making me hotter by the second.

"George, you have no idea how bad this girl wants to be." I sighed as he found that sweet spot on my neck.

Then he pulled back to look in my eyes. "Be my bad girl, Grace," he whispered.

It was like a dam broke.

I lost all control. I roughly pulled his shirt off his body, and my hands moved across his warm skin, desperate to feel him.

I flew through the buttons on my own shirt, letting it fall open to the sides, then I flicked the front clasp on my bra, grabbed his hands, and brought them home, to me.

As his hands surrounded my breasts, I moaned. He bent his head to my collarbone and swept long licks across my skin, making me shiver. He groaned as his mouth found my nipple, and my head fell back as I luxuriated in the feeling of his mouth on me. I began to circle my hips, feeling him rise beneath me, wanting me.

This would not be slow and tender. I needed it too badly.

I slid down to my knees on the floor in a Hamiltonian frenzy. I needed to taste him. I needed him to fill me up. I snapped open his button, unzipped, and had him in my mouth—fast.

His hands came to my hair, guiding me up and down as I sucked him furiously. I heard his groans, and as he said my name, I ached for him. I gave him one last long, strong pull with my lips, then released him and looked up at him from beneath my lashes. He was so beautiful, especially when he was close to coming for me.

I nudged my yoga pants down, kicked off my shoes, and sat next to him. "On your knees, love," I instructed, and his eyes widened. Then a wicked smile crept across his face.

He sank down and pulled my hips to the edge of the seat.

"Take these off," I said, hooking my fingers through the band of my white lace panties, which were already soaked.

He obliged, scooting them down over my hips, my thighs, my knees, and finally my ankles. He threw the panties over his shoulder, then appraised the situation.

I kept my knees firmly locked together, and when I saw him begin to pant heavily at what I was keeping from him, I slowly parted my legs, revealing myself to him. I felt the cool air rush in to hit me and saw his face change to something very close to abject worship.

I wrapped my hands in his hair and brought him down to where I wanted him to go.

"I need to come at least three times before you can fuck me. Can you handle that?" I asked, my breath hitching in my throat as I anticipated the work he was about to do to make me see stars.

Bossy Bad Girl Grace was in full force—my Jack loved a challenge.

"Consider it handled, Crazy," he whispered, grinning that sexy half grin. He roughly pulled me closer, and my hands clutched tightly in his hair as he kissed me, first on the insides of my thighs and then—sweet Lord—right on my gonna-see-God.

Feeling his mouth on me after so long was almost more than I could take, and I bucked up wildly. His fingers swept me open so he could focus more thoroughly on my center, and his tongue fluttered lightly against me, bringing me to the edge quickly. Maybe it had just been too long, or maybe it was all those nights imagining exactly this, but within seconds of that magic tongue touching me, I was coming in his mouth. I screamed, and all the tension that had been building over the last weeks poured forth in a wave that left my brain scrambled and my sex pulsing.

"That's one," he whispered, immediately beginning to work me again. Not letting me down from the first, he pressed his tongue against me, licking me from top to bottom, his lips searching me out. He sucked me into his mouth, encircling me with his lips as his tongue worked feverishly against the tiny bundle of nerves designed for the sole purpose of pleasure.

Now *that* is intelligent design.

I could feel myself building again, and as I pressed his face into me, he moaned, sending the vibration straight into me. I threw my head back against the seat as I came again, thrashing about under his tongue.

He leaned back a little, licking his lips. "That's two, love," he said with a wink.

"I changed my mind—get inside *now*. I need you," I said, trying to get him to crawl up my body.

"Hell no! I need you to really be ready for me, Gracie," he teased. His fingers began to dance around me, and when he grazed me with his knuckle, it was shocking. My back arched into his fingers as one, then two slipped inside.

"Fuck, you're tight," he said, his voice uneven and husky. I panted, and he watched as I began to shake. His fingers, strong and sure, stroked me, and finding that J-spot, he brought me to another hard orgasm.

"And that's three," he said with a triumphant grin.

"Unbelievable, as always. Now get up here, please. I need you inside me," I growled, my face flushed with passion.

"I think my bad girl deserves one more, don't you?" he asked, slipping back down.

As his fingers plunged back into me, his tongue found me once more. His teeth nibbled lightly, and I almost came out of my skin. His fingers stroked me from the inside, manipulating my J-spot as his tongue teased out another earth-shattering orgasm. I could feel this one coming, and it was huge. The combination of textures and rubbing and sucking and licking and stroking and pushing and incredible sweet invasion was too much. I let out a long, lusty scream, which became his name, over and over again.

"Oh, God, Jack! Oohhh!" I screamed, collapsing against the seat. He kissed the inside of both of my thighs, and when his lips found the site of my original Hamilton Brand, he bit down, marking me once again as his. I hissed and dragged him back up to me.

I pushed him into the seat, swung my leg over him, and sat on him. I felt every perfect inch of him as he sank into me, and we both cried out.

"Jesus, I missed you, George," I said as my body clenched around him, never wanting to let him go.

"Fuuuuck," was all he could get out as I began to move my hips, encouraging him to sink deeper into my body. He drove into me as I bounced above him, his mouth capturing my nipple and teasing me with his teeth. I rolled my hips back and forth, letting him feel all of me, his cock exploring me from the inside. His hands were rough on my hips, guiding me, slamming me up and down harder and harder as we both felt the explosion building.

"I missed you, Jack. I missed feeling you inside me," I chanted as he moved me up and down.

"Oh, God, Grace, you feel amazing," he groaned. "You're so warm and wet and tight around me." He sped up, and I matched his rhythm. He looked me in the eye, brow furrowed, jaw clenched. I knew this sweet face. My Jack was about to come.

I squeezed him with all I had, feeling my orgasm begin to rip through me, and we came together.

In the back of a town car, in the middle of Manhattan. What must that poor driver be thinking?

This long weekend was going to be insane.

three

*N*ow that Jack was in New York, things felt right. They felt good. My oonie certainly felt good . . .

As we headed to Jack's hotel, I'm sure the driver was mildly curious about why we didn't spend any time at Grant's Tomb once we got all the way up there, but no matter.

We pulled up to the Four Seasons on Fifty-Seventh Street, and when we climbed out I suddenly remembered we weren't supposed to be seen in public. Especially checking into a hotel. Very bad idea.

"Hey, why don't you get checked in, then call me and let me know what room you're in, and I'll come up," I said quietly, beginning to move off in the direction of Madison Avenue.

"Grace, that's silly. Hey, Grace . . ." he protested, as the bellman took his bag inside and I walked away.

I held up my cell and mouthed, "Call me."

He grimaced, shook his head, and went inside.

I walked around the block, waiting for his call. I knew he

thought I was being stupid, but based on the press coverage he was now getting—ugh. I didn't want the scrutiny that would accompany another "unidentified redhead" sighting.

His premiere was coming up so quickly, and he was about to start a huge press junket. Then he'd be traveling all over the country to make personal appearances. He wasn't sure how many people would actually show up to see him, but I had a feeling it was going to blow his mind. He was going to be freaking swarmed.

And speaking of the premiere, nothing had been said about whether I was invited. I'd mentioned it to Michael, just in case I would *maybe* need to head back to L.A. for a weekend. It would be tricky because our rehearsal time was so limited—the show was set to go up the first week of December. We'd locked in three weeks of performances initially, and then we'd see what kind of response we got.

I was almost around the block when I got a text from the Brit:

Get your sweet ass back here. Room 2104. Don't make me come looking for you—I will make a scene. I will identify this motherfucking redhead.

And I'd thought I was being all subtle and shit. Dammit, he knew me too well.

You are never subtle.

Good point.

I finished my loop, made my way through the front entrance into the beautiful lobby, then found the bank of elevators. I thought fondly of our hotel in Santa Barbara and the fact that the hotel sex had been unfathomably great.

Hmm . . . We might have to sleep here tonight, instead of at my place.

I approached his door and knocked lightly. I could hear him on the phone, and when he opened the door, he smiled and pulled me in, continuing his conversation. I admired the room. It was well appointed and had a great view of the park. I checked out the bathroom: huge. It also had a rain shower like the one in Santa Barbara. Yep, I was definitely staying here with him. I didn't care if I had to enter the building separately every day wrapped in a giant poncho.

I went back into the main room and saw Jack standing by the window, still on the phone. He mouthed the words *I'm sorry*, and I shook my head with a smile. "No problem," I mouthed back.

With a running leap I vaulted myself onto the giant bed, landing smack in the middle with a belly flop. It was soft and inviting, covered in pillows and a silky duvet. I heard a snicker behind me and turned to see Jack looking amused at my acrobatic feat. I curled up on my side and waved at him. He smiled back and mouthed, "Five minutes."

I snickered, getting a delightful idea. I rose up, then sat on the side of the bed, within grasping distance of him. "It's hot in here," I mouthed.

"More AC?" he mouthed back, starting toward the thermostat.

"No, I'm going to get totally naked while you try to carry on your conversation," I whispered. I didn't want him to miss that part.

His eyes widened as I proceeded to do exactly that. First the jacket and scarf came off, then the sneakers. My shirt came off next, followed quickly by my usual yoga pants. I could see him beginning to have trouble following his conversation, so my plan was working. I sat on the edge of the bed in my white panties and white lacy bra, and beckoned him over with one finger. He stalled, trying to decide what to do.

In the end, the boy won out over the man, and he stood in front of me, still on the damn phone. "I'm sorry, love. It shouldn't be much longer," he mouthed.

I smiled sweetly up at him, snaking my hands around his waist and bringing him closer. "It's okay. Take your time," I whispered. "I'm just going to do things to you while you carry on," I said, to his horror and delight.

He attempted to back up, but I quickly unzipped him and had my hand around him through his boxers before he could move very far. His eyes closed quickly, and he hardened completely in my hand.

God, you really had to love a twenty-four-year-old.

Yep, and I really had to love this one in particular.

I stroked him firmly, watching his face contort. He was a little distracted, you see. I pumped him, both hands inside his boxers now, and I could see he was really going to have some trouble soon.

"Mm-hmm, mm-hmm, so I would need to be there for the London premiere on which day? Oh, God . . . I mean, sorry. Oh, God, that's fine. I can be there then . . ." He moaned, and I took pity. His eyes rolled back in his head as I stood up and pushed him gently away.

"Meet me in the shower when you're through," I whispered, removing my bra and throwing it over my shoulder as I walked toward the bathroom. I used to be so concerned about men seeing me naked, always worried about what was sticking out, what was jiggling, what was smushed. But with Jack? I knew all he wanted was me, and he preferred me naked. Totally liberating.

I stopped at the door and slowly slid my panties down, looking behind me.

Jack stood in the middle of the room, mouth hanging slightly open, with his pants around his ankles. He looked totally turned on and slightly mortified at the same time.

I stifled a giggle and twirled my panties around my finger, now totally exposed to him. His eyes traveled down my body and back up to my eyes. "Hurry up," I mouthed, and slipped into the bathroom.

I'd barely gotten the water started and was adjusting the temperature when I heard the door open. I smiled as the water poured over me, steam filling up the large glass enclosure. Then I felt a very warm and very naked Jack press against my back, and my breath caught in my throat.

"You are diabolical," he muttered, dragging his tongue up the side of my neck.

I shivered as he spun me around. "Next time, get off faster," I said, pulling him under the spray with me.

"No one is getting off fast, love. Certainly not you," he promised, dipping his head to kiss the hollow of my neck.

Oh, this was going to be a great weekend.

☆   ☆   ☆

Waterlogged and weak-kneed, we left the shower about an hour later, having thoroughly enjoyed the hotel's giant water heaters. I'd lost track of how many times the Brit made me see stars, and I was a little concerned that I now had a shower-tile imprint permanently etched into my bum.

We were punch-drunk and slaphappy as we stumbled into the bedroom, laughing at the lunacy of our actions.

"Seriously, George, you've only been in New York a few hours, and we're already working through our greatest hits!" I giggled, falling onto the bed and struggling to get under the covers. My hair was wound up in a towel, and I wore a plush Four Seasons robe. He walked around to his side of the bed, pulling the covers down as he went, and climbed in next to me.

"I've been working you in my mind for weeks now, love, and I have a whole set of newest hits for us to try this weekend." He grinned dangerously. I was in for it. We might never leave this hotel. "Besides, I missed you like crazy," he added. "Now that I have you in my clutches, I may not let you go again. And speaking of clutches, bring those fantastic tits over here," he muttered, pulling open my robe as he pressed his body against me. He turned me on my side, his hands finding my breasts, and then . . .

Perfection. All was right with the world.

We were both asleep in minutes.

☆　☆　☆

I woke up groggy and confused, as I often do when I nap in the afternoon. I felt Jack's strong arms around me, and for a second I thought I was back in L.A. But the light was different, and when I looked around, I remembered where we were. My heart stuttered a bit, reminding me we weren't together all the time anymore, but it started up again as I thought about the rest of the long weekend.

Mmm . . .

I rolled away carefully, trying not to wake him, and made

it to the edge of the bed before I felt his hands pull me back to him. I giggled.

"Where do you think you're going, Nuts Girl?" he asked, his voice thick with sleep.

"To brush out my hair. I'm sure it's quite lovely from falling asleep with it wet." I attempted to run my fingers through it, and I could tell it was sticking out every which way. Charming.

"I think it looks cute—sort of a cross between finger-in-the-socket and homeless," he said, pulling me back against him. "Scoot, please," he instructed, pressing me onto my back and laying his head on my chest. He nudged my neck up so he could snuggle into the nook and wiggled about for a minute until he finally settled in.

"Comfortable?" I asked with a quiet smile.

"Incredibly so, yes," he said, wrapping his arms more tightly around my waist.

I glanced at the alarm clock and saw that it was already four thirty. We'd effectively wasted the day on showers and naptime. Just then, my stomach let out a loud growl.

Jack moved lower on my body, kissed my tummy, then looked sternly at my navel. "Shhh, don't be rude."

I giggled when, seconds later, my stomach growled again.

Jack rolled his eyes. "I said quiet down," he ordered, kissing my tummy once more.

"Sweetie, I need to eat something. How are you not hungry? We both skipped lunch, and you flew all night!" I said.

"Actually, I'm starving now that you mention it. Fancy a snack?"

"I fancy a snack," I affirmed, removing his arms from my waist and taking the room-service menu from the nightstand. "Are we going out for dinner tonight?" I asked, flipping through to the snacky stuff.

"That's entirely your call. I made no plans, other than an interview I have to do Saturday morning," he answered, scratching my back.

"Are we in a salty mood or a desserty mood?" I asked, chewing my lip thoughtfully.

"Both. Just order what sounds good to you, and I'll eat whatever," he said, looking at me.

"What're you looking at? No more comments about my hair." I frowned, trying again to run my fingers through it.

"No, it's just . . . it's just really fucking great to see you, Gracie." He smiled softly at me, his eyes bright green.

"I missed you too, George. I really did," I whispered, kissing him gently, breathing in his warm s'more-like smell. There was really no way I would ever eat a s'more again without wanting to have sex with it.

My tummy growled again.

"Okay, I'm calling in this order, and then we're going to plan our evening. And we *are* leaving this room, Hamilton. We're in Manhattan! We aren't staying in all night," I warned, picking up the phone.

"Sheridan, if I wanted to make you stay in all night with me, all I'd have to do is wave some candy in front of you and then kiss on your sweet boobies. You'd be putty in my hands." He grinned sexily.

"There's candy?" I asked, looking around excitedly.

Jack laughed so hard, he fell off the bed.

four

We finally left the hotel around eight, heading for my place so I could show him where I lived and pick up some things. I did want him to sleep at my place. I wanted him in my bed and in my shower and on my couch, even if this was all rented furniture. But sweet damn—I wanted another round in that giant shower, and we had all weekend for me to have him s'more up my place.

Enough with the freaking s'mores.

This distance thing was making me a little insane.

We caught a cab in front of the hotel, and it was so quick I didn't even have time to worry about anyone seeing us. Maybe I did need to relax a little. New York was really different from L.A., and in his ratty jeans and ball cap he looked more college student than famous, so I doubted anyone would recognize him. And he wasn't worried about being seen with me, so what the hell?

We made out like teenagers in the cab on the way to my

apartment. When we arrived, I nodded to the doorman as we walked inside. "Hi, Lou."

"Evening, Lou." Jack nodded as well, and Lou nodded back.

I kept him at arm's length in the elevator, and when we finally made it into my apartment he was like an octopus, arms everywhere. He finally settled in behind me, hands clasped firmly over my tummy, chin planted on my shoulder.

"Okay, give me the grand tour," he said.

"Well, this is pretty much it. It's not big. I don't need a lot of space, and it's close to the rehearsal studio. Kitchen, living room, bathroom down the hall, and bedroom is the last door on the right," I said.

"It's nice," he said, looking over my shoulder.

"Eh, it's okay. It's no Laurel Canyon. That's home to me," I said, leaning back against him.

"But you haven't even lived there yet. How can it be your home when you've only slept one night there?" he questioned, kissing my neck right under my ear.

"Mmm, and what a night it was," I said with a giggle, turning to wrap my arms around his waist.

His hands came to my face, bringing me forward into another soft kiss. "Yes, it was. But really, how can that be home? I mean, do you truly consider L.A. home?" he asked, looking at me with questions in his eyes.

"God, yes. It *does* feel like home. When I first found my house, I knew it would need a lot of work, but I knew it was my home. I could clearly see myself living there. And even though I had to leave for this job, wherever I go, that house is home." I closed my eyes, thinking of the warm California sun, and I could almost smell the lemon trees on my front porch and the honeysuckle in the backyard.

I opened my eyes to see Jack studying me carefully.

"What's that look for?" I asked.

"So you are planning on moving back, right?" he asked, running one hand through his hair.

"Hell yes, ya goofball! I didn't spend all my savings on my house just to sell it again! I don't know how long I'll be out here, and I love New York, but when this is over? I'll be back home." I pulled him against me. "What about you?" I asked, my face pressed into his shirt.

"What about me?" he asked, his breath warm and sweet in my hair.

"Where are you going to live when all this is over? Will you go back to London after the premiere, or are you planning on staying in L.A.?" I asked, a little afraid to hear the answer.

"Well, I don't know, to be honest. That was the plan—London is my home—but there's a film we're in negotiations with that would be filming in L.A. in January."

"Wait, so you're thinking about moving back to London?" I asked, surprised.

"That's where I live, Grace. Who knows what's going to happen after this movie comes out. This could be my swan song. I could peak at twenty-four."

"Oh, please. The world is going to need much more Joshua," I said.

London?

Shhh.

"Hmm, we'll see. Maybe no one'll come and see it. Maybe they'll think it's rubbish," he muttered.

"George, please. It will be amazing. And if nothing else, you're so pretty, they'll pay just to see you romping around half-naked in your period clothing," I teased. I knew how much Jack wanted to be taken seriously as an actor, and I was forever telling him how pretty he was, just to mess with him.

"And I'm sure the men who will be coming to see your show will only be coming to see your acting chops, not your fantastic tits," he teased back, earning him a very grown-up tongue stick-out.

"Oh, love, if you're going to show me your tongue, I may have to give you something to lick," he threatened, wiggling his eyebrows like a villain in an old-timey movie.

"You're sick, Hamilton. Truly sick." I laughed, pulling away from him.

"So we're going to see a movie, yes?" he asked, tooling around my apartment.

"Yes, there's a theater about six blocks from here. I'll check and see what's playing. Then we can grab something after that, sound good?" I pulled my laptop from my bag and sat on the couch.

"Oh, I'll be grabbing something after the movie, that's for certain," he said, winking at me.

"Dirty bird," I muttered as he disappeared down the hall toward the bedroom.

"You love it," he shouted over his shoulder.

I laughed quietly and signed on. My TMZ homepage came up immediately because I was a sucker for all things celebrity gossip. I could hear Jack putzing in the bedroom, so I figured I could indulge in a few minutes of celeb surfing. Guilty pleasure. I scrolled through the pictures of the latest buzz: An actor checking into rehab, another actor leaving rehab. A singer who'd been threatening to retire for twenty years heading back out on tour. I skipped ahead—not a lot of celebrity news. I was about to zip over to the movie times site when an interesting snippet caught my eye:

Jack Hamilton seen out on the town with actress Marcia Veracruz. Are these two on again?

What? Wait a minute. Back up.

Once Time *comes out, maybe he can afford to buy a new car! The two were spotted having lunch in Venice a few days ago before climbing into Jack's old, beat-up MG.*

I felt sick.
Breathe, just breathe.

Ever since he was cast as Joshua, women everywhere have been wondering whether this Brit boy is single. Well, ladies, it appears this time traveler is spoken for! Just two nights ago, Jack Hamilton was spotted driving away from an L.A. nightclub with his latest gal pal, actress Marcia Veracruz. The two were previously in a confirmed relationship, and although they took a break, it appears things are still hot and heavy between them.

I felt really sick. I tried to close the laptop, but I couldn't make my hands move. They were clenched too tightly into fists.
Ask him. Don't flip out. Just ask him.
Hell yes, I was gonna ask him.
I stared at the pictures, examining his face: smiling, ball

cap pulled securely down over his curly hair. Then I forced myself to look at her, really look at her. She was smiling too, her face inclined toward his as they left some club in L.A. together.

She was pretty.

She was really pretty.

Not good . . .

I heard Jack coming down the hallway, and part of me wanted to clear the screen, pull up Moviefone, and shove this Marcia thing in my famous mental drawer—the Drawer, where everything unpleasant goes to be avoided—but we were past that. We were way past that. And if I'd been honest with myself, and not such a chickenshit, we would've dealt with this months ago when I saw her text that night in the dark.

Instead, true to form, I'd refused to deal, letting this build to the point of full meltdown before acknowledging it. Why? Because a battle raged constantly between the cool, tough exterior Grace and the sad, frightened, still-sees-herself-as-the-fat-girl Grace on the inside. Jack'd had a tiny peek or two at Inside Grace, but he had yet to experience the full mess in there.

Hey, why deal with things directly, when they can fester and become an emotional storm of epic proportions? I never claimed to be the mature one in this relationship, that's for sure.

I second that.

"Hey, Gracie, I think we should skip the movie and just stay in and have a shag, what do you say?" he deadpanned, stopping in the archway to the living room. His hands were pressed against either side of the archway, his hair raked back and crazy, his lower lip sucked in between his teeth, and his eyes blazing deep green. He grinned at me, taking my lack of speech as proof that his seduction was working.

He sauntered closer, leaning over my shoulder. "What do you say we close this thing while I take these pesky clothes off you . . ." Then he saw the pictures on the computer.

He froze.

"Explain this, please," I said in a low voice. When I was mad, I was dangerously quiet.

"Shit, Grace, I was going to tell you about this. I know how bad it looks, but really, it's nothing."

"Explain this *now*, please," I asked again, my voice even quieter. I was beginning to shake, I was so angry, but beneath the anger was a profound sadness. This is what I'd been afraid of since the beginning.

"Grace, Marcia is just a friend. I swear. You can ask Holly," he said, moving the laptop away and sitting on the coffee table in front of me, watching my eyes. I think my expression told him to tread lightly.

"Holly knows about this?" I asked, closing my eyes and feeling prickling behind my eyelids.

"Well, yes, she does. We talked about it earlier this week when these pictures first came out. I know this looks bad, Grace, but truly, she is just a friend. And Holly actually thinks we can make this work in our favor, since the pictures are already out there—"

"I know you used to date her, Jack. Don't try to tell me you didn't. What are you doing, going out with your ex-girlfriend? I know I must sound like some crazy bitch, but right now I'm feeling all kinds of crazy, so start talking," I said, my voice getting a little louder.

"Okay, yes, we used to date. But we're just friends now.

47

I promise you there's nothing going on! She knows all about you. I talk about you all the time. That's actually one of the reasons we've been hanging out so much lately. Her boyfriend travels a lot, and she never sees him. So we hang out sometimes. It's harmless. I swear, Grace."

"Y'know, it's not so much that you're hanging out with her, which I can overlook. Hey, we have no claims on each other. You can hang out with whoever you want. But the fact that no one bothered to tell me, and that you and Holly even *discussed* this? I feel sick. I really feel sick," I said, my voice getting louder still.

Jack was quiet, looking at the floor.

My stomach was twisting and turning. "Do you have any idea how this makes me feel? I feel like an old fool. Maybe this is the kind of person you should be with—someone who fits with you better than I ever could.

"And I'm sorry, but a girl does *not* text you in the middle of the night if all she wants is friendship." Tears were beginning to run down my face, and I wiped them angrily away.

Jack's face had grown angry as well, but it flashed confusion when I mentioned the text. "What text? What are you talking about?"

"She texted you in the middle of the night weeks ago, before I left L.A. You were asleep, and I picked up your phone to shut it off. Yes, I read it. I shouldn't have, but I fucking did. I would say I'm sorry, but you know what? I'm not really sorry. I wanted to see who was texting the man asleep in *my* bed, with his hands all over *my* body, at three in the morning.

"And looky what we have here! The same girl you've been

photographed with all over town. Shocking, really," I said sarcastically, getting up and pushing past him to stand in the kitchen.

I was still crying, but these were angry tears, pissed-off tears. All that shit I'd been pushing away for so long was coming home to roost now, and all I could do was hang on and let it come out.

Jack was still quiet. He finally rose and stood in front of me, his face stormy.

"Gracie, I am going to say this once. Was I wrong not to tell you I was hanging out with my ex-girlfriend? Yes, probably. Was I wrong to not tell you sooner about the conversation I had with Holly? Yes, definitely.

"I've never done this before—had a relationship with someone who lives across the country, while I'm going through the biggest thing professionally I'll probably ever go through. And you know what? There will probably be more pictures of Marcia and me together. In fact, I can guarantee it. She has a movie she's promoting, and our managers are milking this thing for all it's worth.

"But even if you don't trust me, which you clearly don't, you *know* Holly would never do anything to hurt you. She was bloody well pissed when she saw these, as she should be. I have my head up my ass sometimes, and I didn't think about what these would look like, or how they might make you feel," he said, breathing heavily.

"Well, I think—" I started, but he put his finger over my lips.

"I'm not finished. You seem to think I'm going to fuck around on you. And these pictures do look terrible if you're thinking about it in that way. You're here, I'm there, and it sucks. But there has to be some trust between us. Do you agree?" he asked, removing his finger.

I glared at him. "Yes, I agree, but—"

"Grace, you either agree or you don't. Yes or no?"

"Yes, I agree, and I do trust you," I said, a fresh wave of tears starting.

"I trust you too. Otherwise I'd be asking you why there are a pair of men's trainers by the front door. A less-trusting boyfriend would wonder about that." He arched an eyebrow at me and looked over my shoulder.

I followed his gaze and saw Michael's sneakers. He'd left them here the other night, changing into boots when it started raining.

Shit.

I looked back at Jack. He seemed curious, and a little . . . apprehensive?

"Grace, you're a beautiful woman. I see how men look at you. I know there are other men who want to be with you. Whose shoes are those?" he asked.

I grabbed a box of Kleenex and blew my nose loudly, getting control again. "They're Michael's. He was here earlier in the week. We were working on a scene, and he changed his shoes. I didn't even notice they were still here until now."

Jack had nothing to worry about; Michael and I were just friends.

Friends who used to have feelings for each other.

But Jack doesn't know about that.

"Did you and Michael ever date, Gracie?" he asked.

"Date? No," I answered quickly. That was true. We never dated.

"Are you sure? You two seem to have more than friendship

50

in your past. I noticed that right away. And when I said I see how other men look at you? He looks at you that way," Jack added, his face going dark.

"No, we never dated. But yes, there were feelings there—years and years ago. That's all over, though. We truly are just friends," I assured him, breathing a little more easily now.

"Ah. Like Marcia and I are just friends."

"Ugh," I said, rubbing my eyes.

"Do you see how much easier this is if we just tell each other what's going on?" he asked, reaching out his hand. I hesitated for a second, then took it.

"How the hell did you get so mature at twenty-four? Seriously, I'm like a basket case next to you," I said, breaking the tension a little.

"I'm British. We're born more mature," he said with the sexy half smile that always turned me to mush. "Feeling better now?" he asked as I blew my nose again.

"Yes. But don't ever let me find out something like that courtesy of TMZ again, okay? I can't take another surprise like that," I said fiercely, as he crushed me against his chest.

"I promise. That was a shitty thing to do. And don't let Michael get too comfortable over here. I don't want to have to piss in the corners to mark my territory, but I will if I need to," he said.

I laughed in spite of myself. "Well, you tell that Marcia I'll be very glad to meet her next time I'm in L.A. And make sure to tell her I said to keep her hands to herself, in the meantime. I can go along with seeing pictures of you two together for publicity's sake, but the second I see her hand on your ass, the bitch is going down." I grabbed his collar and pulled him closer to me.

"Fucking Nuts Girl, how could I love anyone but you? You're insane," he said, lowering his mouth to mine.

I let my hand slip down to his buns and gave him a squeeze. "This sweet ass is mine, and don't you forget it. Now give mama some sugar," I said, and kissed him hard.

We never made it to the movie. But we had made it through another potential shitstorm, and we kept our shit intact. We were an odd couple, to say the least, but for now, all was well in Jack-and-Grace Land.

five

The next morning I woke to the sound of the phone ringing shrilly. Jack groaned and dove deeper under the covers, leaving me to roll across him to answer it.

"No, no, let me get it," I muttered sarcastically as I grabbed the phone on the fourth ring. "Hello?" I asked, yawning deeply.

"Shhh. Too loud, too early," he mumbled from under the covers.

"Good morning. This is your wake-up call," a chipper voice said.

"Great. I love wake-up calls," I said, and hung up. I leaned back against Jack, whose breathing was already evening out again. It was seven fifteen; I had an early rehearsal today.

We hadn't been rehearsing on Saturdays, but as we got closer to the preview and Michael continued making daily changes to the script, he'd ramped up our schedule. Jack had an interview in the morning, but we were both off in the afternoon. The plan was a late lunch and maybe a walk in Central Park—very touristy.

Hmmm . . . I wondered how Jack would feel about a Sheridan Wake-up Call. I certainly enjoyed his Hamiltonian Wake-up Calls.

He will love it . . .

I looked and saw that he'd fallen back asleep, though if I knew my guy, part of him would still be up.

I slid under the covers and stealthily worked my way down, so as not to wake him. Positioning myself right over his boxers, I smiled as I slowly lifted the elastic band and lowered it just enough to sneak my hand in. Then I grasped him softly, easing him out. I took him into my mouth, enveloping him with my lips and tongue, and felt him harden further. He was still asleep, although I heard his breathing change, coming a little faster. I tightened my mouth and felt him grow harder still.

He moaned slightly, and I felt his hands move at his sides, just inches from my head. I moved my mouth around him again, lightly trailing my fingers up and down his stomach, and I finally heard my name.

"Grace," he whispered, his voice still thick with sleep.

I smiled and took him in deeper, feeling him hit the back of my throat. He groaned, his hands moving down to twist in my hair.

"Mmm, Gracie," I heard, and I knew he was enjoying himself. I grasped the base of him with my hands, my mouth creating a beautiful friction as I moved up and down his length, causing his hips to buck, keeping time with my movements. He moaned and held my face in his hands as I continued to pleasure him, hearing him hiss as I altered my grip or sucked harder.

"Grace, oh, God, Grace . . . mmm . . . ahhhhh . . . Graaace!" He exploded in pure pleasure. Loving how I could affect him this way, I kissed him tenderly and he sighed in appreciation. Then I crawled up his body and rested my head on his chest, his arms tightly around me.

"Now that's the kind of wake-up call I don't get enough of," he said with a chuckle.

"I should hope not, love," I giggled, kissing his chest, little hairs there tickling my nose.

We lay like this for a few more minutes, until my cell phone alarm went off. Anticipating a morning romp, I'd set the backup snooze alarm last night. I turned it off, then sank back onto the bed.

"Shower?" I asked, turning to look at him. His hair was all over the place, sheets low on his torso, and it was all I could do not to drool on the one-thousand-thread-count sheets.

"Shower," he agreed. He threw off the covers, stretched, and started walking to the bathroom. "Don't forget the coconuts, love," he called as I watched his cute little tushy cross the room.

How could I possibly forget the coconuts? I giggled into the pillow like a schoolgirl, then grabbed the shower gel from my overnight bag and headed to where a very cute and very wet Brit waited for me in the shower.

☆　☆　☆

In rehearsal later that morning, I saw Jack enter the back of the theater. He walked down to the front as I sang, his face changing as he saw me in my element. I also saw his eyes dart toward Michael, who was watching and taking notes from the front row, looking at me in a way that was becoming more and more familiar.

I finished the song, my voice ringing out clear and strong to the back of the house. "Hi, Sweet Nuts!" I yelled as the other actors began to leave the stage. He smiled sheepishly and raised a hand in greeting as the others gawked. Calling a grown man Sweet Nuts tended to make people look twice.

Leslie grinned at me. She'd grilled me relentlessly all morning, making me tell her every detail about how Jack and I met and how long we'd been dating. I told her everything, except of course the details I preferred to keep to myself. I did tell her we were keeping our relationship out of the public eye—not only for his sake, but for mine. I explained that our friends knew, and that was fine, but if asked in an official way, Jack was single.

She agreed, and as the rest of the cast found out, they also agreed to keep our little secret. Most of them had never even heard of Jack, and only a few were aware of the buzz his film was generating. I knew that would change in the next few weeks, and I was glad they could get to know him now, before he was on every talk show in America.

I jumped off the stage. "Hey." I smiled, closing the distance between us quickly.

"Hey, yourself," he answered, smiling back at me with that sexy grin.

I kissed him swiftly, and I heard Leslie swoon behind me. "Wow, wow, wow, wow . . ."

"Shut it, Leslie." I laughed, kissing on my Brit again.

"Ahem." Michael coughed, and I turned to look at him. "Jack, good to see you again. You having fun in New York?"

"So far, so good. Of course, we've barely left the hotel, but we're definitely having fun," Jack said, his hands drifting down to my ass.

I rolled my eyes, knowing I was in for another round of verbal dick measurement.

"Good, good. Grace, remember I need you Monday," Michael said pointedly.

"You *need her* Monday, do you?" Jack asked. I poked him in the side.

"We're working on one last round of rewrites, and I need her input," Michael said.

"Michael, we already discussed this. Does it have to be Monday? Can't it wait until after Jack leaves?" I said.

"When are you leaving, Jack?" Michael asked. "I mean, so I know when Grace is available."

"I'm leaving Tuesday night. As for whether Grace is available, you'll have to ask her," he said, his voice taking a distinctive tone.

These two . . .

"Okay. Michael, I'm available again Wednesday morning. If it's still cool with you, I'd really like the time until then to spend with Jack. Now, I'm going to get my bag. You two are both pretty, so play nice," I said, walking backstage to get my stuff. Jack gave me a playful swat on the ass as I moved away, earning him a shocked look from me.

Honestly.

Leslie followed, and as soon as we were out of earshot, she started laughing. "Holy shit, girl. Those two are totally fighting over you!"

"Oh, please. Michael's just concentrating on the show right now, and he wants to make sure everything's right when we open."

"Grace, are you fucking kidding me? Are you blind?" she shrieked.

"Hey, quit stirring the pot. There's nothing going on with me and Michael. You know how long we've known each other, and he tends to be a bit territorial. He was like this when we were in college too." I stopped, thinking about what I'd just said.

He was like this whenever I was *dating* anyone in college—every time I brought a new guy into our group of friends.

Oh man . . .

Seriously, Grace. Duh . . .

Leslie must have seen something on my face. "Holy shit, did something happen between you two back then?"

"Um, well—see, the thing is . . ." I started, wondering how to explain exactly what we were back then.

"I knew it. I freaking knew it! He's *totally* still diggin' on you, Grace. And damn, he's such a cutie! Fuck, girl, you have Jack Hamilton on one coast and Michael O'Connell on the other. Seriously, when I grow up, I want to be just like you."

I rolled my eyes. "Leslie, calm down—really. First of all, Jack is my boyfriend, and I love him very much. Michael's a great friend, and someone I'm really glad to have back in my life. As for what happened between us, that was years and years ago, and it isn't a part of what's going on here now. So enough with the love triangle stuff, okay?" I gave her a firm look.

She just smiled in a way that meant she wouldn't be letting this go anytime soon.

I sighed and grabbed my bag.

When I returned to the theater, the two men were engaged

in what looked like a very interesting conversation. I sidled up to them, Leslie in tow. "Okay, dickheads, enough boy talk. Jack, we ready to roll?"

"Ready when you are, love," he answered, taking my outstretched hand.

I said good-bye to Leslie, who was staring at Jack as though she wanted to pounce on him. He smiled at her, and I could tell he enjoyed watching her turn red. He was learning to revel in his new status as a heartbreaker.

I said good-bye to Michael, and as Jack shook his hand and told him he'd see him next visit, I looked at them nervously. I wanted them to be friends, but I wasn't sure that would ever happen.

Jack and I walked out of the theater, hand in hand. Once we were outside, Jack pulled me to him and hugged me tightly.

"Hey, George, what's with the rib cracking?" I laughed, struggling a little in his very tight grasp.

"Gracie, I love you so much."

"Mmm, I love you too," I murmured sweetly in his ear. My hands found their way into his hair, my nails scratching and soothing him. He relaxed his hold on me, but only slightly. I stroked his hair, scratched his scalp, and kissed his neck below his ear, the way I knew he liked.

He sighed, then pulled away from me slightly. "Grace, you've been holding out on me," he said in a warning tone.

"I have? About what?" I asked.

"Why the hell have you never sung like that for me before? That was amazing!"

I blushed. "I sing for you all the time," I protested, trying to make light of it.

"Not like that. I'm truly in awe. Not only are you sexy beyond belief, your talent is just, well, I am actually speechless!" he exclaimed.

"I'm glad you got to see some of what I've been working on. I really hope you can come back for the previews," I said. "They should be between your premieres."

"I wouldn't be anywhere but the front row. Do you think you'll have time to come to L.A. for my premiere?" he asked, sounding a little nervous.

He knew how I felt about all the cameras and paparazzi. He wouldn't be able to walk the red carpet with me, but I was very happy he wanted me there at all.

"You want me to come to your premiere?" I asked, smiling hugely.

"Silly girl, how could you even ask that question? You'll get to meet my family—at least my dad for sure," he said, laughing when he saw my expression change to panic-stricken. "I think it's only appropriate that you meet them. I know they're dying to meet you." He tugged on my arm, as I was now rooted to the spot.

"You want me to meet your family at the premiere of *Time* in Hollywood? And to recap, you're Jack Fucking Hamilton and you claim you're in love with me?" I said, cocking my head to one side.

"I *am* in love with you, Nuts Girl," he said, smiling.

I started pinching myself furiously.

"Hey, Crazy, you're freaking me out a little. Stop doing that." He laughed, holding my wrists at my sides.

"I'm trying to make myself wake up. There's no way in hell this is actually happening. It's too good!" I exclaimed, laughing.

"If you were dreaming, would you be feeling this?" he asked, kissing up my neck toward my ear.

"Mmm, I've had dreams like this, yes," I said, closing my eyes.

"Would you be feeling this?" he asked, sucking my earlobe between his teeth and nibbling. I twisted in his arms, my skin breaking out in goose bumps. He loved when my body reacted to his touch.

"Mmm, this is starting to feel very familiar." I threw my arms around his neck and pulled him closer.

"And if you were dreaming, would we be on our way to get frozen hot chocolate at Serendipity?" he whispered in my ear.

My eyes sprang open, and I shook my head to clear it.

"Thanks for refocusing me, Sweet Nuts. Let's hit it!"

"That's my girl." He laughed at me as I quickly hailed a cab and pushed him into it. He knew to never get in the way of Grace and her sweets.

☆ ☆ ☆

After a lovely lunch followed by some even lovelier frozen hot chocolate, we headed over to the park. I came running here at least three times a week, and although it was a very touristy place to visit, it was a great park. People who'd lived in Manhattan for years used it daily. It was really like everyone's backyard, in a city where hardly anyone *had* a backyard.

It was a gorgeous fall day, and with the leaves crunching underfoot and the smell of autumn in the air, it was easy to feel like we were out in the country. We spent the afternoon just walking and talking and holding hands. I'd relented and let him wear his stupid ball cap today for two reasons: One, it was chilly. Two, the cap made it harder for him to be recognized.

We were relaxed and happy, walking off the enormous amount of chocolate we'd consumed. At one point he laughed at me, saying that during our pig-out I'd been humming "White Christmas" while I slurped. He swore I had a penchant for singing Christmas carols under my breath. I didn't actually remember this, my attention having been totally focused on the delicious concoction. A frozen hot chocolate of that magnitude was a true indulgence, and I didn't miss a drop.

Now I was totally focused on the equally yummy Hamilton. We sat on a bench at the Plaza Hotel end of the park, holding hands and people watching. There were several kids playing by the edge of the little pond, and we laughed as we watched them kick around a soccer ball. Once, it came flying over to where we were sitting, and Jack jumped up to kick it back to them. The kids shouted their thanks, and he came back to sit next to me.

I was still thinking about meeting his family, his father especially. My mind kept bumping into it no matter how I tried to *not* think about it.

"Penny for your thoughts," he said.

"Thought you Brits used shillings and sixpence," I said.

"Do all Americans get their knowledge of British culture from *Mary Poppins*?"

"Yes, although I also got a bit from Dickens."

"Ah, yes. Another reliable source for current culture."

He laughed as I kissed him on the nose and we snuggled together for another moment.

"Nice deflection, Grace, but what are you thinking about?" he pressed.

"Honestly?"

"Yes, please," he encouraged.

"Meeting your family. It makes me a little nervous," I replied.

"Why nervous?"

"I dunno. Take your pick. I'm considerably older than you, you're about to be this huge star, not to mention the fact that I'm a Yank . . ." I trailed off, my words hanging in the air.

Jack was laughing, though. "A Yank? Seriously, where do you come up with this stuff?"

"*European Vacation*, this time. But seriously, Jack. What if your dad doesn't like me?"

"My dad loves any girl who can cook. He always said that was one of the reasons he fell in love with my mum. She used to make this shepherd's pie, and, oh, it was the best. She would—" He stopped, looking sad all of a sudden.

I wrapped my arms around his waist. "You were sixteen when she passed away, right?" I asked quietly.

He nodded.

"I bet she'd be proud of you right now. Look at everything you've accomplished at such a young age," I said, scratching his scalp the way I knew he liked. He leaned into my hand but was still quiet for a while.

"Grace, how come you never talk about your parents?" he asked suddenly. "You never mention them. Where are they?"

My hand stilled. "My mom died when I was a freshman in college—a boating accident. It happened fast. I didn't even make it home from school before she was gone. She was only forty-one." I closed my eyes, remembering how she used to make me scrambled eggs and toast every morning, without fail. All these years, and her breakfasts were still the first thing that came to mind when I thought about her. That and her perfume.

"I'm so sorry," he said, holding me closer.

"I'm sorry too—for you. What a pair we are." I laughed hollowly.

"And your dad? How did he take it?"

"You'd have to ask him, if you can find him. I haven't spoken to him since I was in third grade. He left my mom and me high and dry. No letters, no phone calls, nothing." My skin prickled a bit. I never talked about this stuff. It made me uncomfortable, and I didn't do uncomfortable.

"He just left?"

"Yes, my dad was a deadbeat. Can we talk about something else? No need to discuss," I said, just as the soccer ball came our way again. This time I rose and kicked it back, my foot connecting angrily and sailing the ball over the lot of them. A few of them cheered, and I curtsied. I sat down on the bench again, and we continued to watch.

"Cute kids," he said, watching them play.

"Yes," I replied.

"Do you want kids, Grace?" he asked, turning to look at me.

"What, right now? Today?" I teased, standing up and depositing myself on his lap. He made room for me, tucking me in with his arms around me and his chin on my shoulder.

"Not today, Crazy. Although later on today I'll be glad to demonstrate how babies are made." He laughed, cuddling me to him. "But really, do you want kids someday?"

"I don't know. I don't think so. I mean, I think if I wanted them, I'd probably have thought more seriously about it by now," I said. "What about you? Do you want kids someday?"

"Hmm, I don't think so either. I don't particularly care for children—not in the sense that I want any of my own," he said, kissing my fingertips.

"You might change your mind as you get older," I said.

"Don't you think *you* might change your mind?" he asked, pressing a kiss to my palm.

"I don't have all the years in front of me that you do. My choices are a little more finite. Maybe I will, but I doubt it." I laughed a little, and he looked at me curiously.

"It's funny that you're dating a woman in her thirties and you managed to find the one who doesn't have a biological clock ticking," I said, planting a kiss on top of his head and pulling him to his feet.

We began to walk back toward the Plaza to catch a cab.

"You really don't want kids, Grace? I mean, you seem like you'd make a great mom . . ." He trailed off.

"Yeah, I think I would too. But that doesn't mean I *should* have kids—does that make sense? There are plenty of women who have kids and do great with them, but who maybe in their heart of hearts didn't really want them. Not every woman is made to have a family. My friends feel like my family, and now there's this Brit who I'm taking care of. He takes up a lot of my time." I zipped his jacket up higher against the cold.

"Hmm . . . tell me more about this Brit," he said, wrapping his arm around my waist as we walked.

"He's quite handsome and very sweet. A little on the gay side, but then again, he *is* British," I continued.

"Of course, of course," he agreed.

"And I love him—quite a lot, actually," I finished, leaning my head against his arm as we walked.

"He sounds fantastic, obviously. Does he love you as well?"

"He says he does, and really, how could he not?" I giggled, doing a little pirouette on the path.

He caught my hand and pulled me back to him. "How could he not?" he confirmed, and kissed me.

Neither of us heard the clicking of the camera.

six

The rest of the weekend flew by, and it was Monday night before I knew it.

We'd spent the rest of Saturday afternoon in his hotel, passing more time in that blessed shower. You'd think we were part fish the way we splashed around. Saturday night we went to see a show. I had been saving *Wicked* to see with him. I knew he wasn't so fond of musicals, but I thought this one would hold his interest.

He enjoyed it, although he didn't sob like I did when Elphaba sang "Defying Gravity." Really, no one did. It seemed I would continue to make an ass of myself whenever live theater was concerned. I enjoyed the show so much I actually forgot Jack was there, and I was surprised to find him next to me at the end.

"You were lost in your own little world, Gracie. I watched you as much as I watched the show," he said, holding my hand

and helping me throw away all the crumpled tissues I'd shoved in my pockets and purse.

Sunday morning was chilly and wonderful. We spent the day at MoMA and went to Mott Street in Little Italy for dinner. We sat family style with other diners at a lovely old restaurant, passing plates and plates of food and carafes of cheap red wine.

Monday we had plans to sightsee, but we just couldn't seem to make it out of bed. We tried several times, but in the end gave up and gave in to our insatiable need. We ordered room service for all three meals that day. We didn't even leave the room to have housekeeping come in, although Jack did sneak out into the hallway (wrapped only in a sheet) to steal some chocolates off the maid's cart as she was making up the room across the hall.

Late Monday night, we did something we'd never done before.

Heavens no, not *that* . . .

We filled the giant tub with bubbles, turned on the jets, and took a bath together. Jack sat with his back against the marble, and I tucked contentedly between his legs, lying back against his chest. He ran the sea-wool sponge up and down my arms and squeezed the water and bubbles over my chest. Something about seeing my boobies covered in soap made him all kinds of happy, he said.

I could feel how happy he was.

I snuggled against him, the water lapping gently at my body, not needing anything else in the world. Being kind, I even let him share the lovely ice cream sundae perched on the side of the tub. Since I so rarely indulged like this (although I was kind of on a roll this weekend . . .), I tended to guard my goodies like a mama bear with her cubs. Still, I maneuvered the spoon up behind me and toward his mouth.

"Thank you," he said through a mouthful of ice cream and chocolate sauce.

"I thought I ordered nuts on this. Where are they?" I exclaimed, digging through the concoction.

"You're looking for nuts, miss?" he asked, trying to dip my hand below the water.

I laughed. "Not until we finish this lovely dessert. Then I'll be happy to attend to your personal nuts." Finally finding the hidden nuts I gave him another bite, then settled back to scoop up my own bite.

"Gracie, I don't know how you're not the size of a bus, the way you eat. I love it! Too many girls just eat lettuce and drink bottled water. It's nice to be with a real woman." He smoothed his hands along my skin under the water, along my stomach and hips, beginning to work his way toward my thighs and specifically what was between my thighs.

I stopped cold, the spoon clenched between my teeth. "What?" I asked, my breath stuck in my throat.

"You heard me. It's amazing that as much as you eat, you're not a little butterball—not that you couldn't stand to gain a little weight. I bet your tits would be even more fabulous . . ." He trailed off, kissing the back of my neck.

He must have felt how tense I was, because he stopped. "Grace? What is it?" he asked, trying to turn me around.

I removed the spoon from my mouth and set the ice cream down, then I faced him. "I look the way I do because I work my ass off. Why do you think I'm constantly going for a run, or going to the gym, or running off to another yoga class? You think it's easy to look like this? I have to stay ahead of everything I eat. Don't think for a second that I won't be at the gym as soon as you head back to L.A.," I said, my voice getting low again. I pulled myself out of the tub and shrugged into a robe, bubbles everywhere.

"Where are you going? What the hell just happened?" he asked, his eyes wide at my current state of crazy.

I went into the other room and grabbed my wallet, then came back into the bathroom, where he was looking dazed. I took a picture out and handed it to him. I watched as his eyes grew wide. He looked up at me, then back to the picture, then at me again. His eyes grew thoughtful, then sad.

"Grace," he said quietly, handing me back the picture.

I took it from him, wiping the bubbles off the edges before allowing myself to look at it. It was a picture of me from two years ago. Once I'd started making plans to lose weight, my trainer had taken a picture of me to keep with me in case I ever needed additional inspiration. It was me at my heaviest, and while you could tell it was me, there was a sadness in this picture that always made me refocus when I wanted to skip that early yoga class or get overly indulgent with my desserts. I never wanted to go back to that girl again, but there were days I felt she'd never left.

"So you see, the butterball comments hit a little close to home," I said, shoving the picture in my wallet. I went to put it back in the other room, and when I returned to the bathroom, he was wrapping a towel around his waist.

He sighed heavily. "Grace, this weekend seems to be nothing but miscommunications for both of us. I didn't say that to make you feel bad. How was I supposed to know you had a . . . um . . . well . . . a . . . ." He stammered, searching for the right words.

"A weight problem? A giant ass? Big ol' fatty thighs? You're right; you didn't know. Now you do. Will I always look like this? I hope so—at least for another few years, until gravity starts to take hold and I have to start getting Botox and everything else women have to do nowadays to stay young and beautiful," I said, feeling myself tense.

"You will never need Botox," he scoffed.

"Ha! You want me all frowny and haggard-looking? And what are you going to do when my precious boobs start to droop, huh? When you have rock-in-the-sock to hold on to every night—how sexy will that be?"

"Rock-in-the-what? Crazy, you are crazy," he soothed, crossing to me and pulling on my robe ties when I tried to walk away.

I looked at him for a moment, then hugged him fiercely. "Why the hell do you love me so much? Seriously, I am fucked up and nuts," I said into his chest, still wet from the bath.

I felt him chuckle. "You think I don't know you're nuts? Don't fool yourself. And like I've been telling you, I like nuts girls," he said, kissing the top of my head.

"Well, you sure can pick 'em, if that's what you're in to." I chuckled too. I couldn't believe we'd almost had another argument over something so silly.

Except it wasn't silly. It was part of my past, and it was something I thought about daily: when I tried to skip a run, when I thought about having an extra late-night snack. I was always a bag of Chex Mix away from a full-on food free-for-all, and even though Jack helped by munching the dreaded melba toasts, my need for careful control was always with me. I could never let down my guard, or I'd go back to exactly who I was before. And in this industry, that was as good as suicide.

71

"Hey, Crazy?" he asked, his voice muffled by my hair.

"Mmm-hmm?"

"You know I love your body. I mean, come on, you're beautiful. But it's *you,* my Grace, who I fell in love with—the Chex-eating, foul-mouthed, funny girl. And nothing's going to change that."

Tears pricked at the back of my eyes, and I blinked them away. I looked up at him, wet hair falling in his eyes, strong arms encircling me, smelling like bubble bath and chocolate sauce.

"George, I couldn't possibly love you more."

"Me too, Gracie," he said, kissing me softly.

Our kisses became more urgent, and soon his hands were inside my robe. My skin tightened as it always did when his hands were on me, and I found myself being walked backward over to the bathroom counter.

He spun me about so we both faced the mirror, and our eyes met. He slowly untied my robe and parted it, placed his hands on my hips, and pulled me back against him. I could feel him, and he was more than ready.

With his eyes still locked on mine, he gently removed the robe and let it fall to the ground. I watched him in the mirror as he watched his own hands travel over my body. I flinched slightly, reflexively trying to hide my body from him—the way I would have done years ago. He was having none of it. His hands, sure and strong, urged me to stand tall. He moved them from my hips up to my arms, then gently glided them back down from my shoulders to my elbows, finally grasping my hands and bringing them up over my head to tangle in his hair.

"Beautiful," he murmured as he kissed my ear. I shivered.

He returned his hands to my body. Again he let his hands move across my skin, trailing his fingers down my arms and cupping my breasts in his hands.

"Beautiful," he whispered, kissing my other ear. I moaned softly.

He let his hands move farther down my body, resting on the gentle curves of my hips, his perfect fingers splaying out to capture as much of my skin as he could hold. "Beautiful," he groaned, his lips hovering near the base of my neck as his gaze moved from my hips back up to my eyes.

My skin was on fire from his caresses. His hands began one more trip, gently moving down to my thighs, which he nudged open with his leg. I arched my back, pressing my bottom into him as he brought his hands between my legs and stroked me. We both moaned, feeling how ready I was for him.

"Beautiful," he hissed, and kissed my shoulder.

I watched him in the mirror, his breath getting faster. Pressing back against him again, I watched a wicked grin creep across his face. Hmmm . . .

I let my hands untangle from his hair and slowly placed them on the counter in front of me. Never leaving his gaze, I raised one eyebrow and leaned forward.

He got it.

He pushed my legs open farther, and I leaned farther forward on the counter. He slid inside me, and it felt so wonderful, I struggled not to close my eyes. He filled me completely, and while his fingers worked my sex, he stroked the magnificent spot inside that was named for him again and again.

"You. Are. Beautiful," he whispered in my ear, punctuating each word with a thrust.

"Jack . . . oh, God, Jack . . ." I chanted as I watched the two of us in the mirror. This was totally new. To have him inside me like this felt totally different. And to be able to watch us together was amazingly erotic.

He continued to murmur "beautiful" over and over as he made love to me with such passion and caring. When we were both close, I leaned back against him, feeling his warm skin against mine. I closed my eyes, feeling my insides contract as he crashed into me, bringing my orgasm, sweet and hot.

I cried out his name as he altered his stroke, hitting me in a different place and bringing a second and third orgasm in rapid succession. Then I watched his face through blurry eyes as he came inside me, collapsing against me with the word *beautiful* on his perfect lips.

He leaned on me, breathing heavily as he snuck his hands around, cupping my breasts. "That was—"

"Beautiful," I finished, smiling at him in the mirror.

We stayed up that night watching a *Friends* marathon, laughing uproariously. But when the episode came on with Monica in the fat suit, he clammed up.

"Don't be an idiot," I said. "Monica in the fat suit is hilarious. I'll be offended if you don't laugh," I said, hitting him with a pillow.

He gave in, and we both laughed at her dancing with the sub sandwich. When we finally went to sleep that night—me on my side, him behind me, with boobies in hand—he said, "Grace, explain what rock-in-the-sock has to do with your breasts."

"What?"

I'd been almost asleep.

"When you were talking earlier about your boobs drooping—what do socks have to do with it?" he asked, his chin on my shoulder.

"Picture a sock, and then drop a rock in it. What happens to the sock?" I was glad he couldn't see my rueful smile.

He was quiet a moment, then drew his breath in quickly. "Ew, Grace, that's awful," he muttered, gaining a tighter hold on my still-firm boobies.

I laughed. "Don't worry, love. I'll keep them worthy of your devotion for a long time to come. You don't want to know what I have to do to keep my oonie nice and tight."

"Jesus, Grace. Enough." He cuddled me tighter.

I laughed again, thinking back to the days when push-up bras were just for proms and Kegels were just a myth in *Cosmopolitan*.

☆　☆　☆

And here it was. Tuesday afternoon already. He didn't want me to ride with him to the airport. He said it was silly for me to go all the way there just to turn around and have to ride back into the city.

I protested, but he won. So we waited in my apartment for his car to come, spending the last few minutes cuddled on the couch. I sat on his lap, and he had his arms around me, his head tucked into the space between my neck and shoulder. I played with his hair, and he traced circles on my back as the time ticked by.

"So, you'll be back when you're on the press tour, right? That isn't so far away—only a few weeks."

"Not too long. And then back to L.A. for the premiere, and you'll be there for that, right?" he asked, kissing my neck.

"I already told Michael I might need that weekend off. It's really close to the preview dates, but it should be okay. Even if I have to fly out and back within twenty-four hours, I wouldn't miss your big night." I smiled, kissing the top of his head in return.

"And then I'll be back here for your opening night, and I might even be able to stay an extra day. Holly's coming for your show, right?"

Hmm . . . I hadn't spoken to her this weekend, and there were going to be some choice words when we talked. I was still upset that she hadn't told me about Marcia.

"Yes, she'll be there. She even talked about coming out for Thanksgiving, since I won't be able to make it home."

"That's right, Thanksgiving. You Americans sure do like your holidays, don't you?" He nibbled at my ear.

"Yeah, you'll have to explain Boxing Day to me sometime," I sassed, scrunching into a little ball at the feel of his lips teasing my skin.

"Sorry, I know that tickles. I'll behave." He laughed, tucking me back onto his lap. We were quiet a moment, and then he said, "So I think the worst is over, don't you?"

"The worst?" I asked.

"I mean, we went several weeks without each other, but in the next month or so we'll see each other more often. I think we handled the separation quite well, yes?"

Sometimes I forgot just how young he was, and other times I couldn't forget no matter how hard I tried. He needed reassurance just as much as I did. This was just as tough on him as it was on me.

"Yes, I think we did great. And I do think the worst is over. Think about all the time we'll have together when the promotional stuff is through—you can stay here as long as you want," I said, grinning big.

"Oh—well, as soon as the premieres are over, I'm headed to London for the holidays and probably most of January. When will you be done with your show?" he asked.

"I don't know yet. Depending on the reviews it gets, we could be up throughout the holidays, or we could already be closed. It's all still up in the air."

"Well, we don't have to decide anything right now. It'll all get figured out," he said with an air of finality.

Damn. I missed our days in L.A. together—before he was being shunted off everywhere to promote his film and when all I had to worry about was auditions and turning in my freelance work on time. When we could spend all the time we wanted together. We hadn't fully realized just how much time we'd had. We'd been spoiled.

Everything happening to us professionally was amazing, but personally, I craved a drive up the coast and Fatburger like nobody's business.

Just then his phone beeped. It was the driver waiting downstairs.

My throat tightened. It seemed like I'd just said good-bye to him in L.A., and now I was doing it again. He reached for his bag, but before he could pick it up, I threw my arms around him again for another tight hug.

"I love you," I said, crushing myself to him.

"I love you too, Grace," he replied, lifting my chin to kiss me softly on the lips.

We took the elevator down, holding hands. Actually, I had

threaded my arm through his and had a firm hold on both his hands. I didn't want to let go. When we got outside, I saw a town car waiting. I gestured to the backseat and teased, "Sure you don't want me to come with you?"

His eyes lit up, but then he smiled sadly. "No, love, you stay here. I don't think I could handle the plane ride with a send-off like that. We'll save it for when I come back."

He handed his bag to the driver and pulled me tightly to him, resting his chin on the top of my head, his hands firmly on my hips.

"Miss me, okay? And tell those fangirls to quit grabbing your ass, or I might have to do a little ass kicking," I warned, hugging him as tightly as I could.

I could feel him laughing. "You have no idea how much I will miss you, Crazy." He sighed, pulling back for one last kiss.

"Call me when you land," I called after him.

"I will, love." He slipped into the car.

I watched it pull away, my fingers at my lips—the last place he'd kissed me. Then I went up to my apartment and started to clean furiously, keeping the tears at bay. When I finally finished hours later, it was late. I took a quick shower and climbed into bed. As I settled in, I noticed I'd missed Jack's call while I was in shower.

I dialed voice mail and heard his sweet voice in my ear:

"Hey, Nuts Girl. Just landed and there were actually paparazzi at the airport. Can you believe that? Bizarre. Anyway, you're probably asleep, but I miss you already. Call me in the morning. Love you. Say hi to the boobies for me. Bye."

The tears flowed.

seven

$\mathcal{I}$ woke up the next morning puffy-eyed from crying but determined. Determined to work harder at trusting him and our relationship. Determined to focus on the amazing show I was currently part of. And determined to call out Holly on the Great Marcia Redirect, as I was now calling it in my head. Because I wasn't dramatic at all.

No, not at all . . .

I had an early rehearsal, so with the time difference I wasn't able to call her until we took a midmorning break. I knew I'd catch her at home.

"Hey, asshead," she answered. "How's that fine oonie this morning? Did Jack leave you able to walk?"

I imagined her in her kitchen, still in her pj's, drinking her first cup of coffee. She always checked the entertainment sites on her laptop while she had breakfast to make sure none of her clients had been arrested in the night—or caught without panties climbing out of a limo. That had already happened several times this year. What was with these young starlets and their refusal to wear drawers?

"Yes, dillhole, I can walk. We had a great time. Although we did have a bit of an argument. You want to explain to me why you didn't tell me about this whole Marcia thing? Jack told me your plan," I said, my voice going icy.

She was quiet for a minute, then I heard her exhale slowly.

"I'm sorry I didn't tell you myself. I went back and forth about that, but I thought it should come from Jack. If he didn't tell you, I was going to—"

"He *did* tell me," I interrupted. "But only after I saw the pictures on TMZ. That was awful, Holly." My stomach clenched again as the images played on the inside of my eyelids in CinemaScope.

"Jesus, Grace. I'm so sorry. He promised he would tell you. That's the only reason I didn't. He would've told you anyway; I know he would. You do believe him that there's nothing going on, right? I mean, he's missing you fierce."

She waited to see if I would thaw.

I wasn't ready for that yet. "I believe him; I just don't like it. But I get it. She has a movie; he has a movie—press is press, right?" My lip curled a little.

"It is *exactly* that. Just press," Holly said. "Once I thrashed him for hanging out with her, the only thing we could do was use it. The more his fans are discussing her and whether they're dating, the less attention there'll be on anyone else he might be dating—namely, the unidentified redhead who was photographed with our Mr. Hamilton in New York a few days ago."

Gulp.

"What?" I asked.

"Yep, it's all over TMZ this morning. I can't believe they waited three whole days to post it. Did you two take a walk in Central Park?" she asked, her tone professional now.

"Yes," I said quietly.

"Grace," she sighed.

My anger bubbled over. "Dammit, Holly, there's no reason I can't go for a walk with my boyfriend like anyone else! This isn't fair!" I yelled, grabbing my laptop. I wanted to see these photos for myself.

"Hey, don't yell at me. We discussed this, and for the record, Jack wants you two public. He doesn't care what the press says. He thinks it's 'bollocks' when I tell him he can't talk about you. He doesn't fully understand what that would create for you, though. And if you thought the cougar comment was cruel, they'd go for the jugular with his dating an older woman. If you'll recall, *you* didn't want the press either. *You* wanted to remain the unidentified redhead."

I sighed. "I do." The pictures came up on my computer then. Luckily, they weren't as bad as I feared: one of us holding hands, and the other with his hand on my back as I gazed up at him, smiling. They were great shots true, but I had trouble focusing on that since I noticed right away how giant my ass looked. Bad angle? Let's hope so . . . But I still felt a little sick at the thought of being the unidentified redhead with the large bum.

The pictures made me happy and sad. I loved seeing the two of us together, and it was oddly reassuring that someone could candidly capture what we were really like—obviously in love and full of schmaltz. But—is that *really* what I looked like from the rear? I also hated that we were on a website I checked daily to get a celebrity fix . . . and maybe troll a little for flaws. Now someone could be out there trolling for mine. Karma's a bitch.

Luckily, there were no snarky captions. Just a mention that Jack Hamilton had been spotted in New York's Central Park with a redheaded gal pal. I snorted. Why do they always say "gal pal"? Who talks like that?

"Grace! You still there?" Holly called through the phone.

"Yes, I'm still here. I'm looking at the pictures. Jesus, Holly. What are we going to do?" I asked, despair creeping into my voice.

"Does this mean you aren't mad at me anymore?" she asked.

"Ah, jeez, fucko, I was never mad at you, just pissed you didn't tell me. I know you've got my back. I just hate being surprised by this stuff. It was really bad when I saw those pictures. Then when he told me you two had discussed it—I don't know. It felt like I was being handled or something."

"I know. Next time I'll make sure you know as soon as I know. Deal?" she asked.

"Deal."

"As for what we're going to do. We're not going to do anything. He'll continue to deny he has a girlfriend, and if any other pictures of him and Marcia surface, who cares? You know which side his bread is buttered on—and his crumpet, for that matter. It's probably a good thing you're not in the same city right now. I'd get a call that you'd been caught going at it under the Hollywood sign." She laughed dryly.

I paused a moment. "Holly?"

"Yes?"

"Are you sure there's nothing going on between them?"

"Grace, if I thought for a second there was, he would be short one manager. And two nuts."

"No, no, don't remove the nuts. I've grown rather fond of them," I warned, grateful to be reminded that she would always have my back, first and foremost.

"Pervert. And, girl, you should see how much his fans are hating on her! They can't stand Marcia. They're crucifying her online. Poor thing. I wonder if her management team will rethink this—although more people definitely know who she is now."

"Pfft. No more Marcia talk. It's giving me heartburn."

Besides, I had other things to worry about. Like the way my butt looked in those pictures. I shifted in my chair a little. Was I imagining it, or did my pants feel a little snug this morning?

"Take some Tums and suck it up, ya little fruitcake."

And so it went. Holly and I were fine, and she started sending me early press releases and pictures from the photo shoots Jack had been doing for months. As the pre-movie hype machine began to roll, all the photos Holly had been hoarding were slowly released to the press. It had quickly become clear that when Jack was featured in a magazine, sales went up. Simple as that. He was going to be quite a hot commodity, and Holly had her hands full with new press inquiries and requests for additional interviews—not to mention the demand for photos, photos, photos! I was amazed at Holly's savvy in stockpiling them earlier, since there weren't enough hours in the day for Jack to pose for all the photos now. Brilliant. And I was lucky: I got a sneak peek at a lot of the images before they were released.

My goodness, he was pretty.

I especially liked the ones from a shoot in Santa Barbara. Maybe it was wishful thinking, but I swear I saw something different in those pictures. He always looked perfectly shagable, but in those pictures? Mmm . . . They were taken the day after we had our first boom-boom, and I swear on that he looked . . .

Pleased.

Sated.

Wicked.

Freshly done.

In love?

Sigh. Yes. In love. He looked in love.

And still impossibly horny . . .

Holly also sent me the interviews he was doing. Most evenings just before bed, I went through all the new Jack goodies she'd sent me, followed by a check to see what was where on the Internet. Some of his interviews were just priceless; they really captured him. The female reporters often got quite flirty (who could blame them?), and once, when asked whether he preferred blondes or brunettes, Jack replied, "It depends."

"Depends on what?" the reporter asked, leaning forward and seeming to forget she was on live TV.

"Well, are they all lined up and I get to choose, like a buffet? What are my options?" Jack asked seriously.

She didn't get the joke, poor thing, but after that, the buffet line was the most-downloaded sound bite on the Internet for three weeks straight.

See what I mean? Priceless.

Jack and I had agreed that I was never to take things personally when he said he wasn't seeing anyone. And, in fact, he was now using the interviews to talk directly to me.

"Listen up, Nuts Girl. When I say, 'I don't have a girlfriend,' what I want you to hear in that head of yours is, 'I love you, Grace,'" he instructed on the phone late one night. "When you hear me say, 'No, I'm not seeing anyone right now,' what you need to hear is, 'Yes, I am, and she has the best tits in the free world.' Can you do that, please?"

"Yes, sir. I'll listen for your secret messages. Jeez, this is so cloak-and-dagger. You'd think you were a spy or something." I laughed.

"Maybe we can role-play that scenario next time I see you—although I'm not sure how you'd take to being dipped entirely in gold."

This quickly turned into a discussion of whether I would indulge his Bond fantasies in the future, although frankly I think he just enjoyed torturing me with the words *Pussy Galore.*

He really got into the girlfriend question now, and he relished finding new ways to make sure I knew he was thinking of me. I found I could tell when he was really missing me, because he'd deny it more forcefully, sometimes adding, "Girls never talk to me."

I made sure to give him a little more phone boom-boom on those nights.

Rehearsals were going really well, and the show was coming together. Michael was finally pleased with the tone of the script, and his rewrites were limited now to simple phrasing changes. It was a real show.

We worked exclusively in a small black-box theater, using a limited stage since we weren't putting up a full production. The show relied heavily on its music and the work of the actors to demonstrate what it could be, if it were to receive full backing. The process was thrilling, and as we approached the preview dates, I became more and more nervous.

I was relying heavily on Michael for guidance, as his vision for my character, Mabel, was absolute. He leaned on me for moral support as well, since this was his first attempt at a musical of any kind. He had a writing partner for the score, but the spoken words, the lyrics, the melodies, were all Michael O'Connell.

We'd slipped back into our old college ways. The shorthand we used made it infuriating for anyone else to try to get a word in edgewise when we were on one of our tangents, cracking each other up. We argued about music, movies, politics—oh boy, did we argue about politics. This subject almost caused an actual fight one day at lunch, when I threatened to remove his Adam's apple with my spork if he didn't agree with what I said about healthcare. Needless to say, people stopped wanting to dine with us.

I'd forgotten how thoroughly I used to rely on him back then: he was like my own cute little moral compass. He called me on my shit, he extolled my virtues when I needed propping up, and he knocked me down a few pegs when I got too big for my britches. Now that we were adults, we'd both mellowed, and I realized the quirky emo boy I knew in my twenties had evolved into a fully formed, wonderfully smart and funny man in his thirties. Although he'd kept the idiosyncrasies that would forever link him to that boy in the Ministry T-shirt, he was all grown up.

He was a brilliant businessman who conducted his business in old Timberland boots, faded jeans, and a North Face hoodie—while chewing Fruit Stripe gum. He had investors lining up to consider backing this show, and he did it all with the same charm and subtlety that had won over the girls back in the day. He was incredibly charming, and the years had only intensified his draw on the opposite sex.

Hot guy? Of course. Funny hot guy? All the more enticing.

I was his gut check when he needed a reminder that the show was fantastic—and he really had written an amazing show. He was my gut check when I got nervous about all the investors and critics coming to see the show (and me) in mere weeks.

Christ in a sidecar—critics!

But he handled me, and I handled him. That's what friends do. Our friendship was symbiotic, complementary— and, I slowly realized, becoming a wee bit blurry around the edges.

I knew what had been going on when Jack was in town. It just took Leslie to drag it out of the Drawer and into my face. The fact that I pushed my own shit to the side meant sometimes I pushed other people's fairly obvious shit off to the side too. Back in the day, Michael had been a little territorial when it came to me, and we'd fallen into our old ways so quickly when I came to New York that it seemed perfectly logical that he would react that way to Jack. But now I was forced to face the fact that there was clearly more going on.

☆　☆　☆

Michael's sister, Keili, came to town about a week after Jack's visit, and I was thrilled to see her. She was a few years older than us, but she had gone to the same college. Holly and I used to spend the night at her apartment freshman year when we needed to get out of the dorm. This usually meant Michael would spend the night too, and since it was college, this meant we all ended up snuggling on Keili's futon in the living room. We passed the bong, ate ramen, listened to Alanis, and talked about what we wanted to be when we grew up.

I was running a little late for rehearsal and came dashing in babbling apologies. I saw a pretty brunette talking to Michael at the front of the theater, and when she turned, I saw that it was Keili. She looked the same: sparkling brown eyes, sweet loving face . . . and a giant belly. My eyes flew open in astonishment as I raced down the aisle.

"Keili!" I exclaimed, hugging her fiercely.

"Grace, it's so good to see you," she said, with an equally forceful hug.

"Jesus, you're huge!" I said, taking in her very pregnant state.

"Ugh, I know. Four more weeks and then he's out of me." She grimaced.

"He? It's a boy?" I asked, smiling at her glowing-but-frowning face.

"Oh yeah. Add that to the two kids we already have at

home, and you'll see why I'm never allowing my husband to have *S-E-X* with me again." She laughed ruefully.

"You might want to check with Shane on that one, sis. I don't know that any man is happy when you take away the *S-E-X*," Michael said, and I turned to see him, arms full of toddler.

"Who is this?" I asked, walking over to see.

"This little rugrat is my niece Abigail," he said, turning her upside down as she giggled and squealed.

"Stop it, Uncle Michael. You stop it!" she said, red-faced.

He turned her right side up and placed her on the ground. She ran away, spinning slightly as she caught her balance, and then continued on her path, weaving back and forth between the rows.

"So what is she, like, six?" I asked.

"She's three," Michael chided, looking at me incredulously.

"Oh, shit, anyone under fourth grade looks the same to me. Can they read at that age?" I frowned, crinkling my nose. I truly was clueless.

"Shit, shit, shit, shit . . ." I heard Abigail chattering as she ran back and forth.

Michael raised his eyebrows at me. "Grace, you can't swear around kids. Either spell it or, better yet, just think before you speak."

Keili laughed, watching the exchange.

"Sorry, I didn't mean it." I blushed furiously.

"Don't let him fool you," said Keili. "Who do you think taught her the word *asshole*?" She mouthed the last word.

Now that I was not the only one blushing, I turned back to Keili. "So you have another at home too?"

"Yes, Oliver is almost five. He stayed at home with Daddy today. He's getting over a bad cold," she explained. Her ears perked up as we all heard a big bang from the end of a row. Seven seconds later, we heard Abigail cry.

"That's the I'm-more-scared-than-hurt cry. I'll get her," Michael said, walking briskly in the direction of Abigail's newly red face as it appeared over the back of the last chair.

We watched him go to her and pick her up. He held her tight against his chest and told the nasty chair that bonked her in the head to leave his Abigail alone.

I smiled, watching him with her. Keili caught me and smiled her own secret grin. The two of us caught up for a few minutes, and she was very pleased to learn Michael and I had become close again. The whole family was thrilled he was working in New York. They hailed from Connecticut and were glad to have him close to home.

"And, Grace, he was so totally floored when you turned up for that audition. It worked out perfectly. I always hated how you two ended things," she said.

Keili had heard the entire story from both sides. Ultimately, as Michael and I lost touch, she and I had as well. But she was always a fan of the two of us, and one of the few who saw our friendship for what it truly was back then: more than friendship.

"I hated how we ended things too. But that's all in the past. I'm just glad we can work together now. It's been so long since I've had a great guy friend, and it's been wonderful to go through this process with him," I said, watching as Michael now showed Abigail the lighting above the stage and how to move the follow spot.

He was so great with her: calm and attentive, relaxed and happy. And she adored her uncle Michael. I found myself watching her as well. She was really funny, curious about everything, asking question after question. Michael was patient, answering every question with the same careful detail he gave everyone else. He caught me watching them and smiled over the top of her head as he carried her across the back of the theater.

"And now you live here in New York! That's so great. We'll get to spend so much more time together. Once I have this baby I'll be able to come into the city more often," Keili prattled on.

"Well, I wouldn't say I *live* here. I live in L.A. In fact, I just finished remodeling a house there that I bought last spring, and I can't wait to get back to it when this is all over. It's still a work in progress, but I love it." I sighed, my face breaking into the smile I always got when I thought of my cozy bungalow in the canyon.

"Oh, I thought you were living here now. At least that's what Michael said."

"Well, that's mostly true. I mean, I'm here until the show is over, and then we'll have to wait and see what happens with it. I'm having a blast out here, but I love L.A. It's my home," I said.

She looked at me for a moment, then suddenly grimaced and rolled her eyes. "Jeez, guy, settle down in there," she warned, taking a sip of her water and patting her stomach.

"Is he . . . what is it that they do? Kick?" I asked, looking at her stomach nervously.

"Yeah, you can say that again. He kicks and kicks so much, I must be cooking up a soccer player in here. Oof!" She rubbed her belly.

I watched her hand curiously, wondering what it felt like to have a baby rolling around inside you, kicking. Weird.

"Yes, you can." She smiled.

"Huh?" I asked, my eyes snapping up to hers.

"You want to feel, right?"

"Oh, I don't know. I mean . . . would that be strange?" I asked, backing away a little.

"Grace, you used to stand guard while I peed on the side of the road. Nothing is strange." She laughed, grabbing my hand and placing it on her belly.

"Wait, I don't know if I should— Whoa. Wait, is that . . . is that a . . . kick?" I asked, eyes wide. It didn't feel like a kick exactly but more like a flutter. I imagine it would feel like a kick if it were my bladder taking the beating, though. Fascinating.

This felt strange.

I'd seen pregnant women walking around every day of my life, and not once did I ever feel the compulsion to put my hand on there and *feel*. But this felt strangely normal. Stranger than that, it felt . . . nice?

"Feels cool, doesn't it?" I heard Michael ask. I looked at him with the deer-in-the-headlights eyes and nodded.

He stood close to me, Abigail in his arms. He smiled.

I smiled back.

"That's my brother in there," Abigail explained, looking from my hand to my face.

"It is? Does that mean you're going to be a big sister?" I asked her, smiling.

"Yep," she answered.

"Abigail, this is my friend Grace. Can you say hi?" Michael asked, leaning her toward me.

I offered her my hand, and she shook it like a little grown-up.

"Hi, Abigail," I said.

"Hi, Grace. Your hair is red," she said promptly, pulling at a curl that had fallen out of my bun.

"Yes it is, and your hair is blond. You have very pretty hair, Miss Abigail." I laughed, crossing my eyes at her.

She giggled. "You're funny," she said, looking at Michael for approval. "She's funny, Uncle Michael."

"Yeah, she's pretty funny," he said, then winked at me.

"She's *pretty*, too," Abigail crooned.

Michael flushed and cleared his throat, suddenly flustered. "Yes, Abigail, she's very . . . pretty." He hesitated, then finished with, "Just like *you!*" and gave her a raspberry on the cheek.

She screamed and kicked to be let down. Off she ran, back to playing in the rows.

"She's supersweet, Keili. And you, Uncle Michael, you sure have a way with her. Although you always have preferred blondes," I joked, poking the hair back into my clip.

"Not so much blondes," he said softly, smiling his shy smile. Then he went to help Abigail investigate a coloring book.

Again, I was caught up in watching the two together. I became vaguely aware of someone calling my name.

"Grace! Hey, Grace!"

"What's that?" I answered, distractedly.

"Didn't you hear me? I was asking if you ever thought about having kids," Keili said.

"Wow, that's twice in as many weeks. What's going on with the universe?"

"Someone else was asking you about having kids?" she asked, digging through her bag to find crayons for Abigail, who then took them to Michael.

"Yes, actually my boyfriend and I were talking about it," I

said, smiling as I always did when I used the word *boyfriend* to describe Jack.

"Oh yes, Michael mentioned you were seeing some guy. Quite a bit younger than you, I hear?" she asked, her face very curious.

"He's younger than me, but it's actually pretty great. He's an actor too. He's—well, I hate to use this word, but he's *awesome*." I smiled again, thinking of my George.

"How much younger?" she prompted.

I sighed, irritated that everyone was so preoccupied with this—including myself.

"Twenty-four."

"Oh, well, hell—have your fun then, girl! For now . . ."

"For now? What does that mean?" I asked, looking at her carefully.

"Exactly what I said. Have fun! I'm a little envious of a fling with a young guy—wow. But I mean, what can you possibly have in common with a twenty-four-year-old? Other than S-E-X . . ." She sighed, smiling at the thought of S-E-X with a twenty-four-year-old, no doubt.

I knew what she meant, and since I'd known her so long, I didn't take offense. But Jack and I had more in common than just the S-E-X, didn't we? Sure we did.

Keili stayed for rehearsal, and we spent a little more time together over lunch. She promised to e-mail and keep me updated on the baby. She was due right before the show went up, so it was doubtful she'd make it back to the city before she gave birth.

I was very glad to have seen her, but she'd planted a seed.

She'd planted several.

eight

*J*ack had started his worldwide promotional tour for *Time*. He was truly amazed at how many fans turned up to see him everywhere he went—and he was more than a little freaked out by it.

"Grace, it was just this blast of screaming. I could barely tell which end was up. I couldn't even tell where it was coming from. And then the outside doors opened while I was going through the hotel, and there they all were," he explained late one night, calling from his hotel in Chicago.

"I'm not surprised, love. You're their Joshua. They love you." I sighed, wishing I were there with him.

"It's just so weird. I mean, last year I could barely get into a casting director's office, and now?"

"Hey, you're about to have Hollywood by the balls. When this movie opens you'll be *bankable*. Everyone's gonna want to work with you. Wait and see."

"I know, I just . . . Jesus, if they only knew—" he started to say.

"If they only knew what? If they only knew you were an amazing musician? If they only knew you're the funniest motherfucker this side of London? If they only knew how much you love your Fatburger?"

"Please. No one cares that I like Fatburger." He chuckled.

"Oh, really? I know how the minds of teen girls operate. I guarantee, if you mention your favorite fast food, at some point it will be mentioned again. Us girls love that stuff. I still remember who Joey McIntyre's favorite singer was from back in 1991." I laughed, remembering how I used to read *BOP* and *Teen Beat* cover to cover.

"Girls are all mental. And somehow I ended up with the craziest one of all," he teased.

"Tread carefully there, or I'll make you watch my *Hangin' Tough Live* tape."

"Tape? Like an actual videotape? Wow, like, from the eighties?"

"You're on thin ice, fucko." I tried to stifle a yawn, but he caught it.

"You need to get some sleep, love. You sound exhausted. How are the rehearsals going?"

"They're good. Everything is pretty well set. No more rewrites, so it's getting easier." I snuggled under the covers. This was the time of night I missed him most.

"You'll be ready to open?" he asked, covering his own yawn.

"Yes, I think so. Sweet Nuts, you sound tired too. Why don't we go to sleep?"

"That sounds good. If I were there, what do you think we'd be doing now?" he asked.

I heard his covers rustling. Somehow, knowing we were both doing the same thing made me feel better. "Hmm, right about now you'd be turning me on my side."

"Yes?"

"And sneaking your hands under my shirt."

"Mmm-hmm."

"And now you'd probably be surrounding my boobies with your hands."

"Definitely."

"And now you'd be groaning."

"Because your boobies feel so fantastic?"

"No, because I just turned on *Golden Girls*, and it's the episode where Rose tells Dorothy and Blanche about the Great Herring War."

"And on that note, I will say good night. Say good night, Gracie."

"Good night, Gracie."

I could hear a click as he turned out his light.

"I love you, Jack."

"I love you too, Grace."

☆　☆　☆

The next week was hell for both of us. I was in daily rehearsals all day and usually well into the night. He was on his monster promo tour all over the country. I checked in on him each day via the Internet, and my Sweet Nuts looked exhausted. But he was having fun too. As a great tie-in to the time-traveling aspect of the film, the studio had booked personal appearances for Jack in the science centers and museums across the country. These places had never seen such giddy crowds! This was truly the most exciting thing he'd ever gone through, and when he told me how nervous he was, or how much it freaked him out when everyone screamed at him, I simply reminded him that this was awesome.

He was experiencing something hardly anyone in the world could appreciate, and the more he gave to his fans, the more they loved him. They loved that he said whatever he wanted, that he was self-deprecating, that he was funny and silly—and, boy, did they love that he was British.

"I'm just about to get in the shower. What's your schedule like today?" I asked one day when he called to check in. He was somewhere in the Midwest, although he wasn't sure exactly where. Different city, different hotel every day.

"Mmm, taking a shower are you?"

"Yes, George, settle down. Although I do miss showering with you," I said, knowing the reaction I'd get.

"Stop it. Killing me!"

"You know how much I love to wash your hair. It makes me a little crazy," I purred into the phone, grinning like a cat. "That's something only I get to do."

"Maybe I should include that in the interview I have this afternoon. I can tell them all about this nuts girl that gets off washing my hair while I hold on to her boobies—for balancing purposes only," he teased.

"You wouldn't dare. That hair and those coconuts are mine and mine alone," I laughed.

"Mmm, don't remind me, Grace. Not right now. I have a meet and greet in twenty minutes, and I don't think I could explain away my current state of excitement."

"Easy there, trigger. Only two more days and then you can channel your excitement my way."

He was going to be in town for literally twenty-four hours, at least sixteen of which were taken up by promotional and press obligations. I would be in rehearsals. The only time we'd have together would be the night. Which was fine by me; I'd take what I could get.

I'd watched daily as his confidence grew and the mobs increased. He'd had to start traveling with security, since each night his hotel was crawling with Joshua lovers. He used aliases at each hotel, never checking in under Jack Hamilton. Once he used my name—a dangerous little game. A few times he used a combination of Holly's name and mine, and then? Then he really starting having fun with it.

In the same week, in different cities across the country, if you were looking for Jack Hamilton, you could have found him under the names:

> George McHair
> Johnny Nuts
> Sheridan McGeorge

And, my personal favorite:

> Sophia Patrillo

Finally, he was in New York. I was on pins and needles all day, not only because he was here but also because I didn't know *when* exactly I was going to get to see him. His costar Rebecca was in town as well for this part of the movie tour, and we'd all planned to meet at an Italian restaurant for dinner. This time he was staying at the Plaza.

Nice.

We texted most of the day. He was all over town—on *Today* at *Seventeen* magazine, MTV Studios, radio stations—you name it and he was there, ending the day with a Super Sexy Scientist Guy event at the American Museum of Natural History. One of his last texts made me blush . . . a lot.

Grace, I'm going to fuck you until you can't see straight tonight. Are you ready for that, Crazy?

Sweet mother-of-pearl . . .

George, Get. Over. Here. As. Soon. As. You. Can. Make me see God!

Last one:

Grace, will pick you up at the theater at 9 for dinner. Will be in a black town car. Panties are unnecessary.

That motherfucker. I still had four hours of rehearsal. How the hell was I going to get through this?

I clicked my phone off, giggling, my face flushing. He never failed to get a reaction out of me, which was exactly his intent. As I smiled to myself, I noticed Michael watching me. He nodded to my phone.

"What?" I asked, still flushed.

"Hot date?" he asked, taking the seat next to mine.

"Um, well, yes. He's only in town for a day, so we're going out for dinner. You should see the schedule they have him on." I brushed my hair back from my face and tucked it into a sloppy bun, my constant hairstyle these days. One piece didn't make it in, and I fussed with it.

"That's good. I mean, good that you get to see him for a night," Michael said, watching me futz with my hair. "Your schedule's been pretty busy too. Is he going to make it back out for the show?"

The curl fell out again. I pushed it back. "He says yes, but who knows, with the amount of press he's doing? He's heading to England for the London premiere, and then to France. So I don't know if he's going to make it for our opening. I know he'll try." I sighed, slumping in my chair a little.

"Well, you're going to be amazing. I know he'll want to see that."

"Thanks. We'll see. I'm starting to get really nervous," I admitted, making my eyes huge to mask how nervous I truly was.

"You're not going to ruin another pair of my shoes are you?" he asked.

I immediately laughed. When we were in college, I had the lead in a musical—my biggest role since junior high. Michael was running the light board for the show, so he watched us rehearse each day. He'd offer me his critique each night as we walked home, and his opinion was always important to me. Because as much as he enjoyed my singing, he was never a yes-man; he always gave honest feedback.

Opening night I showed up at his apartment, shaking. I was so nervous that when he opened the door, I threw up on his shoe. After he removed the unfortunate Adidas, we sat on his couch and listened to Toad the Wet Sprocket. He wrapped his arms around me and told me everything would be fine. That I would kick ass and take names. That I should never second-guess my talent. To trust myself.

In the end, I did kick ass. But I still tend to get nervous on opening night.

"Well, we'll see, won't we?" I said, smiling as I returned to the present. "It's been almost ten years since I've been on any real kind of stage, so I'd steer clear of my mouth." I laughed, and the curl fell out one more time. "Blasted hair," I muttered.

We both reached for it at the same time. He got there first. As I stared, he tucked it back into my bun, his hand lingering maybe just one second too long.

In that second, things began to change for us.

He looked at me with those brown eyes I remembered from all those years ago. Those brown eyes that used to light up when we'd laugh together. Those brown eyes that would deepen when we argued.

We'd been such great friends. We spent countless hours alone together—doing laundry, watching movies, cooking dinner—but the friendship we had was never anything more. Although I had very strong feelings for him that were definitely more than friendly, he seemed not at all interested in me romantically, so I kept them to myself.

But when I was onstage, it was a different matter entirely. Every so often I would catch him looking at me, when his guard was down. The way he looked at me when I was singing gave me hope that someday he might come to return my feelings. I was head over heels in love with my friend Michael, and I wanted nothing more than for him to want me in the same way.

And then, that night came. In those brown eyes I had once, just once, seen my love for him mirrored back. Those brown eyes had closed tightly in passion during our one night together.

I'd thought of those brown eyes occasionally over the years, wondering what had happened to him and where he was. And now I'd come to know those brown eyes, trust those brown eyes, all over again.

Those eyes now looked back at me with confusion and trepidation and . . . something else. Was I imagining it? Was I just seeing what I wanted to see?

Wait—did I *want* to see that?

My phone beeped, and his eyes changed. He pulled his hand back as I looked at my phone.

I smiled sheepishly. "Holly."

He nodded and stood up. He started to walk away, then paused for a split second before continuing on. I pressed IGNORE on my phone and sat back into my chair, stunned by the rush of emotions I felt.

What the hell was going on? Michael was looking at me in a way that, well, I would have loved to have him look at me ten years ago.

Not now.

Right?

I shook it off. I had to. I threw myself into the last part of rehearsal, losing myself in the show and the work of creating Mabel. This ate up the rest of the evening, and All Things Michael were locked safely in the Drawer to be forgotten.

When we finally broke for the night, it was almost nine, and I was anxious to see Jack. I'd brought along some clothes for dinner, and I quickly changed into the heather-gray wool wraparound dress Leslie and I had found at Bergdorf's a few weeks ago. I paired it with knee-high black boots, giant hoop earrings, sassy red lipstick, and a huge smile.

I waited for him in the lobby of the theater, saying good-bye to the other cast members as they left. Several of the guys from the crew wolf-whistled at me, and I grinned. It was nice to know I could still clean up pretty well.

Michael walked out and said good-bye quickly, then stopped at the door. He looked back as if he were about to say something but continued through the doors.

As I pondered this development, my phone buzzed. It was the Brit.

"Hi," I answered.

"Hi, yourself. Are you ready?" he asked in a low voice.

"I'm ready. Where are you?" I asked, smoothing my dress.

"I'm outside in the car. I can see you in the lobby, Grace," he said, his voice almost a whisper.

"You can see me, can you? What am I doing?" I asked, bending over to pick up my purse from the bench, making sure to stand up slowly, arching my back and pushing my chest forward.

"Mmm, I love it when you bend." He chuckled darkly.

"Now, that's one I haven't heard before." I laughed as I buttoned my calf-length camel leather coat over my dress and wrapped a red cashmere scarf around my neck.

"Fucking Nuts Girl, you know what it does to me when I see you in red." He groaned.

"Well, then, you'll love what's underneath this dress," I said, loving that he could see me and I couldn't see him.

I put a little extra bounce and sway in my hips as I walked across the lobby toward the glass doors. They automatically swished open, and as the crosstown bus pulled away from the curb, I saw him.

He was leaning against the town car, looking like a wet dream come true. Black jeans, black V-neck sweater, leather jacket. He gave great lean . . .

"You look beautiful, Crazy," he murmured as I walked toward him.

"You look crazy beautiful," I answered.

I took the cell phone from his hand and closed it. I shut mine off and placed them both in my bag. Then I leaned in, placing my mouth very close to his right ear. "There'll be no need for phones tonight. I plan on engaging in a little personal, one-on-one communication, yes?" I kissed the spot right below his ear that I knew drove him out of his mind.

He groaned, hands coming up to pull me the rest of the way to him. He was already hard, and I moaned.

"I missed you," he growled, his hands on the small of my back, pressing his body against mine.

I smiled and wrapped my arms around his neck. "George, you have no idea," I said, kissing him greedily on his perfect lips.

"How fast can you eat dinner?" he asked between kisses.

"That depends, but pretty freaking fast. Why?" I asked, as he began to kiss my neck. My hands dug into his hair with wild abandon.

"Because as soon as we're done with dinner, I'm taking you straight to my hotel, taking everything off this glorious body, and ravaging you until you're incoherent," he said, licking the little hollow at the base of my neck.

I actually shook as my brain processed what he'd just said. "Hell, love, all I really need are some crackers and a glass of water. Then we can have the hotel boom-boom," I said, my eyes rolling back in my head as he began to unbutton my coat, his mouth never leaving my skin.

Then I became aware that we were standing in the middle of a very crowded sidewalk only blocks from a *Time* billboard. Leslie and I had seen it when we went for coffee.

A crowded sidewalk, and I am making out with Jack Fucking Hamilton. I pulled away—his lips actually still attached to my neck, hands busily prying at the buttons on my coat. "No, no, Sweet Nuts. Dinner first, buttons later. Besides, isn't Rebecca meeting us there?" I asked, struggling to maintain control. I could feel my resolve slip a little when he stuck two fingers between the buttons on my coat to graze my breast through the dress.

"Yes, she is. But she'd understand. She knows how much I've been missing my Grace," he whispered in my ear—in the Queen's English, for pity's sake.

As much as my body wanted to simply have him ravage me up against the side of the car, my brain still functioned just enough to pull away again and hold up one hand.

"Okay, Pony Boy. Listen up. We'll drive to dinner, and we'll have dinner with Rebecca. We'll decline dessert, we'll decline any after-dinner drinks, and then we'll leave. We'll go straight to your hotel, and I'll let you begin to do things to me in the elevator on the way up to your room. Deal?" I watched his eyes light up as I spoke.

"Okay, deal. But no appetizers," he said, holding open the car door.

"No appetizers," I agreed, stepping in.

Once we were situated, he told the driver where to take us, then raised the divider separating us from the front seat.

"Grace?" he said, sliding closer to me on the leather seat. He smelled uncommonly good. The Hamilton would be hard to keep away tonight.

But who wanted to keep away the Hamilton? Certainly not this girl.

"Yes?" I answered, reaching out to stroke his cheek.

"You said nothing about the car ride to the restaurant and whether I can do things to you in here." He grinned.

"No, I certainly didn't." I sighed in pleasure, his hands already moving under my dress. My breath hitched as his fingers traced a circle on my upper thigh.

"We have about twenty-five blocks to play. Up for a little slap and tickle?" He eased his hand higher, closer.

"Hell, love, you never need to ask. *Always* yes." I kissed him deeply.

We may have been a little late for dinner.

nine

*R*ebecca and I had a blast getting caught up over dinner. She told me all about the stalkers, the *Time* fans coming to Jack's appearances, and the paparazzi trailing him constantly now. Because he'd had me otherwise occupied in the car, I hadn't noticed the car following us, carrying his new security guard. The guard now went out with Jack for high-profile events, and even not-so-high-profile events like a simple dinner. That would take some getting used to.

We got to the restaurant rather quickly, so there was no chance for actual sexy times, just the promise of sexy times. The panties had very nearly come off, though, and I was now hypersexual. Everything was turning me on: the way he drank his wine, the way he twirled his pasta, the way he licked his lips to catch a drop of sauce. And was it me, or was he massaging that breadstick?

I had to excuse myself from the table. I needed some air; he was seriously driving me crazy.

Rebecca followed me to the ladies' room. "Is he *trying* to make you self-combust?" she asked, raising an all-knowing eyebrow in the mirror.

"Jesus, yes! You noticed it too?"

"Oh shit, girl, he is *on*. He misses you so much. I almost feel dirty, watching the display of table sexing going on . . . but I'm totally going to watch." She laughed at my expression.

"He's killing me. I almost can't stand it," I admitted, fanning myself.

"Grace, I have to tell you, he's so in love with you," she said, reapplying her lipstick.

I stopped fanning and looked at her.

"Why do you say that?" I asked, really interested in what she was going to say.

"He talks about you all the time. And he really misses you. You should've seen him in his interviews today. He was bouncing out of his seat, checking his watch. Y'know, he tries to play it so cool, but he's just an idiot. Those fangirls think he's all sexy scientist man, but he's really just a British goober who adores his girlfriend."

I was so glad he had a friend like her. She really got him.

"He is kind of an idiot, isn't he?" I laughed, thinking of him back at the table. Massaging his breadstick.

But he's your idiot.

Yes, he really just is.

"All boys are idiots when they're in blue-ball hell. You need to make sure he gets plenty tonight. I can barely contain myself, with all the sex vibes being thrown around, and he's like a brother to me!" She laughed as we walked back to the table.

We arrived to find the security guard, talking quietly to Jack. I slid into my chair, grasping Jack's hand on the way and kissing his knuckles as he curled his hand around mine.

"Hey, love. Miss me?" he asked quietly.

"I did, actually. Are we leaving soon?" I waggled my eyebrows suggestively.

He exchanged a glance with Joe, then looked back at me.

"Well, yes. Soon. But you should know there are a bunch of photographers outside. You okay with that?" His concern for me showed on his face.

I took a deep breath.

"Grace, you can walk out with me," Rebecca said. "We'll play this off. They don't need to know you were here with *the* Jack Hamilton. You were here with the slightly-less-well-known-but-equally-hot Rebecca Lake," she said, fluffing her hair and striking a pose.

I took another deep breath.

This was going to happen eventually. It was surprising that it hadn't happened yet. If I hadn't moved to New York, I probably would've been identified long before now. But Rebecca was right. I could walk out with her and meet Jack back at the hotel.

"It's cool. I'll do whatever you want, Jack. You know that." I placed a finger over his lips as he started to comment on my very easily misinterpreted statement. "But for everyone involved, it's probably better if I walk out with Rebecca, don't you think?" I giggled as he tried to nibble on my finger.

"Yes, yes, it would be better, I suppose." He sighed heavily.

"I'll get a cab and meet you at the hotel."

"Don't be ridiculous, Grace," he said. "We can all ride in the same car. Just don't let them photograph us together."

I rolled my eyes, but decided to let him have this one. We stood up and made our way to the front of the restaurant. Rebecca went out first, with me following, but when I saw the flashes, I froze a little. She smiled, took my arm, and guided me to the car. I tried to hide my face without looking like I was trying to, but who knows if I actually pulled it off. Jack followed a moment later, grinning for the cameras.

We all piled into a black Suburban with tinted windows and sped away toward the Plaza. Jack and I held hands in the backseat, talking quietly. We dropped Rebecca off first, then once we got near the Plaza, I insisted he drop me off in front of Bergdorf's so I could walk the last block or so.

"Now you're just being silly, Grace," Jack pouted.

"No, I'm being realistic. Your movie comes out in less than two weeks, and the last thing you need is to make your fans think you're unavailable. We can discuss this again once things have mellowed a bit."

This brief encounter with what he went through on a daily basis had confirmed what I already knew about how I'd be treated if the press found out he was dating someone—especially someone older.

He pulled me to him for one last kiss. "Room 1309. And, Grace?"

"Yes?"

"Don't wait too long," he whispered, kissing me slowly.

I kissed him back, then slipped from the car. The cool air did nothing to cool me down as I walked around the block, dodging the still-thick pedestrian traffic on the sidewalks. After circling once, I figured enough time had gone by, and I headed toward the Plaza.

☆ ☆ ☆

When I got to his room, I found the door slightly ajar. When I entered, I saw that my Brit had been busy. There were candles lit throughout the room, and he was waiting. He still wore his black pants, but the sweater had come off, revealing a long-sleeved white T-shirt, untucked and slightly slouchy.

"Hey," I said, setting my bag down.

"Hey yourself," he answered, taking a sip of his wine. He had a bottle of red open on the sideboard, and he'd poured a glass for me.

I crossed to him, picking up my wine. He didn't move, but his eyes followed me. I raised the glass to my lips, sipping slowly. I felt the warmth slip down the back of my throat and rolled the taste around on my tongue. A slow smile crept across my face.

He ran his hand through his hair and grinned sexily at me.

I began to unbutton my coat, and he said, "Slower."

My eyes widened, and then I understood.

"Slower, huh?" I asked in a low voice.

He nodded.

I set my glass down, biting back a smile, and let my hands return to the buttons on my long coat. I slipped each one of them open, slowly and methodically. I watched as he watched me, his eyes following my movements. Once the coat was unbuttoned, I allowed the leather to slide down my arms, then laid it on a chair. His eyes traveled the length of my body and back again, the green noticeably darker once they returned to mine.

I smiled, enjoying his reaction. I tugged on my scarf and

the ends trailed down my skin as it unwound, the fringe catching on the edge of my low neckline. His breath was coming faster now.

I was breathing rather heavily too, and I could feel my cheeks flushing. I bent over slowly, allowing the V-neck of my dress to fall open for a little peek. I removed one boot, then the other, unzipping at an almost unbearably slow pace. He took another sip of his wine, then hooked his thumbs in his belt loops and leaned back against the dresser.

His eyes were dark, dark green now.

I untied the bow holding my dress together but kept it closed, covering myself as long as we could stand it. That turned out to be not much longer, as he finally pushed himself off the dresser and came to me. His hands went to my hips, causing the dress to open slightly, revealing what I had on underneath.

"Mmm, Gracie. That's my bad girl," he whispered as his now almost-black eyes took in the deep-red lace bra and panties I was wearing especially for him.

"You like?" I teased, letting my dress puddle on the floor at my feet.

"Very much," he said breathlessly, his fingers tracing a path from my collarbone to my navel.

My breath caught and my back arched to keep contact with his touch. My hands quickly came up behind him and pulled off his shirt, tossing it over my shoulder.

"I like it very much too," I purred, running my hands over his chest and down to his navel, circling it with my fingertips. He twitched, and I looked at his mouth. His teeth were biting down slightly on his lower lip, and I knew I needed to kiss him, now.

But before I had a chance, he sank to his knees in front of me. His hands moved to the small of my back, pulling my body closer to his. My hands tucked into his silky curls, and I ran my fingers through them and made them stand straight up. I pressed his face into my tummy, hearing him sigh as his lips made contact with my skin.

His fingers slipped under the band of my panties and slowly dragged them down, revealing my body to him. He gazed at me once I was bare before him, then looked up at me, his eyes shining.

"Brilliant," he said, running a hand from my bottom to my knee and hooking my leg over his shoulder.

I caressed his face as my body tensed in anticipation of his touch. He nuzzled at me, and I gripped him for balance. His lips found the space where my leg joined my hip, and he kissed me.

"Fucking brilliant," he whispered, letting his tongue trace where my panties had been.

I moaned at the feel of him, at the sweet fluttering of his tongue and lips as he swept me open. His soft lips met me, and as he probed me with his tongue, I could feel the want and need I had for him, that was always there, begin to build.

He stood quickly and lifted me, removing my bra as he carried me to the bed.

The sight of him, shirtless and about to make me see God, was something I'd never tire of seeing, and I panted at the thought of what was about to happen.

He laid me down and stood over me, his hands sweeping across my body. My shoulders, my breasts, my tummy, my hips, my thighs, and finally his fingers found me, nudging my legs open, revealing me to him.

"You're so beautiful, Gracie," he murmured, and bent his head to me. His tongue found me instantly, and as he stroked me, I cried out at the perfection that was him.

No one would ever know my body as well as he did, and no one would ever make me feel the way he could.

His hands held me on the bed as my body thrashed. His mouth and lips and tongue brought wave after wave crashing over me, making me moan, groan, sigh, cry, and finally scream his name.

"Oh, God, mmm, Jack, Jack, Jack!" I screamed, feeling as though my insides were bursting. He hovered over my body, the intense pleasure beginning to ebb as he took me down slowly, his tongue gently sweeping, lips kissing, teeth nibbling, as he made his way to my inner thigh.

"Hmm, this appears to be fading. Can't have that." He chuckled and bit down, making his Hamilton Brand stronger.

The combination of the crazy orgasms he'd just given me and the exquisite pain of his teeth brought me out of my dream state and back into reality.

A reality where Jack was still wearing pants.

I pulled him up my body and flipped him on his back. His surprise at my sudden attack quickly turned to passion as I kissed him fiercely, almost bruising his lips. I struggled to remove his pants, and he finally lay naked before me, gloriously naked.

And gloriously hard.

I grasped his hands in mine, kicked one leg over him, and positioned myself.

His eyes watched me in the same way he'd watched me remove my clothes earlier—with lust and want.

I winked and slid down on top of him. We both groaned at

the feel of him filling me up again. His hips thrust upward as I rocked backward, and he hit me so deep I almost cried right there.

"Jesus, Grace, I missed you," he moaned as I began to move up and down on him, his hands unclasping from mine so he could hold on to my hips and grind farther into me.

"I know, I missed you too," I answered, my pace beginning to quicken as I felt myself getting close again.

He sat up, pulling my legs around his waist so he could thrust deeper into me, then bent his head to my neck, kissing and sucking as I threw my head back and held on tightly to his shoulders.

"You are so sexy," he growled, pumping into me fiercely.

I loved Aggressive Jack. "I'm only sexy because you're so good to me," I moaned in his ear, knowing how he liked it when I talked to him.

He growled again, lifting my hips and slamming me back into him, causing me to scream out his name once more. He hit that spot, that J-Spot, and then I was coming all around him.

"Fuck yes, Grace. That's so good," he moaned, and then my beautiful man made the beautiful face that he alone can make: jaw clenched, eyes shut tightly, lips parted, and brow furrowed as he came in me.

"Brilliant," I whispered, clutching him to me, taking in his deep breaths as he collapsed against my chest. He rested his head on my shoulder as I held him.

"I love you, sweet girl," he whispered, kissing the space between my breasts.

"I love you too, Jack." I kissed his forehead.

We slept together all night, tangled in the sheets.

And his hands? Where do you think?

☆ ☆ ☆

Jack flew back to L.A. the next morning after we had naked pancakes and naked waffles. I put him in a cab for the airport, knowing I would see him very soon. It was getting easier to say good-bye.

He spent the next few days doing interviews, photo shoots, and TV shows. He interviewed with *The Tonight Show* and *Ellen* and all the others, and he consistently sent me secret messages through the inane answers he gave the interviewers. Nice . . .

Countless photos began to appear in magazines, and he was truly becoming the next big thing. His name was on everyone's lips, his face was on every cover, and he spent his evenings alone in his hotel room, giggling like a boy on the phone with me as we talked for hours and hours. The sexiest man alive was a closet *Golden Girls* fan.

The next week in rehearsals, I made sure everything was as it should be so I could justify taking a weekend off right before the final touches were put on the show. A few members of the local theater press showed up at the last day of rehearsal, specially invited by Michael, and I actually spent a few minutes being interviewed about the show and my role! No one had ever interviewed me before, and though it was nowhere near the stratospheric level (and climbing) of Jack's success, it was a victory for little ol' me. I was proud of the work I was doing, and any time spent talking about the show was time well spent. I even had a "pinch-me" moment when a reporter asked me to spell my name for him: I might soon see it in print! I marveled at the life I was living and the good fortune I'd been granted for a second shot at this career.

As Jack geared up for the biggest night of his life, Leslie and I shopped for a dress worthy of a red-carpet premiere, and—although I don't know if it was him or me—Michael and I spent no time alone together all week.

Finally, it was the day of my flight back to L.A. I was packed and ready to go. I took a cab to the airport, with my dress folded carefully away.

I was going home.

ten

*M*y flight landed around 3:00 p.m. on Thursday, the day before the premiere. I was practically jumping out of my seat by the time we neared LAX, energized by the nap I'd managed to catch on the plane.

I looked out my window, watching as the desert gave way to that decidedly Southern Californian terrain. When I glimpsed the ocean, I knew I was home.

Jack wanted so badly to pick me up at the airport, but he couldn't for two reasons: one, he was booked solid with interviews and promotion, and two, there was no way he'd be able to dodge the paparazzi at the airport. There was always someone at the airport waiting to catch a star looking terrible after a transcontinental flight, and they'd be ecstatic to catch Jack picking up his unidentified redhead, whose legs would be locked firmly around his waist as he kissed her as only he could. Welcome home, indeed.

Since Holly was also occupied with All Things Premiere,

we'd decided I'd catch a cab straight to my house. Jack had agreed to meet me there after his last interview and after he'd said good night to his father. His dad had flown in for the premiere, and while I was looking forward to meeting him tomorrow night, I was also severely nervous about such a big event. Jack had gotten tonight off from most of his "familial obligations," as he called them, to "welcome me home in style." Who was I to argue with that?

As I walked outside to the line of cabs, I was pleasantly surprised to hear my name, then see my very own car! Leaning on it, sunglasses firmly planted on his face and wearing a huge grin, was the cutest thing I'd ever seen: Nick. One of the sweetest guys Holly and I had ever known, he was a screenwriter with an even bigger crush on Jack than mine.

"Hey, bitch. I heard you needed a ride," he deadpanned.

"I really do." I laughed, hugging him fiercely. I'd missed my buddy.

After he threw my bag in the backseat, he headed to the driver's side, but I held my hand out.

"No way. I've been riding on a subway and in cabs for weeks now. I need to drive my motherfucking car. Keys, please," I instructed.

He handed them over. "I figured as much. Sunglasses?" he asked as I settled in.

"Sunglasses, check. Let's go home."

We drove the long way, avoiding the highways so I could soak up as much Cali weather as I could. With the top down in true Southern California style, we got caught up on everything as we drove PCH north, then turned east on Sunset for one of my favorite drives—the one Jack and I took months ago. I could feel the sun on my face, smell the tangy sea air, and I knew I'd never want to live anywhere else for the rest of my life.

We finally made it to Laurel Canyon, and just as I pulled up in front of my beautiful little bungalow, my phone rang. It was Jack. Nick kissed me on the cheek and hopped out as I answered the phone.

"Hey, love, hang on a second," I said, and waved Nick back over to the car. "Thanks for coming to get me. It's so good to be back! Will I see you tomorrow?"

"Oh, please, girl, I'm your date! I'm the beard who's escorting you to the premiere and hoping I can get close to that costar Lane. Have you seen the body on that guy?" He trotted back to his car and sped out of the driveway.

I knew all eyes would be on Jack at the premiere, and with Holly managing every aspect of his career, I'd be more likely to sew my head to that red carpet than walk it with him. But I still wished I could walk with the man I loved on his special night.

"Who's that you're talking to, Grace?" Jack's voice asked in my ear. "Back in town less than an hour and you're picking up guys?" He laughed, and I smiled. Just the thought that Jack and I were back in the same city made my head swim.

"Ha-ha. That was Nick. He picked me up at the airport. Where are you?" I asked, schlepping my stuff toward the house.

Mmm, the lemon trees by my front door smelled intoxicating. I'd had a gardening service come by periodically to do some basic maintenance while I was away, and I was glad I had stood the expense—everything looked green, green, green.

"I'm just finishing up my last interview of the day, and

you'll be interested to know that one of these teeny bopper magazines has analyzed a sample of my handwriting. They've deduced from it that I'm artistic, highly motivated, and loyal." He chuckled.

I turned the key, unlocking my home. "All true. Once you decided to woo me, you didn't stop until you had me. Pretty motivated, as I recall." I pushed through the door and walked inside. The smell of still-new construction, Pine-Sol, and my favorite white tea candles greeted me.

"Me, woo you? I think you have that backward, Nuts Girl. You were clearly throwing yourself at me from the moment I met you. You with your boobies talk and your saltines. You were on the prowl."

"Yes, saltine spit-up is a wooing trick I've been using for years and years." I laughed as I set my bag down and began opening windows. The light poured in, and I could feel the late-afternoon sun on my skin. I didn't even realize how much I'd missed it until I sighed out loud.

"Glad to be home?" he asked.

"You have no idea, George. When are you coming over?" I sank into one of my fluffy couches in the living room.

"Right after I have an early dinner with my dad. I'm not planning on eating much, so I'll have a late dinner with you, if you like," he said.

"Mmm, that sounds good. I may just catch a quick nap while I wait for you," I said, stretching my arms over my head and hugging my couch pillow. I felt a flash of nerves at the mention of his father but pushed it back down. I could deal with this. What was I so afraid of?

"Did you check out the fridge yet?" he asked.

"No, I just got here. Why? I didn't leave anything in there."
Puzzled, I got up and headed into the kitchen.

On the fridge, right under the Post-it note I'd left myself,
was a picture of me and Jack. It was from Santa Barbara, taken
by the photographer who'd done the *InStyle* shoot. I sat on
Jack's lap, looking at him with an intensity I'd never seen on
my face before, as he smiled back.

We looked crazy in love. And since I was sitting on his lap,
there was no need to worry about the way my ass looked.

"Oh," I said, my hands coming to my face. It was the only
picture I had of the two of us, since I'd refused to print any of
the ones from TMZ.

"Like it?" he asked.

"I love it. Thank you." I smiled from ear to ear.

"I thought you might." He chuckled, then I heard someone
talking in the background. "Hey, I need to get going, but I'll
come by later, yes?"

"God, yes. And Jack?"

"Mmm-hmm?"

"Have I told you I loved you today?"

"Not yet, you haven't." I could hear his grin.

"I love you so much. Truly I do." My fingers touched his
face in the picture.

"I love you too, Grace. I'll see you tonight!"

I clicked off my phone and walked back through my house.
I unpacked quickly and hung my dress for tomorrow night in
the guest room closet. Safely inside a garment bag mind you,
I didn't want Jack peeking. Leslie and I had finally found the
perfect dress, and I couldn't wait to wear it for him.

I was hungry, as it was dinner time in New York. Looking

out at the backyard, I saw that my avocado trees were full of fruit. So in pure Southern California fashion, for a snack I had an avocado, dressed simply with salt, pepper, and fresh lemon juice from my own trees. It was accompanied by a dirty martini, which Jack had thoughtfully purchased the ingredients for. He'd even put the vodka in the freezer. I truly did not deserve this man.

After checking in with Holly and inviting her to breakfast the next morning, I made my way to my bedroom, thinking of the one and only night I'd slept here.

Then I lay down on my bed, crawled under the soft sheets, and let myself take a blessed nap. It was good to be home, even for only one weekend.

☆　☆　☆

"Hey, sweet girl. Wake up."

I sighed into my pillow, my dream of Jack spilling over as I swear I heard his voice right next to me. I waited for horns honking and the hustle and bustle of the city to remind me where I was.

Instead, I heard birds and wind chimes. I smelled—wait, s'mores? I cautiously opened one eye, not able to believe I was really home. My eye took in a beautiful sight: Jack perched next to me on the bed. White waffle-weave long-sleeve T-shirt, shredded black jeans. He looked exhausted but happy as he leaned down to kiss my forehead.

"Hey, yourself," I mumbled, opening both eyes and stretching my arms over my head. I'd slept hard and fast, and I was sure there were pillow wrinkles on my face.

"You have pillow wrinkles on your face," he said, his fingers tracing along my cheek.

"Can't you let one slip by? We're not all one of *People*'s Most Beautiful," I teased, rolling over on my back and curling my legs beneath me.

"What are you prattling on about? I'm not on that list." He frowned, swinging his own legs up onto the bed after kicking off his shoes. He lay next to me on top of the covers, leaning his head on his elbow.

"Not yet, maybe, but you will be. Mark my words, people will be lining up to market the pretty. Make sure no one steals my Hamilton Brand, though. That's mine alone." I laughed, and he looked confused.

"What the hell is a Hamilton Brand? Holly was talking about branding the other day in a meeting with a PR rep. Why the hell do I need a brand?"

"Actually, I was thinking of a brand of a different kind, and I'll tell you about it at just the right time." I scooted closer and snuggled into his warm body. I could tell he hadn't been eating well on the road; he'd been losing weight steadily since I left him in September. I'd have to start cooking for him again, once my show and his film schedule settled down.

I looked up at him, and he smiled at me. "Lips, please," he said.

"What's that?" I asked.

"Lips, please. You haven't properly kissed your man yet," he said, and I leaned in to comply. I kissed him softly and sighed as I felt his warm mouth. I kissed him again more firmly, and then snuggled into the Hamilton Nook.

We lay in silence for a few minutes, and he stroked my

hair and shoulders. It was so comfortable and peaceful; I was reluctant to ever get up. But my tummy decided for us, and when it began to rumble so loud it was impossible to ignore, I giggled.

"Well, I guess we should decide what we're doing for dinner," I said, sitting up and stretching.

"What are you hungry for, love?"

"I've been craving Gladstones since I passed so close to it today on my way home from the airport. Too public?" I asked, wondering about the brilliance of eating somewhere so touristy the night before his premiere.

"Oh, fuck it, Nuts Girl. Let's just go. They have great fish and chips, and we can take a drive up the coast." But he looked so tired, I thought he could fall asleep right here.

"Are you sure? We can stay in and order something. You look tired."

"That's a nice way of saying I look like shit, Grace," he answered with a rueful smile.

"Not possible. You're too pretty." I laughed, giving him a light slap on the cheek.

He mimed outrage and was about to pounce when his phone rang. "Sorry, love, it's Holly. I need to take this."

"It's cool. I need to run through the shower real quick, and then we can go."

"Damn. I hate the idea of you showering alone when I'm so close." He looked at me, then the phone, then back at me again, torn.

I laughed and opened the phone for him, put it in his hand, and kissed him on the cheek. I gathered what I needed quickly and stepped into the bathroom. I was washing my hair when I heard him open the door, still on the phone.

"Gracie, can I use your computer?" he asked.

"Yeah, it's in my bag in the front hallway."

"Thanks," he said, and I heard the door close.

I finished up, stomach growling loudly now, and began toweling off. I couldn't wait until the day we could shower together all the time again. I pulled on my jeans and was buttoning my shirt when I heard him coming down the hall.

"Gra-ace," he sang, and my skin grew hot at the sound of his voice.

I might as well stop buttoning right now. I knew that tone.

☆　☆　☆

He'd attacked me in the bathroom, and I quickly gave myself over to our impromptu sexing. It was hot.

Once I untangled myself, the Brit grinned at me sheepishly while I tried to button my shirt again. But since he'd removed most of the buttons when he ripped it off, no such luck. I looked in my bag for something else to wear, and he laughed when I asked him if he'd found what he needed on the computer.

"Yes, Gracie. I sure did. And thanks," he said in a low voice, thick with sex. I could feel myself getting worked up again, and I made a mad dash for the front door, pulling him along with me.

"Come on, love. The crab cakes are calling," I quipped, locking the door and then tossing him the keys.

We drove back the way I'd come this afternoon. The sun had almost set and cast a silvery light along the cliffs as we drove toward Malibu. The radio was loud, the top was down, his hand was on my leg, and I was smiling big.

When we got there, it was crowded, and I felt a little panicked. I suggested we just hit a drive-through, but he insisted it would be okay. He tried to take my hand, but on this one I did stand firm. He frowned, and I tried to gently assure him.

"Love, you know why. Let's just get through your film premiere, and then we can discuss the potential of ruining your fan base over me, huh?" I tried to joke, as he ran his hands through his hair.

"Whatever you want, Grace," he said, sighing heavily.

I knew this was tough on him. It was tough on me too. But we'd promised Holly we'd remain inconspicuous, and I intended to keep my promise. Besides, I knew how much they'd hate me, and I tended to think Jack was being a little naive in his opinion that his female fan base would be so accepting of his dating any woman at all, let alone one in her thirties.

I shook my head. *Not tonight, Sheridan. No bad thoughts tonight. Put it in the Drawer.*

We got a table outside so we could relax and watch the tide roll in. The evening air was cool but refreshing, and I was glad I'd pulled on the red flannel shirt Jack always had with him. We spent the evening laughing and drinking beer, getting him ready for the onslaught tomorrow evening would bring. There was a huge crowd expected at the premiere, and although he was getting more used to dealing with crowds, it still made him nervous. He still didn't truly grasp how much his fans loved him, or why they loved him, for that matter. He insisted it was just because of the series; that they were in love with the character. I tried to explain that yes, that was probably it at first, but the pandemonium that ensued with each public appearance could only be explained by his innate charm and self-effacing personality. Not to mention that the boy was stunning.

And the fact that he didn't get that? Even hotter.

We made it through dinner with no paparazzi and only two autographs, which, according to him, was a light day. Then we drove back to my house, the moon shining brightly over the canyons as we played each other songs.

When we got to the house, I went around turning off lights while he made sure we were locked in for the night. I was in the bedroom plugging in my phone charger when he came in with his own bag.

"Is it cool if I hang a few things in the closet?" he asked, pausing by the closet door.

"Of course. You don't have to ask, you silly Brit," I answered as I placed a few more clothes in an almost-empty dresser. The ones I hadn't taken to New York were still in boxes or in storage.

He disappeared into the closet, and I was tempted to follow him in there, but I wanted us to have some quiet time tonight—not another repeat of closet sex, Santa Barbara style. Although that was highly enjoyable.

I realized I hadn't brought my nightshirt with me, but I spied one of his many T-shirts and slipped that on instead. I was surrounded by his scent, which made my head swim a little. Hard to explain why that was so comforting. When you don't see someone for weeks at a time, it's weird what you fixate on. I was enthralled by the scent of him. I'd roll around in it like a kitten in catnip, if it were an option. I missed it that much.

We talked while we got ready for bed, falling back into the pattern we'd established when we spent all our nights together. He brushed his teeth while I put on my lotion, then he sat on the counter while I brushed my teeth and handed me my little cup of Scope when I was done. We talked about everything and nothing, catching each other up. He discussed his plans to remodel my house to make room for the giant shower he still insisted upon, which I informed him sounded great. Provided he pay for it.

I told him about the *Time* billboard Leslie and I walked by each day when we went for coffee. We discussed at length the fish and chips he had at dinner that night, and the difference between porpoise and dolphins. A pod of *something* swam by during dinner, and we continued our argument about what made the two different and which we'd seen.

This discussion finally came to a close when I climbed into bed and he shut off the lights. He wore his normal bedtime clothing: boxers. Tonight they were a dark charcoal gray. I wondered if he'd noticed I had trouble keeping my toothbrush steady when I saw him strip down. He walked across the room toward the bed and, with a graceful turn, slipped beneath the sheets. He'd grown thoughtful in the last few minutes, no longer responding to my Flipper jokes.

"Hey, George. You still with me?" I poked him with my big toe as he settled under the covers.

"Sorry, Gracie. Yes, I'm still with you." He smiled, but something wasn't right.

"What's wrong?" I asked, sweeping his hair back. He relaxed under my touch and scooted closer to me in bed.

"Nothing's wrong. I'm just glad you're here," he said as he snuggled up against me. He laid his head on my chest, and when he was comfortable, I began to play with his hair the way I knew he liked. I scratched his scalp and worked the knots out, making his curls soft and silky.

He sighed contentedly. "I'm glad you could make it back here for this."

"Wouldn't miss it," I whispered into his hair, kissing it softly.

"It's going to be crazy, I'll warn you now," he said, his voice darkening.

"Well, lucky for you, I happen to know all about crazy." I smiled and resumed my stroking.

We were quiet for a few minutes as I scratched his head and kissed him every so often. His breathing deepened, and before I knew it, he was fast asleep. I looked down at him, his eyes closed. He looked so young in that moment, like a kid almost. He looked perfectly peaceful. I shifted slightly to turn off the TV.

As he felt me move, his green eyes flickered open long enough to meet mine, and he smiled sleepily. "Love you, Gracie." He yawned and rolled me over onto my side. He pressed his body against mine, and his hands crept under my shirt and up to my breasts. With one in each hand, he kissed the side of my neck, sighed once, and said, "Fantastic."

Then he promptly fell back asleep. I felt his warm chest through the thin cotton of my (his) T-shirt and his gentle yet possessive grip, and I smiled as well.

"Love you too," I whispered, but the only response was the tiny snore he always had when he was first asleep. I was out within five minutes, wrapped in Jack.

eleven

The next morning we woke to the sound of phones ringing. Mine rang first, then his, and in the confusion we bonked heads in the middle of the bed.

"Ow!" I rubbed my forehead while I answered the phone. He mumbled a similar hello into his.

"It's a big day for your boy, so wake the fuck up," I heard Holly's merry voice say.

"Asshead. So good to hear from you so early in the morning. Exactly how early is it?" I settled back against my pillow and squinted my eyes at the alarm clock. Jack had a perplexed and still-half-asleep look on his face, his curls everywhere.

"Holls," I mouthed to him, and he rolled his eyes.

"Holly, why are you calling both our phones at— Christ, woman, it's seven a.m.!" he exclaimed, lying back on his pillow as well. He yawned and rolled on his side to look at me. I smiled at him, rolling my eyes too.

Holly's loud morning voice came through both phones. "This is a big, big day, and there's no time for sleeping in. Besides, I need to be sure you're up before I come over for breakfast. I'm bringing bagels and coffee, since I know you have nothing in the house," she continued.

Jack chose that moment to hang up on her.

"Did he just hang up on me? I swear that boy is getting too big for his britches," she said.

Jack chuckled, still able to hear her chirping. He let his eyes travel down my body, and they stopped on my leg, exposed by the tangled sheets. He grinned sexily, then danced his hand across my skin, starting at my ankle and working his way up. His hand dragged up my leg, making circles on my knee. My skin tingled.

I shook my finger at him as I attempted to listen to Holly. It was getting very hard to concentrate. His hand moved higher, ghosting across my thigh. Then he slipped lower on the bed, bringing his head down to my tummy and pushing up my shirt. I gasped as I felt his mouth brush my skin. It felt wonderful.

Holly heard me. "You okay, Grace? What's going on?"

"Hmm? Nothing's wrong. I'm fine," I sputtered, as he grinned into my skin. He was determined to push it.

He looked back up at me, his chin resting on my belly as his hands snuck to the band of my panties and began to slowly push them down my legs. I shook my head at him, and he nodded his head right back.

Demon . . .

He settled down lower on the bed and nudged my knees apart with his nose, grinning wickedly.

I mouthed "No," but he just rolled his eyes as if to say, "Oh, please." His tongue touched me, and my back arched immediately.

That motherfucker.

Holly had switched topics and was now going on about the dress she was wearing to the premiere. I really tried to listen, but between the tongue and the fingers and the lips and the vibrating moans he was directing at my oonie, I never stood a chance.

"Holls, I need to . . . wow . . . I need to call you . . . fuuuuck . . . back . . . I . . . God *damn!*"

"Ah jeez, while I'm on the phone, Grace? I'll be there in thirty minutes. Knock it the fuck off by then," she instructed.

"Better make it . . . unhh . . . shit, that's good . . . Make it an . . . hour—hour—hour—Jack!" I dropped the phone and my hands plunged into his hair as he made me come four mother-loving times in a row. It was so good, I almost blacked out.

When he finally finished, he looked so damn proud.

As well he should be.

"Jesus, George. What the hell?" I moaned as he crawled back up my body, laughing at my noodle arms as I tried to hold him close.

"Don't die on me now, love. Climb on up here," he said, rolling onto his back and tucking his hands back behind his head.

I gamely pushed myself up, rolled my neck, and cracked my knuckles. "Climb on up here? Is this what you want me to climb up on?" I asked, gesturing to the very prominent Nice-to-See-You beneath his boxers. I brought him out to see the world on this fine morning. I gave him a quick stroke, then poked Mr. Hamilton with my finger to watch him wag back and forth.

"Are you kidding me with this shit?" Jack asked, raising one eyebrow at my shenanigans.

I sighed, then cracked my back, rolling my neck again. I really was trying to get some blood moving through my system again after those annihilating orgasms, but I also enjoyed torturing him.

He rolled his eyes. "Grace, you're not a gladiator going into an arena, you're about to shag your man. Who, by the way, just made you come several times. Now get on top like a good girl," he said, his fingers still laced behind his head.

"I'm coming, I'm coming," I fake-grumbled, planting a knee on either side of his waist.

"That's what she said," he teased, and I started to lower myself.

"Wait!" he cried.

"What the fuck, George? I'm trying to get my groove on here." Oonie had sensed her Mr. Hamilton, and she was anxious to be reunited.

"Shirt off, please. I need to see those fantastic tits."

I obliged. He hissed as he caught sight of them, then laughed as I got stuck when my T-shirt caught on one of my earrings. The shirt was stuck halfway up my face, my nose propped up in a very Miss Piggy–like way. His laughter grew, and as he laughed, his hips rose. I shifted my weight, trying to get a better angle on my cotton prison, and Mr. Hamilton and Oonie took that very moment to *embrace*.

I was on top of him, naked, T-shirt stuck around my head. I must have looked like a cross between a Muppet, Jenna

Jameson, and the Flying Nun. Jack couldn't stop laughing, even as he groaned and pressed into me farther.

"A little help here, please? And don't start without me," I said, trying to be fierce.

He finally reached out to gently pull off the shirt. My nose was released, then my eyes. My ear was still caught, but when the shirt cleared my eyebrows, he let go. He was laughing too hard.

"Stop it. Come on!" I said, the T-shirt now sticking up and out behind me like Erykah Badu.

"Fucking Nuts Girl," he gasped between chortles. Tears streamed down his face.

"You think I won't sex you up good with this on my head? Watch me," I threatened, rolling my hips in a tantalizing way that was made less impressive by the current ridiculousness.

"What the hell else would I watch? This is the best show I've ever seen," he said, resting his hands on my hips as I began to ride him.

"I will totally fuck you exactly like this," I said, fluffing the shirt out like my hair.

"You're already fucking me. Less talk. More fucking." He groaned as I began to move faster.

Jack thrust into me with conviction.

I rose up on my knees, then sat back down fast, taking him into me hard. I felt him go deep, really deep, and I began to moan with him.

It soon became too ridiculous even for us to have this thing on my head, so we managed to get it off before we got off, throwing it on the floor, his hands quickly returning to my hips, urging and guiding me.

"You feel so good, Gracie. Just . . . like . . . that . . . God . . ." he said, his eyes smoldering as he watched me.

"Mmm, Jack. Tell me I'm your good girl," I said breathlessly, watching his eyes widen.

"Fucking hell, Grace, you're my *only* good girl," he whispered, his left hand leaving my hips to palm my breast.

He rolled my nipple between his fingers and pinched it slightly. I cried out at the touch, and he increased his pressure. My skin was hot, crazy hot as the morning sun poured in the windows. His body was slick with sweat, and my hands snuck down to tease where we were joined. He watched as I stroked myself, grunting his approval.

"Jack, oh, God, so good . . . I . . . mmm . . . please . . . Jack!" I screamed as I came hard around him, clamping down and shaking as I threw my head back. He caught me, sitting up beneath me, driving deeper and farther into me as his own orgasm made him cry out.

"Grace," he murmured as his body shook with rapture.

I cradled him to my chest, feeling him pulse inside me. I wrapped my legs firmly behind his back, making sure to keep him where I wanted him. My hands slid across his back and into his damp hair, rocking him slowly as we settled in. I was thoroughly overwhelmed with feeling for him, this man who was so dear to me. He felt so close, so warm, so mine.

I kissed his cheek, pressing my forehead against his as he smiled. "I love you so much. You know that, right?" I looked him dead in the eye, suddenly serious. I was overcome with a longing to hold him here, in this bed, in this room, and never come out. We were perfect, in this bed, in this room.

"I do know that. I love you too, sweet girl." He sighed, crushing me to him, face tight against my chest.

We were quiet. We were still. We were content. It was the calm before the storm.

☆　☆　☆

The rest of that day was surreal.

It began with Holly's arrival with bagels and the laughing judgment of our performance she'd heard over the phone. She was a dirty girl and hadn't hung up right away, instead enjoying the free phone sex we so thoughtfully provided.

Jack took a long shower while we had some girl time. She complimented me again on the colors I'd chosen for my kitchen as we sat and talked. It was the first time I'd seen her since I'd left for New York.

"I love how you laid out this kitchen, Grace. It's perfect. I'm thinking of redoing mine. Maybe next year," she said thoughtfully, swirling cream cheese on her Asiago bagel.

"Don't you dare! Your kitchen is perfect. You just miss me cooking in it, which I'll do as soon as I get home. Michael and I cook all the time in my kitchen in New York, but it's nothing like this one," I added, spreading butter on my own everything bagel.

"When do you think you'll be coming home?" she asked, looking around.

"Jack's in the shower, why? What's up?" I looked at her carefully.

"Well, do you think the show's going to be picked up? If it does, are you ready to move across the country? If it does well, you could be there a year, maybe even longer," she said, taking an obnoxiously big bite. Cream cheese oozed out the side of her mouth.

"You're disgusting. You know that, right?" I frowned as I handed her a napkin.

"Shut it, and don't change the subject. What will you do? Are you prepared for that? You sure this is what you want?" she asked again, wiping her chin.

I sighed and leaned on my elbow. I'd been thinking a lot about this lately. When I first got to New York, it was just so busy and exciting and thrilling. But now that we were getting close to the previews, and there was a real shot at this becoming a fully mounted production, I realized things could change. For real.

"This is the single most amazing thing that's ever happened to me. I'd be an idiot to turn my back and walk away," I answered, putting down my bagel and laying my head on the counter. My stomach had felt strange all morning, and now it was fluttering like crazy. Must be nerves about tonight.

"Grace?" Holly asked, placing a hand on my shoulder and shaking me a little.

"How could I walk away?" I asked, almost to myself.

"From the show or from Jack?" she asked quietly. Her bagel *thunked* down on the plate.

"What does Jack have to do with this?" I asked the countertop sharply.

"Grace, look at me," she commanded.

I peeked at her through my arms.

"Where's your head? Why does it sound like you're making a choice all of a sudden?"

"Well, don't I have to? I mean, it's going to come down to

that eventually, right? How the hell can we keep this going like this? This is insane . . ." I was surprised by the words coming out of my mouth.

Where was this coming from?

Where do you think? You have a giant mental drawer of I'll-think-about-you-tomorrows you've piled up and never gone through. Someone asks you one little question, and Now It Will Rain Shit.

"Grace? You really want to do this now? What else is going on?" she asked.

I looked at my best friend. The one who'd taken care of me so many times, looked out for me, and opened her home to me. The one who helped me get back on track and never, ever asked for anything in return. She knew me better than almost anyone else, and the knowledge that I wouldn't be able to hide anything from her made me lose it.

The tears came in a rush, flooding my eyes and dripping onto my cheeks and my shirt—his shirt. He'd cut a slit in each side of the neck hole so it would never get stuck again, making it mine now. When I'd said something about it, he smiled and said, "Heh-heh, you said neck hole."

I sobbed silently, with no idea exactly why I was crying. All I knew was it had to come out. My thoughts were swirling, not letting me take a breath.

Holly just patted my hand—neither of us was big on the sister hug—then handed me a napkin to wipe my nose with when I began to calm down.

"Okay, start at the beginning," she said, her eyes kind.

"I don't even know where the beginning is! I didn't even know I was *upset*! I—I—" I began to wail again.

"Grace! Grace, get control. Calm down, ya dillhole," she instructed.

Her words broke through and made me laugh a little. I took some deep breaths and laid my head back down on the cool granite.

"Just talk, fruitcake, and we'll see what sticks to the wall," she said.

So I talked. And I talked. And I was *terrified* at what came out of me. I talked about how amazing the show was and how happy I was in New York. I talked about how glad I was to be back up on a stage again, thrilled to be working with such amazing people. I talked about Michael and how glad I was we were friends. I talked about Michael and how close we'd gotten again.

I closed my eyes in sudden exhaustion. I was frightened by the images playing on the inside of my brain. My own little highlight reel:

Snapshots of Jack and me driving up the coast, happy and carefree.

Michael and me arguing over lunch. Him stealing my fries when he thought I wasn't looking.

Jack and me sexing it up on the floor of the closet together.

Michael walking away with Abigail, her tiny hand in his.

I stopped suddenly.

"Holly, do you ever think about having kids?"

"What?" she asked, her face astonished. Neither of us had ever wanted kids. It was one of the things we'd bonded over right away. We both promised we'd never turn into breeders.

"I mean it. Do you ever think about it?"

"Umm, no. Why? Is there something you want to tell me? You're not . . ."

"*No!* I mean, no. But don't you ever think about it?"

"Do *you* ever think about it?" she asked.

I chewed my lip. I hadn't thought about having kids for years. I always assumed it meant something, that I'd made it this far in life without an inkling of thought toward the subject. It meant I wasn't meant to have children. I'd decided something at twenty-two, slapped a sticker on it that said DECIDED, and filed it away in The Drawer.

I would have wanted them by now, right?

Kids made me uncomfortable. I didn't know how to talk to them; they were weird, and they smelled funny. I hated baby talk, and I never went ass-over-apple cart when I saw a stroller go by, trying to peek inside. Isn't that what women did when they wanted kids?

Not all women behave that way. That doesn't mean you wouldn't be a great mom. No one would be more entertaining.

Had I made a decision about this too young, not allowing myself to even consider a different life, a different path? Did I need to think about whether I wanted kids? Could I allow myself to think about it?

I *was* thinking about it . . .

Let's timeline this. You're thirty-three, about to turn thirty-four. If you want kids and marriage and that life—well, hell! Let's pretend, just for a second, that you're with someone other than Jack, someone who wants kids.

I flinched, thinking about it not being Jack.

You'd need to get married, and that would mean dating for at least a year. Engaged at thirty-five. Then, depending on how long the engagement lasts, maybe married at thirty-six. You wouldn't want to have kids right away—be a wife for a while. So, maybe Baby Number One at thirty-seven.

Baby Number One?

Wouldn't you want more than one?

I flashed to a picture in my head that I didn't even know I'd stored away. It was a family on the beach: a toddler walking in front of the parents, a little one in Daddy's arms, Mommy smiling. A family of four.

Yes. Yes, I would. I'll have two hypothetical children with my hypothetical husband. Mr. and Mrs. Hypothetical.

So Baby Number Two at thirty-nine, maybe even forty.

Fucking hell. Pregnant at forty . . . when did I get so damn old?

"I *am* thinking about it," I finally responded. "Not in the sense that I want them, but in the sense that I need to consider things very carefully now. I'm not getting any younger. And neither are you, by the way," I said slowly.

"Yes, but you look so much older than I do. It's natural that you'd be there and not me," she said, deadpan.

I stuck my tongue out halfheartedly, feeling the room begin to spin. "Seriously, Holly. If we want kids, we have to think about this. Maybe not now, maybe not next year. But we have a finite amount of time to consider this shit," I said, surprising myself.

That Drawer is full of stuff you haven't dealt with. You sure you want to shed light on all *of it right now?*

"Where does Michael factor in to all this?"

I smiled involuntarily, thinking of him with Abigail in his arms. Her questions and his patience. His good, good heart and his strong arms.

Holly caught the smile. "Where does *Jack* factor in to all this?" she asked.

My stomach clenched at the thought of him. I loved him

so much. Did we want different things? Maybe. Maybe we did. Could I spend my last baby-making years with a man who was too young for babies? And didn't want babies? Do *I* want babies?

"I love Jack. That's not in question," I stated firmly, and my body immediately betrayed me. Fresh tears rained onto my cheeks, and Holly watched in horror as I hunched over, my stomach convulsing.

"What *is* in question, Grace?" she asked, her voice a whisper.

"Whether what we have is enough," I heard my voice say, and then my body took over. I made it to the sink just in time, my bagel and coffee rushing back up at the realization of what I'd said. My brain and my heart needed a moment to fight. Holly held my hair.

As I rinsed my mouth out, I heard the shower shut off. I could hear Jack moving in the bathroom, and he was singing "People Will Say We're in Love." I wiped my face quickly, splashing water. Holly watched in silent resignation.

"Hey, sweet girl! Have you seen my jeans from last night?" Jack bellowed.

I looked at Holly with panic in my eyes, shaking my head furiously. Then I backed away and ran for the door.

She walked toward the bathroom. "You better have some clothes on, Hamilton. I'm coming in to help you find your jeans. Do you know how many women I could have here in two minutes to help you with that?" she said.

I heard the beginning of Jack's protesting yell as she pushed her way into my bedroom.

Then I didn't hear anything else. I was in my car and out of the driveway.

twelve

When I got back to the house, Holly and Jack were holed up in my home office, which they'd turned into Premiere Central. He was on the phone, she was on the phone, and they both looked up when I came in.

"Hey, love, where'd you run off to?" he asked, covering the phone and gesturing me over. I went to him, sinking into his lap as he sat at the desk. He was talking to his dad, making plans to meet at the theater tonight.

Holly was trying to get a seamstress over to the house to take up her hemline a little bit more. The entire day was taking on the feeling of prom: heightened expectations, limo drivers, updos, and just-under-the-surface tension.

"I had to run to the drugstore to pick up a few things," I lied smoothly. The thirty-minute drive had put me in a calm mood. I was very good at squelching things down, and after my breakdown and potentially scary realizations this morning, I was calling on all my squelch-down skills to keep things in check. Were these very skills part of the morning's problem? Perhaps. But no time for that now. I was in melt-down-management mode.

Holly had one eye on us and one eye on her computer screen as she tried to manage every aspect of the day from this ill-equipped office. My house wasn't yet ready for someone to be in it on more than a temporary basis. No DSL. No Wi-Fi. And her air card wasn't working for some reason. It was driving her batty.

Finally, she'd had enough and threw her cell phone into her bag in disgust. "That's it! I'm heading back to my house. That's now the command center for this entire operation. Grace, you're in charge of bringing your dress, your lunch, and your Brit to my house by noon, got it?" she yelled, getting that wild look in her eye that often appeared just before a big event.

"Yes. No problem," I said, somewhat numbly. I was curled into Jack's lap, his arms around me while he talked on the phone. I could barely feel him.

She rolled her eyes at me and waved at Jack. "I'll see you at my house in a little while," she told him, then nodded at me. "Walk me out?"

I peeled myself off Jack. He kissed me on the cheek as I pulled away, and I followed Holly to the front door. Outside there, she rounded on me.

"Now, look. Whatever you're planning on doing, *do not do it tonight!* Not on *his* night. He's nervous enough as it is. And I'm not convinced of this anyway. You need to really sit down and think about all this, before you say or do anything," she added, hands firmly on my shoulders as if she were physically trying to ground me.

"I won't. It's fine. I'm fine," I said.

"And promise me you won't talk to Michael today?" she said, slinging her bag over her shoulder.

"Not that he has anything to do with this, but whatever," I said, rolling my eyes.

"Mmm-hmm. Sure, Grace. I'll see you at noon. Go take a shower. Remember, *not tonight*," she shot back as she walked to her car.

I gave her the finger and turned back inside. I could hear Jack still on the phone, so I headed toward the bathroom. If we were going to pick up lunch, we'd need to get a move on.

I grabbed my things, my mind still racing. Hearing Jack coming toward the bedroom, I quickly locked the bathroom door. I stood, eyes wide in the mirror as I heard him come into the bedroom and walk across the floor. Then I saw the door-knob turn—once, twice, a third time, followed by a tentative knock.

"Gracie?"

"Yes?" I answered, eyes clinched tight.

"Why did you lock the door?"

He was right to question it. I'd never locked him out before. "Sorry. Habit from New York, I guess," I said leaning against the door. I took a deep breath. Why was this suddenly so hard? I loved him. I knew this completely.

I could hear him breathing on the other side, probably wondering what was going on.

"Are you going to open it?" he asked, his voice teasing, but laced with something else.

I choked back a sob that had formed quickly and said, "Can you give me a minute? My tummy is a little upset."

"Oh, hey, do you need anything? I can run and grab something for you. Ginger ale?" I could tell from his voice that his eyebrows were knit together, and he probably stared at the door with a curious look.

"No, no. I'll be okay. Start thinking about what you want for lunch, and we can pick it up on the way to Holly's," I said before the tears began to fall again.

I turned on the water and was instantly underneath, the water and my tears mixing together. Everything I'd thought before this morning—and the carefully constructed calm I'd felt when I first returned from my getaway drive—was crumbling like a house of cards. The very foundations of everything I thought I knew had been thoroughly shaken, and it was me who had shaken them! I needed to get this under control fast, if I was going to be in any kind of shape to make it through tonight. This was going to be a long evening.

Ninety minutes later, we were at Holly's. We'd picked up sandwiches from Nate 'n Al in Beverly Hills for later. Her place was a circus, and as we brought everything in, we saw car after car arrive, including Nick's. Holly had hired hair and makeup for the two of us, and we'd be getting ready here. Jack had brought his suit with him last night to my house and now had it draped over his arm along with my dress, still hidden in a garment bag.

We all ate, and then Holly put Jack on the phone to do a few last-minute interviews. I'd managed to avoid any more mini-meltdowns, and was feeling a little calmer. I was going to be there for Jack tonight. This was the man I loved. I'd figure the rest out later.

As the day progressed, everything seemed to simultaneously speed up and slow down. Jack and I had no time alone together, and before I knew it, I was in my old room, in my bra and underwear, with rollers in my hair and a woman applying my makeup. Holly showed up in the doorway looking similar, although she'd had the taste to put on a robe.

She plopped down on the bed and watched me get primped. "You ready for this?" she asked.

"Yes, why?"

"Okay, then, I'll give you the ground rules. Jack, get your British ass in here!" she yelled.

Almost instantly, he popped his head into the room. He raised his eyebrows at my skimpy attire, and I giggled in spite of myself. He made me melt like a thirteen-year-old every time he did that.

"Here are the rules, you two. No hand-holding, no touch-ing, no kissing of any kind, obviously. You'll arrive separately, and Grace, you'll walk the red carpet with Nick. I'll have one of my assistants working the line ahead of time, and if there's too much speculation about whether Jack will be bringing a date, or any mention at all of an unidentified redhead, you'll skip the red carpet altogether. Got it?"

At this, Nick stuck his head around the corner. "But I'll still get to walk it by myself even if this little whore ruins it for herself, right?" he asked, outrage on his face.

"Nice, Nick," Jack muttered.

"I would never take a red carpet from you, Nick. You can walk it alone if I can't." I laughed, seeing his eyes light up.

"So we can't touch or kiss. Are we allowed to talk?" Jack said with a heavily sarcastic tone.

The tone was ignored by Holly as she considered his ques-tion. "Yes, you may talk. But only after everyone is inside, and only once the press clears out," she answered, in full manage-ment mode now.

I was a little scared of her. Jack just looked scared period.

The stylist finished taking the rollers out of my hair, and the makeup artist gave me a final touch-up. Holly was next.

"Can you guys give us a few minutes, please?" I asked Holly and Nick.

"Yeah, let's get me beautiful in my room," Holly said. "Come on, Nick." She winked at me, and they all filed out, leaving Jack behind.

"Nervous?" Jack asked.

"Yep, you?"

"Yep, a little," he answered. He looked more than a little nervous.

"Come here," I said, pulling him over to my side of the bed and opening my arms. He scooped me up and sat me on his lap. His arms went around me, and I cradled him to my chest, letting his head nestle into my nook. I scratched his scalp and kissed his hair, and hummed something, maybe a Christmas tune. I wasn't really thinking about it. I could feel him relaxing as the band around my heart got tighter and tighter until I felt like bursting.

"Your heart is beating so fast," he whispered, and I closed my eyes.

I kissed his cheeks, his forehead, his eyelids, his nose, and finally his sweet lips. "I love you, George. You know this, right?" I asked, my gaze fierce.

"I *do* know this, Gracie. Why do you keep asking me that?" He smiled that sexy little half grin, and I almost went to pieces. I heard Holly coming back down the hall, saying something about needing bobby pins from the bathroom.

"I better finish getting ready. See you downstairs in a little while," I said, standing up and leaving the safety of his arms.

"I'll see you downstairs, love." He pulled me in for one last kiss.

I took a deep breath, centered myself, and began to get ready.

The dress Leslie and I'd found at Bergdorf's clung to me like a second skin. I'd been going for extra-long runs each day for the last two weeks, not to mention banishing anything that even looked like a carb to the curb to get ready for this night, this morning's bagel aside. I was relieved to see it had paid off. The dress was silk, shaded between champagne and gold with a gathered, plunging neckline. It was tight to the waist, then flared out in a bubble. Thin spaghetti straps kept my cleavage hiked up miraculously to my chin, and the tiny belt with a small emerald-green rhinestone-encrusted clasp made my waist look practically nonexistent.

I thanked Jesus that I hadn't made a mess with the self-tanner, and my skin glowed. My hair fell in soft curls all around my face. Jack loved it when I wore my hair down and wild, although it was carefully tamed for this evening.

But the kicker? My kicks. Manolo. Jeweled d'Orsay.

I felt like a princess as I sailed down the hall to find Holly. She was looking hot herself in a little black strapless number paired with tall red heels. When someone mentioned Lane earlier, she'd suddenly decided to change from the more sensible black kitten heels she'd initially been wearing. I was going to have to ask her about that . . .

As we approached the stairs, I could hear Jack in the kitchen laughing with Nick. He was still trying to convince Jack they should at least kiss to make sure he was, in fact, straight.

"Nick, will you please quit molesting the Brit?" I called down. I stopped a few steps from the bottom. Nick stopped and smiled. Jack's back was to me, and as he turned, I took a moment to admire him in profile. Gray suit, black tie. Strong jawline, messy hair, great stubble. Guinness in hand. He ran his fingers through his hair, and I once again admired his hands. He completed his half turn, which took at least an hour, and his green eyes pored over me.

"Beautiful," he said breathlessly, and came to stand in front of me at the bottom of the stairs. Holly waited in the wings to give us our moment.

"You like?" I asked, struggling to keep myself from launching down the last few steps and throwing myself at him.

"I like," he whispered, and my eyes filled with tears for the millionth time today. Waterworks, freaking waterworks.

He held his hand out to me and I took it, stepping down so we were on the same level. On even ground. He spun me like a ballerina, watching as my skirt puffed out. When I came back around, he was smiling.

"Fucking Nuts Girl," he said, the same half grin on his face. He led me by the hand toward the kitchen where everyone was gathered. Holly came downstairs and commenced running around like a chicken with her head cut off. A chicken with fabulous shoes.

She noticed mine. "New Manolos?" she asked, pointing.

"Yep. You?"

"Of course," she laughed, then cocked her head like a dog, listening for something.

"The limos are here," she said, and raced outside.

"Wait, we have to get pictures!" Nick cried, looking resplendent in his own right in a charcoal gray suit.

Jesus, it *is* prom.

At his insistence, we found ourselves lined up on the stairs like the New Kids in their *Step by Step* video.

"This is stupid," I said.

"Oh, come on, it's cute," Holly said, posing a few steps below me.

"All we need is a corsage and a Vanilla Ice song and I'm back in high school," I muttered.

Jack nudged me from behind and said in my ear, "Shut the fuck up and enjoy this, Crazy."

I rolled my eyes and let the makeup artist finish taking pictures of all of us.

Finally, we piled into the limos. I was to ride with Nick, and the cars would be staggered by about an hour, so Jack would arrive well after me. Just as I was about to get in, he pulled me back against him for a passionate kiss.

I kissed him back with all the force I could, without actually mounting him in the driveway. No matter what may have transpired this morning, I loved him dearly, and my body could never resist him. "I'm so proud of you, George. You deserve all the success that's about to come to you," I said, kissing him just below his ear, then hurriedly wiping it off before Holly could yell at us.

"Is it crazy that I want to skip this whole thing and go back to your place?" he asked.

We did cocoon really well. If there was one thing we knew how to do, it was hide away from the world.

"No, love. It's not crazy, but it's impossible. I'll see you there."

"Yes, but not too close, now. We can't have anyone thinking Jack Hamilton is actually getting laid. Can you imagine?" he said mockingly.

"I heard that," Holly said, clicking across the driveway to talk to the driver of the car she and Jack were taking.

I kissed him again and squeezed his hand once more. He smacked me on the ass as I got into the car, and I squealed.

Nick made a big show of getting into the car really slowly, keeping his bum in the air and pointed toward Jack as long as possible. Jack sighed and smacked Nick on the ass as well. Nick squealed too.

As we pulled away, Jack was smiling.

"Are you excited to be meeting Jack's dad?" Nick asked as he straightened my dress around me.

"Oh, fuck!" I exclaimed. I'd forgotten about Jack's dad.

I started drinking in the limo. Vodka. Bad idea. As soon as I made that decision, the stage was set.

A little while later we approached the theater, and Jack was right when he said the sound was petrifying. I'd never heard this sound before. No, that's not entirely true. I'd heard it, but prior to now I was always one of the people making the noise. I'd screamed my ass off at a concert or two, and when Holly and I went to see the New Kids last summer, we'd screamed like teenagers.

It is an entirely different thing to be on the outside watching the pandemonium than it is to be inside it, part of it. No wonder Jack had started using security.

Nick and I stared at the hundreds, maybe even thousands, of women standing and screaming and waving signs that said things like MARRY ME, JACK, and TAKE ME BACK IN TIME, and, my favorite, LIE ON TOP OF ME, JOSHUA.

Nice.

I took one last slug of vodka, and our limo pulled up to the red carpet. We were early enough that none of the cast was here yet, but that didn't stop the crowd from screaming when they saw the door open, and the cameras immediately started flashing. Nick strutted a bit before turning to help me out of the car. I was semigraceful, managing not to flash my business at the crowd. Jack had asked several times if I would please go commando, which I steadfastly refused to do. But he made sure to tell me *he* was going commando. *Jesus.*

Holly had made me show her my panties to be sure I had some on.

When the press realized we weren't anyone, the flashes stopped almost instantly, but a few asked who we were. Nick had been down the carpet a few times and gave his name. Someone asked for mine and without thinking, I gave it as well. Then I noticed a few of the photographers looking at me more carefully, and I heard the word *redhead*. I saw a few more flashes in my direction, and my flight instinct kicked in. I hurried Nick down the carpet.

"Why're you rushing me, girl? I am shining," he said, a smirk on his face. The women in the crowd were actually cheering for him. They were so amped up, anyone with a penis would make them shriek.

"I'll meet you inside. I need to get off this carpet," I said, glancing at a photographer. This one was following me. I could see him peripherally, and he was continuing to take pictures. I looked the other way, trying to hide my face.

"How will I find you?" Nick asked.

"Just find the bar. That's where I'll be," I answered and made for the door.

Right before I got there, the photographer got close enough for a tight shot. He said my name, and I turned. Someone says your name, you look.

"Are you the redhead we've seen with Jack?" he yelled over the noise.

I tried to shake my head, not willing to say anything.

He looked at me carefully. His eyes widened as he put it

together. "Fuck me, you are! You're the redhead! Jesus, how old *are* you?" He snapped a few more pictures as I almost ran inside.

Unbelievable.

Once in the lobby, I found the bar directly. This was exactly what I'd been afraid of—that someone would recognize me from the pictures taken of us over the summer and in New York. I was shaking. It was naive of me to think I could come here and not ruin this for Jack. *Fuck*.

I ordered a double dirty martini, light on the dirty.

I tried to calm down, foolishly thinking maybe the photographer would forget my name in the chaos quickly developing outside. So what if he had my name? No one knew who I was. But he had my picture, and he'd identified me as the redhead.

Shit, this was bad.

And clearly there was no question about whether I looked older than Jack. I sucked down the booze. I wasn't usually much of a drinker—strictly a two-cocktail limit—but tonight I needed all the liquid courage I could get.

I watched from my vantage point as the venue became more and more crowded. There were movie posters everywhere, and the mob was growing more and more wound.

I was working through my second double martini (to say nothing of at least three shots on the drive over) when I heard the crowd hit fever pitch. Nick had found me by then, and we made our way to the window to watch the show before the show.

The cast was arriving, actors with smaller roles first. It was a carefully orchestrated event. Rebecca soon appeared, and I was happy I'd get to spend time with her. She was a very cool chick. And then Lane was so cute. He was a natural on the red carpet, chatting with reporters and fans alike.

Suddenly, everyone got quiet. There was only one star not there, and one last limo had just pulled up.

And then Jack opened his door.

Utter. And. Total. Pandemonium. Ensued.

Women cried. Women fainted. Women yelled. Women screamed.

Jack stood and took it all in.

He was my Jack, and he was their Jack. He was Hollywood's Jack. He was a movie star.

He worked the red carpet with a mix of self-deprecation and cocky strut. He owned that freaking crowd. He was a natural because he was not a natural.

He took pictures with the cast and kept really close to Rebecca. These two were going through something so specific and stylized, and I was glad they had each other. I was grateful to her for helping him. And I had a feeling he calmed her as well.

Eventually he made it inside. I watched him work the room, looking around. For me? For his dad? Before I had a chance to get to him, someone else found him.

Marcia.

She was beautiful in person. She was poured into a gorgeous black dress, and her legs may have been six feet in length. She was radiant; she was stunning; she was young.

I was feeling no pain.

I watched her make eye contact with him from across the room. It was like freaking *West Side Story*. His eyes lit up as he saw her. They walked through the crowd toward each other, and I was frozen to the spot, unable to tear my eyes away.

Just friends. Just friends. Just friends.

My aunt Fannie.

You don't even have an aunt Fannie . . .

Shut it.

Have another cocktail, why don't you?

Great idea.

I was kidding.

They hugged like old friends. Old friends who'd shared something profound.

He caught my eye over her shoulder, and I raised my glass and an eyebrow to him.

He flinched and actually had the decency to look a little embarrassed.

I saw him talking to her, and I saw her turn to meet my eyes. She smiled warmly, and I smiled back. What is the opposite of warmly?

Coldly.

Yeah, yeah. I like that.

This is going to end badly, isn't it?

Saddle up.

thirteen

$\mathcal{A}$s Jack walked Marcia over to meet me, I set my empty glass down and tried hard not to fidget. But I was a fidgeter from way back. Even Jack had noticed it, and he knew when I was nervous.

Upon arrival, he immediately took my hand and squeezed it. "Don't fidget, Crazy. You look beautiful," he whispered.

I smiled at him and turned to Marcia. She was still smiling brightly at me.

"Marcia, this is Grace," he said, and my heart actually stopped when I heard him say her name. At one point he'd probably said it the way he said mine.

"Grace, I'm so happy to finally meet you. He talks about you all the time," she said, and leaned in to kiss both my cheeks.

Ah, shit. I don't want to like this bitch.

Jack smiled. He was enjoying this.

I kissed her back and smiled.

"Yes. I've heard a lot about you recently as well," I said, and she blushed a little.

"I know. Can you believe the rumors that get started?" she said.

Jack smirked as if to say "I told you so." I gave him a sharp look, and he just rolled his eyes.

"I need to talk to you," I whispered in a low voice, trying to convey urgency. I needed to tell him what had happened with the photographer.

"Oh, I already know what you want to talk about. That was the topic of conversation on the carpet out there," he whispered back, arching an eyebrow and staring down at me.

"I don't know what happened. I was just trying to get inside and—" I started, then Marcia interrupted me.

"Your dress is beautiful. Where'd your stylist find it?" she asked.

"Oh, I, uh, I found it myself. Bergdorf's. New York," I stammered. This child was freaking me out, and I hated that. I wished I had another drink.

"Oh, that's right. How are you enjoying Manhattan? It's a wonderful place to live, isn't it? Are you planning to sell your house here?" she asked, locking eyes with me.

Hmmm. She knew an awful lot about my plans.

"I don't know yet what I'm going to do. It all depends on what happens with the show, doesn't it, Sweet Nuts?" I asked, leaning farther into his arm as he wrapped it around my waist.

"Sweet Nuts?" she asked, wrinkling her nose.

"Private joke," I said, kissing on Jack's neck.

With radar as good as the military, Holly swooped in just at that moment and took Jack's arm. "I need you for a few minutes before the film starts," she told him. "Come with me please? Ladies," she said in parting, shooting me the hairy eye-ball.

"Ladies, I'll see you in there," Jack echoed. "Grace, we'll talk about this later. Don't worry." He tried to lean in to kiss me, but Holly Go-Cockblocker was right there.

"Please," she said, and pulled him away with a furious glance at me.

"I'm sorry," I mouthed, then realized I was alone with Marcia.

"So," I started, and she looked at me expectantly.

But the universe was kind and sent me an angel. I felt giant pawlike hands wrap around my waist and lift me into the air.

"I wondered if you'd make it back for this circus," a sexy voice purred, and I turned to look into a pair of ice-blue eyes.

"Lane!" I cried and gave him a big hug.

"Fuck, you look hot, Grace," he said, stepping back to give me the once-over.

"Thank you, dear. And you are always pretty." I laughed.

Just then Lane noticed who I was standing with, and he choked back a laugh. "Well, this looks interesting. What's the topic of conversation, girls?"

We laughed a little uncomfortably, and then Marcia spoke up. "You know, everyone expects we wouldn't get along simply because of a media-created story, but I can tell I like you already, Grace." She smiled warmly.

Again with the warmly.

And how the hell did all these twentysomethings get so damn mature? When I was her age, I was struggling with college math and trying to figure out how to buy a new Jeep Wrangler. They were like mini adults.

Lane burped.

Thank Christ. Now I smiled warmly.

"Marcia, I'm sure once we get to know each other we'll get along just fine. Now I'm going to find my date—a gay man, since I can't be seen in public with my real boyfriend. I should leave before someone takes our picture and writes a story about *you* with an unidentified redhead," I said with a wicked grin.

"Ah, good idea. It was wonderful to meet you, Grace. You're just as pretty as he said you were." With a smile and a graceful turn, Marcia walked back through the crowd. Not a hair out of place, not a wrinkle on her dress.

I really didn't want to like her, but I knew I would.

"Lane, Lane, Lane." I sighed and leaned back against him. I motioned to the bartender for another.

"We gettin' shitty tonight, Sheridan?" he asked, winking devilishly at me.

"Lane, I'm a grown-ass woman with a mortgage and a huge Bergdorf's bill. I don't get 'shitty.' But I *am* getting knee-walkin' drunk." I lifted my glass toward him. "You in?"

"Shall we drink to your newly outed relationship?"

"How the hell do you know about that?" I asked, eyes going all buggy.

"That's all anyone is talking about out there. Three reporters asked me if I knew about you, and how long Jack had been with the older redhead," he said.

"Great. I went from unidentified redhead to older redhead."

Next thing you know, you'll be the portly pepper-pot redhead.

Shut it.

I sipped my drink and looked expectantly at him.

"Hell, yes. Let's get it on!" He laughed and asked for a shot.

We joked and talked as he attempted to calm me down. He felt certain this would totally blow over.

"So, where's that hottie friend of yours—Holly?" he asked.

Again with the freaking radar, Holly instantly appeared at my side, taking notice of my third cocktail. What she didn't know was it was my third just since *getting here*.

"Breaking the two-drink rule tonight, are we?" she asked, then ordered one for herself.

"Holly, how are you?" Lane asked.

Holly's eyes went wide as she noticed my drinking buddy. "Lane. Nice to see you again. I'm well, thank you. And you?" Her voice seemed a little quivery.

What the hell?

"I'm great. Nice shoes," he murmured, looking down at her red heels. She blushed all the way to the roots of her hair, then turned back to me.

"Listen, Jack saved seats for you and Nick right behind him and his dad. You should go in before they do, though, so you aren't walking in together. We'll continue to deny this as long as we can, although you giving your name to the paparazzi was not too smart," she admonished.

"I didn't mean—"

"Let's not talk about it tonight. We'll play this off. I just need to think about how," she said.

"Where are *you* sitting, Holly?" Lane asked.

"I'm sitting with my client," she said, and turned back to me. "Scoot. Nick's waiting for you." She gave me a little push.

I drained the rest from my glass and set it on the bar. I was starting to feel a little unsteady on my feet, but I kept it together—in exactly the way someone who's been drinking thinks they're fooling everyone. I heard Lane say something to Holly in a low voice, then Holly shot back, "Later!" But I couldn't miss the excited flush to her skin when she said it.

This was a weird night.

I circled the room looking for Nick and found myself semi-hidden behind a potted palm. I noticed a well-dressed older man talking with Marcia, and as I heard his accent, I realized he was likely Jack's father. He was tall and very distinguished, and I caught a glimpse of Jack in thirty years or so. Classy. And here I was hiding behind a potted palm.

Jesus, could I get any more *After School Special*?

He definitely knew Marcia, though. They were having quite a chat.

I totally listened. Their talk wasn't so small.

"I like her. I think she's good for him," Marcia said. My chest burned.

"She is lovely, but I do wish he'd mentioned how much older she was."

"Well, Jack's kind of an old soul, and she seems to have a positive effect on him. I haven't seen him this happy in a while," Marcia said, suddenly my biggest fan.

I was such an asshole . . .

"You haven't met her yet?" Marcia continued, leaning in.

"No, not yet. I thought Jack might introduce her last night, but at the last minute he canceled our dinner and decided to eat with her instead. I suppose I'll meet her later. I wonder if Jack will make it through the film, though. You know how he feels about watching himself on-screen."

They both laughed.

I headed for the theater before I could hear anything else about my being an old bag, and I finally spied Nick by the door.

"Where the hell have you been? Holly's ready to have a cow," he said, hands on hips.

"Oh, would you settle down, please?" I said, listing slightly.

"Grace, you're drunk," he said, sniffing me.

Very nearly.

"I'm just pleasantly lit, so back the fuck up, pretty boy," I said, loudly enough to attract the attention of a few people walking in to take their seats.

"Oookay, let's get you inside," he said and took my arm.

We went down almost to the front, then slipped into the second row. I saw Rebecca talking to the director and waved exuberantly. She smiled and waved back, then whispered to him. I could tell she said the word *girlfriend*, and they turned to look at me.

Ah, well.

I saw Jack enter the theater with his father and Holly, and they all walked down to the front row. He winked at me as he passed and gestured me over. Nick helped me out of my chair, and I leaned across the back of the front row.

Jack stopped in front of me and went through the introductions with his father. This was now officially the most fucked-up night of my life. I was meeting my twenty-four-year-old boyfriend's father at the Hollywood premiere of a movie in which he had the starring role. And I was well on my way to public intoxication.

"So, I finally get to meet the mysterious Grace who has my son so thoroughly charmed," Jack's father said as he reached for my hand, which he quickly brought to his lips.

I was the one thoroughly charmed. "And I get to meet the man from whom Jack obviously got his good looks. I can't tell you how pleased I am to meet you, Mr. Hamilton."

"You must call me Alex. I must be on a first-name basis with any woman who has swept my son off his feet the way you have, yes? Although I daresay that if I'd met you first, my son would have had a little competition." He chuckled, and Jack rolled his eyes.

"Well, Alex, I daresay that I've always had a thing for older men, especially those from across the pond," I bantered back. Jack's father was still holding my hand.

"Well, there's something to be said for those of us who have a little more life experience, isn't there? Something Jack will no doubt learn as he gets a little older as well." He smiled again and released my hand to slap Jack on the back.

I might be more than a little tipsy, but I could still small talk with the best of them. At least, as far as I knew. According to my internal drunk-o-meter, I was cool as a cucumber and not at all showing the effects of my numerous cocktails. No effects at all . . .

The three of us chatted warmly for a few more minutes until the director headed up to the stage to make a little speech before the movie began. I accepted a kiss on the cheek from Alex before returning to my seat in the second row, behind Jack. He turned and leaned in just as I was about to sit down.

"I got this for you. I know you like a little snack while you watch a movie." He smiled and handed me a box of Milk Duds.

"Candy!" I exclaimed, ripping the box out of his hands with a little too much enthusiasm. I heard Nick sigh next to me as I tried to open the box. Then Jack offered to help me.

"I got it, I got it!" I insisted. I finally wrenched the top off and spilled Milk Duds all over the place. I smiled to everyone sitting around us. "Sorry, I just thought you might all like some candy," I joked, finding myself hilarious.

"Funny, I thought you never shared candy," Jack said, looking at me more carefully.

"Nope, I just don't share candy with you." I laughed loudly, and Holly turned from talking to Jack's father.

"What the fuck?" she mouthed at me, and I dropped into my chair.

I saw her and Nick exchange glances, and that pissed me off. I wasn't going to be handled. I started to stand up and say something to Holly to that very effect when the lights dimmed. The film was about to start.

"Are you okay?" Jack asked.

"Fine, love. I'm fine," I said, shoving a Milk Dud in my mouth.

He glanced at Nick as well, and now I was really starting to get pissed. He sat down directly in front of me.

I was sitting *behind* my boyfriend on the biggest night of his life. I couldn't even hold his hand, whisper to him, or give him a congratulatory kiss—although apparently the entire entertainment news community now knew Jack Hamilton had a granny fetish.

I sighed loudly and slipped off my shoes.

Nick leaned over and whispered, "Are you sure you're okay?"

"The next person who asks me that will get their balls handed to them. I'm not kidding," I whispered back through clenched, caramel-coated teeth.

He backed off.

The movie started.

I watched the back of Jack's head watch his movie.

Ten minutes in, after fussing about in his seat the entire time, he took off. Literally. As soon as Jack saw himself on the screen, he bailed.

I'd tentatively reached out with my fingertip to touch the back of his neck when I saw him begin to fidget, but Nick had slapped my hand down. He was well versed in Holly's rules for the night.

For fuck's sake. I'd had about enough.

When he stood to get up, I almost did too. I had to force myself to wait five whole minutes before I stole out of the theater. Nick tried to grab my arm to stop me, but I was the one slapping his hand now. I was going to follow my Brit.

I found him by the bar. He was not alone. Marcia had already found him, and they looked to be sharing a cocktail. They were laughing. He looked calmer already. She was calming him. I saw a rogue photographer draw close but I no longer cared.

I turned and walked swiftly toward the ladies' room, the sounds of their mixed laughter following me.

The lighting in the bathroom would have worked equally well for interrogation. The bags under my eyes were highlighted nicely, as were my laugh lines, which were suddenly not as funny as they used to be. My faced look haggard, tired, and sad.

So sad.

As I looked in the mirror, I saw a different image than earlier in the evening. My skin that I'd thought looked tanned and glowy now looked streaky and orange. My hair that I'd thought looked curly and wavy now looked frizzy and obnoxious. My eyes were puffy from the cocktails and had begun to resemble the cabbages they'd surely turn into tomorrow. They always did.

My phone beeped. It was a text from Jack.

Gracie
Where are you?
George

I also had a text from earlier. I hadn't heard it come through.

Grace
The Village Voice is raving about you! New York misses you. When are you coming home?
Michael

I smiled. It was the only thing that had made me smile in more than an hour. New York was a world away from where I was tonight. And New York was a world I understood. A world I was kind of rising to the top of, actually. Not this ridiculous charade. I smiled again in spite of myself, and the door to the ladies' room opened. It was Marcia.

"There you are. Jack's looking for you," she said, coming to stand next to me at the counter, under the same lighting.

Her skin was perfect. Her hair was perfect. Her face was smooth and unlined. *She* was a star. My smile faded. I belonged in some kind of dietary fiber commercial.

I turned to her. "Well, I saw him leave, so of course I went to follow him—you know, offer a little comfort to my one and only. But look at that, someone else beat me to the punch. I seemed a little unnecessary." My voice was cutting and sarcastic.

"Grace, I didn't follow him out there. I saw him out in the lobby and we just—"

173

I cut her off. "Enough. I'm too old for this crap. I don't have the energy. Please tell *Jack* that I'm not feeling well, and I went home." I barely managed to get the words out, the drunk tears starting to build. This was too much. I'd reached my limit. I was nearly out of control but wise enough to remove myself from the situation. I spun on my heel and made for the door.

"Grace?" she called after me.

My hand on the door, I turned wearily back toward her. She was still lovely.

"There's something on your dress, on the back. It looks like, well, it looks like you sat in something," she said, her face bright red.

I turned to look.

Fucking Milk Dud.

Right in the middle of my ass. It looked like I had a little turd stuck to me.

Of course you do.

You know when you just have one of those really shitty days? When nothing works, when it just gets worse and worse, and you think you're going to burst into tears over and over again? But you keep it together. You don't know how you do it, but you maintain. Then you do something stupid like stub your toe or drop your coffee, and that's the last straw. And you lose your fucking mind.

I saw it clearly now. This was not my world. This was never my world. Jack needed someone better suited for this life. And it was not me. I didn't deserve someone as wonderful and amazing as Jack. It didn't matter that I loved him more than anyone in my entire life.

The writing was on the wall, the Milk Duds were on the

chair. And I sat smack dab in the middle of them. I sighed heavily, my shoulders hunching over.

"Please don't take this personally, Marcia, because I can tell you are honestly a nice person. And I know Jack would never be friends with a jerk, so I know you're not. But you strike me as the kind of girl who has never, and would never, sit on a motherfucking Milk Dud. And I really can't be around that kind of girl right now. It was nice to meet you. Take care of him, please." I left the ladies' room.

I walked straight through the lobby, not even bothering to hide my ass and the remnants of the Dud. I kept my head down as I made my way to the street, and, forgetting about trying to find my limo, I went through the line of fans, crossed the street, and hailed a cab.

☆ ☆ ☆

I went back to my house, took off my dress, and left it in a puddle on the kitchen floor. I threw my shoes at the wall. I stood under the shower for a solid hour while my phone rang and rang and rang on the bathroom counter. When I got out of the shower, I put it in the freezer without even checking messages, and I grabbed the Absolut.

I sat on a lawn chair on the patio, drinking icy vodka from an "I Got Lei'd in Hawaii" shot glass shaped like a hula dancer.

After a while I heard a car pull up. I heard keys in the door. I heard loud footsteps clunking through the house, and I heard him yelling for me.

I didn't answer.

I heard his voice getting closer and angrier. He finally came to the French doors on the patio and looked out into the darkness. He couldn't see me, and he clicked on the floodlights.

They illuminated everything. My wet hair, the mascara all over, my vodka bottle. My tearstained face. My defeated face. My resigned and determined face.

"What the fuck, Grace?" he asked, face angry.

We stared at each other across the patio.

I set down the bottle and stood to face him. I was shockingly sober, considering the amount of alcohol I'd consumed.

"Jack, first let me apologize for leaving you tonight. I had to get out of there—"

"Why the hell did you leave?" he interrupted. "What—"

I held up my hand. "I'm not finished. Please let me say this. I'm sorry I left you tonight," I began again, my voice very low and controlled.

He waited, then nodded for me to continue.

"This isn't going to work, Jack," I said, and I felt my body tense.

"What's not going to work? What are you talking about?" He stepped out of the doorway and down onto the flagstone.

"This. Us. This isn't going to work. We need to cut our losses now, before either of us gets in any deeper." I was amazed at the sound of my voice. I sounded so in control.

A better word for it would be dead. *You sound dead.*

I felt dead.

"Are you kidding me with this shit? What the fuck is wrong with you, Grace?" he yelled. He actually yelled at me. He crossed the patio in three long strides and grabbed me by the arms. I flopped like a rag doll, lifeless.

"We should never have started this in the first place. We want totally different things, and we should stop this now. This has to stop," I heard myself say. It was like I was underwater and could hear myself talking. The words were murky and thick. It didn't even sound like me.

"You're crazy, you know that? How in the world can you even think about ending things with me? You know we're perfect together," he said, his eyes pained. He knew I was serious.

His eyes pierced my veil, and I began to feel some things. Hurt. Sickness. Panic. Anger.

"Don't say that. I see perfection, but I don't see it here. Do you know how I felt, seeing you and her together tonight?" My voice began to rise.

"Oh, please, Grace. Is that what this is about? How many times can I tell you there's nothing going on between Marcia and me?" His voice matched mine in intensity.

I ignored the way my stomach contracted when he said her name. "Oh, I believe you. I know you're just friends. But that's the kind of girl you *should* be with. A *girl*—not some geezery woman like me. And now that the press knows who I am, how old I am, they'll fucking crucify me. We've been fooling ourselves to think this could work outside the little sex bubble we've been living in."

He was quiet. He was so angry. I'd never seen him so angry. When he let go of my arms, I had little Jack-prints on my skin.

"I've never in my life seen someone deliberately run in the opposite direction of happiness more than you do," he said, staring daggers into my eyes.

"What?"

"You heard me. You push it away as hard as you can. You and I both know there's no one on the planet better suited for you than me, no one better equipped to handle all your shit, and yet here you are. Throwing it away like you don't care."

"I do care! I love you! But I just know in my heart this is wrong. You don't need all my shit. It isn't fair to you. That doesn't mean I don't love you, but this just isn't the right time for us. You don't realize how they're going to blow this up, you dating a much older woman—they're going to crucify you," I said, my voice beginning to crack.

"Would you please let me decide what I can and can't handle? God*damn*, Grace. You act like you're *so* difficult. Did you ever stop to think that I need you, too? That you're perfect for me? That you put up with my shit as well? You can't just give me your love and then take it away without asking. It doesn't work like that!" he snapped. He ran both hands through his hair, stopping with them on either side of his face.

I softened when I saw him look so sad, and he saw me weaken. He moved in fast.

He pressed his body into mine and kissed me hungrily, his hands finding their way inside my robe. I moaned in spite of myself, my body reacting the way it always did with his hands on me. It wasn't enough, though.

I pushed away.

His face looked broken.

I placed my own hands on either side of his face, cradling it. We both had tears now.

"When you're a little older, you'll see this more clearly," I said, and he closed his eyes.

When he opened them, they were cold.

"Don't you dare bring my age into this when you're the one acting like a child," he glowered.

That was what I needed. I backed away, closing my robe and my heart to him. "I need you to leave," I said, my voice as cold as his eyes. I was back in control, and I was making the right choice.

"Don't do this, Gracie," he pleaded, his voice softer now.

I turned away. I couldn't look at him. "I have to. I need some time. I'll call you when I can," I said, effectively ending the conversation.

And us.

He walked away without another word.

I waited until I heard the car leave, and then I fell apart.

Eventually, I went inside and packed up my shit. I couldn't look at our bed. I got my phone out of the freezer. I barely saw the Post-it and the picture.

I went to Holly's. She took me in, fed me ice cream and aspirin, and didn't yell at me for ruining her client's big night.

She put me on a plane back to New York the next day.

Broken.

What had I just done?

fourteen

$\mathcal{I}$t had been six days since I left L.A. Six days since I'd seen Jack. Six days since I'd talked to Jack. Six days since I broke both our hearts.

I was miserable. I literally did not know what to do.

I'd been through bad breakups before, and the first days are the worst. All you want to do is avoid reminders of the boy in question. But imagine you've just broken up with the new It Boy.

The day after the premiere, the entertainment shows and online blogs were full of pictures of me and Jack. I scrutinized the images of me solo on the red carpet, and I looked better than I'd thought. Seeing myself without dirty-martini glasses (which were evidently the fancy girl's beer goggles, but with a tragically opposite effect) certainly improved things. I still saw the flaws, though. The curves that maybe shouldn't be quite so curvy. The hair that was a little too frizzy.

The media also re-posted the pictures from last summer,

including the one from our first date at Gladstones where I was pointing with a shrimp. That one tugged at my heart a lot. That was the day he kissed me for the first time. They brought back pictures from our outings in Los Angeles last summer and this fall in New York. Now there was a name with them: Grace Sheridan, age thirty-three.

Holly had confirmed that I was a client, as well as her friend. She denied the rumor that Jack and I had been dating, explaining simply that we were good friends and had gotten to know each other when I was staying with her last summer.

Conveniently, pictures of Jack and Marcia had surfaced as well, including a new batch of the two at lunch in L.A. Holly was a master at spin, and the Grace and Jack story was quickly dropped by the mainstream media when Jack refused to comment.

On the fan websites, though? The story ran rampant and wouldn't go away. My reviews were decidedly mixed. Rumors and speculation ran wild as to whether I was really his girlfriend. I was called Grace Sheridon't, Grace McOldAss, and That Redheaded Hamilton Fucker. That last one was pretty funny, actually.

And there was a small group who seemed to really like the idea that Jack was maybe, possibly dating an older woman. I had a feeling these women were all in their thirties . . .

I allowed myself a peek that first day, and then I stopped looking. It was too hard to see the pictures, and it was too hard to see how happy Jack had been that night—his big night. Before I broke his heart.

I was in the final weeks of rehearsal, as the first week of previews had been pushed up to the week after Thanksgiving. I was in a black funk most of the time and not looking forward to celebrating a holiday right now. Which was fine, because the rehearsal schedule left no time for cooking or cavorting, and Holly had ended up stuck in L.A. The entertainment industry never slows down, even for a holiday. The cast had turkey sandwiches and cranberries from a can for lunch break on Thanksgiving Day, but otherwise the day slipped by unnoticed.

Leslie knew I'd broken up with Jack, and while she looked at me like I was the most insane person on the planet, she didn't ask me about it. Poor Michael didn't know what to do with himself.

He knew I was devastated, but I don't think he quite understood what I'd done, or why I'd done it in such a dramatic, all-or-nothing fashion. I was questioning it myself, but my decision was based in self-preservation, and as much as I was in total and complete hell, I was pushing through it. I'd had to end it, before it ended us.

Now I focused all my energy on the show and on Mabel, the aging beauty queen. She became the conduit through which my frustration flowed, and it all came out onstage. I was powerful. I was broken.

Late at night after rehearsal, I roamed the streets of Manhattan, losing myself in the city. New York was beautiful and totally unlike any other city I'd lived in. It seemed to be enormous and untouchable, a giant. But it was really lovely and warm when you broke it down neighborhood by neighborhood, street by street. Because there were so many people there, I relished the anonymity. Everyone was bundled in coats and hats, and no one knew anyone. You could be anyone or no one in this town. I walked and walked, trying to beat back the voices in my head.

Jack's movie opened. I'd tried to avoid all things *Time* since the night of the premiere, but it was nearly impossible to do. I damn near stomped on my laptop when I saw his face on my Yahoo! homepage. I broke into tears when I walked past the posters on every street corner or saw the magazines on every newsstand.

Women everywhere wanted him. I'd had him. Had been loved by him. And I pushed him away *like it was my job*. What the hell was wrong with me? I picked up the phone to call him a dozen times, but I just couldn't.

Holly was oddly silent on the matter, choosing to keep our conversations light and airy. We had only one discussion about Jack. She'd been telling me a story about another of her assistant's celebrity freak-outs. Sara had tried so hard to play it cool, but it became too much for her and she cried, laughed, and damn near pissed herself when Lane came into the offices.

I laughed so hard at the image I had tears in my eyes. "Oh man, you know Lane is riding high on his *Time* fame!"

I was just about to ask why he'd been at Holly's offices when she said quietly, "Aren't you going to ask me how he's doing?"

I stopped laughing almost instantly, but the tears remained. She didn't mean Lane.

"How is he?" I whispered.

"Miserable," she said.

I was quiet, taking it in.

"Grace, you know I love you, and I will support every decision you make. But I think, well . . ."

"Well, what?"

"I think you might have been wrong on this one."

I sighed heavily. "I know you love me, but I just need this right now, okay? I know you don't understand why I did what I did—hell, I barely do. But right now, I just need some time. Please, let's not talk about this again until some more time has passed."

She waited a moment, then agreed. We talked a few more minutes, then she told me she loved me, and we said good-bye.

This whirlwind romance with Jack had brought up every insecurity I'd ever had. Sure, we were great when it was just us, but when you put it in the context of real life? It had to end. I didn't know what I wanted in my romantic life, but it no longer made sense for me to be playing house with a twenty-four-year-old. No matter how much I loved him.

And Michael? He was my rock.

We spent even more time together. A few nights, he walked me home from rehearsal, and we talked about anything and everything—avoiding all things Hamilton, but anything else was fair game. We let some feelings out that had been carefully walled up for weeks, years even. Did it make me forget about Jack? No, but it did help. Spending time with Michael and remembering how good and simple things once had been was incredibly helpful. It eased some of my guilt over the terrible way I'd ended things with Jack.

One night, when rehearsal had ended early for a change, I heard Michael call after me as I headed out the door.

"Hey, Grace!"

"Hey, what?" I smiled as I turned around.

"Great rehearsal today. I didn't think you could get any better, but, man, lately you're really on fire!" His whole face lit up. He stood next to me in the doorway, hair wild. His warm brown eyes gazed into mine.

Those damn eyes. I'd thought about them for years.

"Yes, well, breakups are great for creativity, aren't they?" I chuckled ruefully.

He stopped smiling instantly. "Oh shit, Grace. I'm sorry. I know this is tough right now. If there's something I can do . . ." He trailed off.

"No, it's okay. You just gotta go through it, right? I'll see you tomorrow." I patted him on the arm and turned to walk out.

"Grace?"

"Now this is getting ridiculous." I laughed, looking over my shoulder.

"What are you doing tonight?"

"I was going to take a walk, then grab some dinner on the way home. Why? What's up?"

"Well, I was thinking we could grab dinner and maybe a movie?"

No movies. Time *posters everywhere. You can't handle that.*

"Ugh, no movies," I said, shaking my head vigorously and pointing at the poster on the bus stop across the street.

"Oh, right! Of course. That was rude. I just thought . . . I don't know . . ." His head tilted down toward the ground.

On impulse, I reached out and raised his chin. "How about just dinner?"

I surprised myself.

I definitely surprised him.

We'd eaten dinner together countless times since I'd moved to New York, but this was different. We both knew what I was asking.

My fingers felt the scruff of his whiskers. He hadn't shaved today. His hand tentatively reached up and took mine, raising his eyebrows to see if this was okay. It was the first time we'd physically acknowledged each other this way since being thrown back together. Up until now it had been playful hugs and punching.

"Dinner sounds great," he said, grinning.

My heart beat a mile a minute. "Let's go." I opened the door and led him out into the street. Into the city.

As we walked, we kept our hands clasped. At one point, he noticed me glancing down at our entwined fingers.

"Is this okay?" he asked.

"Yes, it's okay." I nodded, shivering a little in the night air. I had on my leather coat, but it was November on the East Coast, and it was cold.

He let go of my hand and wrapped an arm around me, pulling me closer. He looked at me, questioning again, and I nodded once more, although the Drawer was rattling a little.

Had enough time passed since the end with Jack?

It's been weeks.

It was time to explore these feelings I was having. It was a little strange being so close to another man, but this was Michael, after all. Still, my thoughts strayed to Jack. I wondered what he was doing tonight. I wondered if he'd ever understand what I was doing.

I wondered if *I'd* ever understand what I was doing.

Michael smelled different than Jack, but good. Like wool and sage and lemons. And Right Guard. He smelled the same as he had in college, when I fell in love with him. This felt odd but right.

We ended up at a small sushi bar on the Upper West Side,

close to my apartment. I'd become a frequent patron of this restaurant—fantastic spicy tuna rolls. We squeezed into a booth at the back and ordered hot sake. As we sipped, I realized we could very well be on our first-ever date.

I was suddenly nervous, and it seemed he was as well. I'd look at him, then he'd look away. He'd stare at me, and I'd look down at the table. We were in a constant state of blush. He was red to the tips of his ears, and I could feel my chest burning bright.

When we both looked away for the tenth time, I reached across the table and grasped his hand. "We're being silly, aren't we?"

"Yes," he said, letting his breath out all at once. He looked instantly more relaxed, and I giggled.

His eyes twinkled. "It's silly that after all the time we've known each other we're so nervous," he said, picking up his sake with the hand that wasn't clasping mine.

"As I recall, you used to make me nervous all the time," I said, sipping from my own tiny cup.

"You nervous? Ha. You didn't seem so nervous the night you attacked me," he teased, setting down his cup and holding my hand in both of his. He traced the inside of my wrist with his fingertips, and my skin reacted with goose bumps.

"I really did attack you, didn't I?" I laughed as the waitress set down our tray, and we began to eat.

"Yes, you really did. You actually knocked my head into the wall behind me so hard I saw stars," he said, mixing wasabi and soy sauce with his chopstick.

"I did? Well, I wanted to get your attention, and I figured shoving my tongue down your throat would do the job pretty quickly." I laughed, suddenly feeling a little less at ease.

"You always had my attention, Grace," he said quietly, looking up at me through his long eyelashes.

My heart leaped, then my stomach clenched. I thought of Jack.

Michael picked up a piece of salmon with his chopsticks and raised it into the air. "Well, Grace, here's to you. And to the show. And to Mabel, who I now think I created expressly to bring you back into my life." He smiled, those damnable brown eyes warm.

"To Mabel," I added, raising my own chopsticks in celebration.

We spent the evening enjoying each other. I felt more and more relaxed as the night went on, and despite some momentary pangs for enjoying dinner with another man, I pushed through it.

This is what you wanted, remember?

"Do you ever think about that night, Grace?" Michael asked as we lazily sipped the last of our sake, waiting for the check.

"Yes. Sometimes. Do you?" I asked, knowing instantly what he was referring to, my voice steady. His gaze met mine, and neither of us looked away this time.

"Yes. More so lately. Over the years I thought about you and wondered where you were, what you were up to. I missed you sometimes," he said.

"I missed you too," I whispered, my voice no longer steady.

The check came and he put his credit card down without even looking at the waitress. She took it away while we stared at each other.

He licked his lips.

I tugged at my hair.

Our eyes never left each other.

The check came back to the table, and our gaze finally broke as he signed the receipt.

He stood and helped me with my coat. I was fighting with my scarf, trying to get my hair out from underneath it when he leaned in to help. I felt his fingers graze the back of my neck, and the instant spark from his touch made me take an extra breath. He brushed my hair out of the way and straightened it out. I stared up at him, the scent of warm wool and lemons thick in the air between us.

"You ready?" he asked, his voice low.

"I think so," I answered, looking deep into his eyes.

He led me to the door, and we walked the few blocks to my apartment. We didn't talk. I kept my arm looped through his, and he kept me close. We stopped in front of my door, and he looked at me.

"Well, I'll see you in the morning, eight a.m."

"Yep, eight a.m.," I answered, swinging my arms nervously.

"Grace, I'm really glad we did this. It was really . . . nice," he said. I felt a wave of nostalgia crash through me, as I remembered what had made me fall in love with him back in the day.

"Me too," I replied, focusing all my attention on that bottom lip.

"So, good night," he said, and turned to walk away.

I closed my eyes and took a deep breath. That bottom lip, that lip. My entire world was tied to that bottom lip. Why were all the men in my life constantly biting on their lower lip? And why did I find it so sexy?

I saw Jack—Johnny Bite Down—in my head, his face broken and sad that last night in L.A. I saw Michael holding my hand as we walked the streets of New York.

You can do this.

"Wait, Michael!" I called.

He turned back, an expectant look on his face.

"Do you want to come up for a while?" I asked, smiling.

He looked at me, eyes full of questions.

I nodded in affirmation.

"You sure?" he asked, walking toward me.

"Yes."

He came back to me. "Then, yes. I'll come up." He took my hand and brought it to his mouth. His warm lips pressed to my skin, and I stared at the man I'd let get away from me when I was twenty-one.

The man who broke your heart, you mean?

Yes, yes. Whatever.

But he was here now. Again. And I knew we were perfect for each other. All the signs pointed to it. I mean, people float in and out of your life for a reason. Michael and I were meant to fix what we should've never let break in the first place, all those years ago. I knew he wanted me. I knew that for certain now.

I took another deep breath and squelched the image that kept rising in my head: my George.

I pushed it aside with all my might, slammed the Drawer, and reached for Michael's other hand. Walking backward into my building, I pulled him with me. "Come on," I said, and we went inside.

fifteen

*M*ichael followed me into the elevator without another word. I took a deep breath as I pressed the button for my floor. My head was whirling—from the sake, from the closeness of Michael, from the distance from Jack.

When the door *pinged* open, I looked at Michael and was overcome by the warmth in his eyes. He smiled hesitantly at me, and I smiled back. I extended my hand once more to him and pulled him out into the hallway. We walked silently down the hall to my door, and when I pulled my keys out, he took them and opened the door for me. He nodded and let me walk in before him. As I passed him, I took another hit of wool and lemons, and my eyes crossed a little. It was intoxicating.

I took off my coat. He removed his. I asked him if he wanted anything to drink. He declined. I started to say something about the mess in my apartment. There was no mess.

And then he came to me, all comfort and safe haven, and opened his arms.

I fell into them, my face nuzzling against the soft fleece covering his chest. I could feel his breathing speed up as mine did, and I felt his arms around me, his face buried in my hair, his breath hot in my ear.

I was spun backward in time to a futon and a boy and a girl discovering each other. My hands clutched at his fleece as his hands dug into the small of my back.

"Grace," I heard him say, and I shivered.

I pulled away to look up and was momentarily blinded by the feeling shining from his eyes. I smiled shyly at him, and he bent his head. He pressed his lips to mine as softly and shyly as my smile. My stomach tightened as I allowed myself to feel everything coursing through me at that moment.

His hands moved across my back, gently pressing me into his body. I deepened our kiss, tracing my tongue across his bottom lip and sucking it into my mouth. He sighed, his breath fanning across my face in a heavenly way.

He answered my kiss with a deeper one of his own, his hands now tangled in my hair. My hands slipped around to his back, sliding up under his pullover, touching his skin for the first time.

We pulled apart for one second, the space between us crackling. Our foreheads met.

His hands moved restlessly from my hair to my back, continuing to press me farther into him. I felt his excitement at our closeness. It was thrilling.

I trailed my nails down his back, and he groaned.

"Grace, you're killing me." He laughed, and I smiled in response.

"Let me," I whispered.

His hands crept between us, and he slipped my shirt out of

my pants. My skin was on fire as I felt his knuckles graze my tummy, and I inhaled quickly.

He stopped, bending his head to meet my eyes. "Is this okay?" he asked, concern in his face.

You sure about this?

Shhhh.

"It's okay, Michael. Really." I brought my hands back around front and slipped them under his shirt.

He grinned, then closed his eyes at the sensation of my hands exploring his chest and abdomen. I pushed up his shirt and kissed his skin. His scent was stronger here, the heat concentrated. I kissed across his chest and felt his hands raise my shirt. He began to undress me. I let him.

We made our way to the bedroom, and as we walked, me backward and him forward, shirts were removed. We smiled and laughed a little, in the way that young kids do when they discover something new and exciting, but a little scary.

We paused at the edge of the bed, neither of us quite sure who would make the first move, beyond simple exploration and into something much more serious. I closed my eyes, took a breath, and pushed him down onto the comforter. He quickly rolled so that I was beneath him, and held my face in his hands as he gazed down at me.

"I've thought about having you this way again for so long, Grace," he murmured, sweeping kisses across my forehead and down across my face.

He bent his head to me, his curly hair tickling as he made his way down my body, kisses becoming more and more urgent. It felt wonderful and surreal and warm and comforting and weird and strange and *too much.*

My brain and my heart began to fight, and my body waited to see who would win.

His mouth sought me, nuzzled at my breast, and his wonderfully kind hands reached my bra, beginning to touch the skin underneath. I closed my eyes and felt his warm tongue touch me. My body reacted, and I arched underneath him. I heard him groan, and felt his lips encircle my breast. I opened my eyes and looked down to see his looking up at me.

His eyes were warm.

My body was cold.

His rich, cozy scent of wool and lemons was now too thick, too much, too *there*.

Lemons. My lemon trees. Home.

Home is where your heart is. Where is your heart, Grace?

This was wrong. Grace and Michael lived perpetually back in college, in what might have been. As lovely as this idea was, it was now all wrong.

I felt my eyes burning. My heart had won. Tears rolled down my cheeks, and all I could see was my sweet Jack—the pain in his eyes when I closed my heart to him.

"Michael, please," I begged.

"Grace, I know, I know," he whispered, kissing me intimately.

"No, Michael, I can't. I just can't," I said, pulling him back up my body.

"Gracie, what's wrong?" he asked, sitting up and caressing my face.

You are not his Gracie.

"Please don't call me that," I said, tears running freely now.

Horrified, he sat back on the side of the bed. I sat up, pulling my shirt back in place to cover myself.

Tears ran down my face as I tried to explain to my dear, sweet friend why this couldn't happen. "Michael, I'm so sorry, but I just can't," I said, brushing his hair back from his face. He'd slipped his shirt back on, and now sat with me, his arm around my shoulders. I'd wrapped myself tightly in a blanket.

"I knew this was too soon," he said. "I should never have come up here. This was too soon after, well . . ." He rocked me back and forth.

"I don't want to hurt you. Oh, Michael, I just adore you," I cried, throwing my arms around him again. I felt safe, now that I'd stopped what this was about to become. I still had alarm bells going off in my head, but they were starting to quiet down.

"We just need to slow down. I'm not going anywhere," he replied.

I stopped short. I needed to be clear. I couldn't leave him behind as another casualty.

"No, Michael, I can't do this. Ever," I started, as he stared at me, blinking. "You're too good a friend to me, but I think . . . I think our time has passed. Don't you feel it? Doesn't this feel too much like we're trying too hard?" I begged him with my eyes, wanting him to see it, feel it too.

"Aw, Grace. You're too crazy for me. What the hell?" he slumped back on the bed, covering his face with his arm.

"I know. I'm so sorry. I never meant to lead you on. This just isn't—it isn't right."

This wasn't about two old friends who should have. This was about two reinvented friends who should not.

He studied my face carefully, not speaking for several minutes. I blushed under his scrutinizing gaze.

Hurricane Grace: another victim.

Jeez, I'm an asshole . . .

"I really wish you could've figured this out before I was almost naked." He grimaced, winking at me.

I threw back my head and laughed. That felt really good. "Is this okay? I'm so sorry, Michael."

"Grace, just don't. I'll be fine. I'm not gonna say I'm not upset, but I'll be fine. You need to get your shit figured out, though. 'Cuz damn, woman. You're fucked-up."

After wiping the tears from my eyes with the sleeve of his fleece, he got up to leave. I followed him to the front door.

He turned to me again, shrugging into his jacket and buttoning up. "Grace, for what it's worth, I love you," he said, his face serious, but kind.

"I know. I love you too. Friends?" I asked, wrapping his scarf around his neck.

"Of course, friends. 'Night, Grace," he said, and leaned in to kiss me softly.

I let him.

"'Night. See you tomorrow."

He nodded and was gone.

I went back to my room, put on my white polo, and got into my now-unmade bed. I turned on the TV and watched the end of *The Wizard of Oz*. My favorite part has always been when Dorothy realizes she's had the power all along. She can go home whenever she's ready.

I cried myself to sleep.

☆ ☆ ☆

The next day we had rehearsal only in the morning, finishing by one. Michael and I seemed surprisingly okay. My worries about an uncomfortable repeat performance of our previous morning-after behavior were quickly put to rest when he asked me to grab a quick coffee. I smiled and agreed, and we headed to a coffee shop around the corner.

"So this is awkward, huh?" I asked, as we settled into a booth.

"It doesn't have to be. So what if you ruined me last night and I had to lift a few cars on the way home? I'll manage," he teased, and I banged my head on the table.

"I really am sorry, Michael. Truly," I managed, talking to the Formica tabletop.

"I know you are, Grace. But you could've at least given me a little hand action before you sent me on my way," he said, eyes twinkling.

"Shut up. You know, not for nothing, but I really did think you and I were going to end up together," I admitted.

"I did too," he answered thoughtfully.

"You and me in college together, now back in each other's lives—I feel like it means something . . ." I said, my voice trailing off.

"It does. It just isn't going to be the way I wanted it to be. But it's good. We're good." He smiled and took a bite of his bagel.

I munched along with him.

"I have to ask, why the hell did you break up with that guy? What did he do?"

"He didn't do anything," I said helplessly. "It was all me. I lost my shit and let my head take over. And your sister didn't help matters either, planting all these seeds in my head about kids."

He laughed.

"What? Why are you laughing?" I asked, kicking him in the shin.

"She says that to everyone! She thinks everyone should have kids. That doesn't mean she knows what the hell she's talking about, though."

"Yeah, yeah, now you tell me. But really, she got me thinking. What if I *do* want kids someday? I can't have them with a twenty-four-year-old. That's ridiculous." I laughed, an image springing to mind of Jack pushing a baby carriage.

Funny.

"Why not? Have you asked him?"

"No. Yes. I mean, I don't know! We talked about it once, in a very random way, and he said he didn't want kids—for sure he didn't want kids. And I thought I didn't either. I still don't know, I just— Jesus this is a mess," I said, shaking my head.

"So, you broke up with a guy you're in love with because of kids you don't even know if you want, and you didn't even tell him that? Wow, did I dodge a bullet last night." He raised his eyebrows at me.

"Shut up, O'Connell!" I threatened, kicking him a little higher. He quickly moved his legs out of the line of fire, then looked at me seriously.

"Besides, Grace, no guy wants kids when he's—how old did you say he is?"

"Twenty-four. He's twenty-four." I sighed.

"For the record, when I was twenty-four, the last thing on my mind was having kids. If you'd asked me then, I would probably have said no way."

☆　☆　☆

That afternoon, as I traipsed through the city on one of my walks, I thought about what Michael had said. I really never *did* explain things to Jack.

No shit.

I found myself in front of a movie theater, and on impulse I bought a ticket and went in to see *Time*. I was overcome when I saw Jack on-screen. He was larger than life, and beautiful and sweet and funny and brilliant.

I would like to say that I paid attention to the plot and the story, but all I could see was my Jack. I cried and cried, and ate an entire bucket of popcorn.

As I left the theater, I thought again about whether I wanted kids, and what I really was giving up. I walked back to my apartment, changed into a pair of leggings and a fleece, and went out for a run. I had to work off all that popcorn.

I ran over to Central Park and followed my normal path, up to the reservoir and back again. I cursed myself for forgetting my iPod. For the last few weeks, whenever I ran I made sure to turn my old-school gangsta rap up loud. That way Eazy-E, NWA, and Ice T kept my thoughts at bay.

As I ran today, I thought about Jack and his grin. His hands and his lips. His humor and wit. His good heart. I thought about how much he loved me.

Flashes of *The Wizard of Oz* kept coming to me, and I thought of Dorothy, who had to go all the way to Oz and back before she realized she had everything she truly wanted right in her own backyard.

I came upon a family walking together. The man held a baby, and the woman pushed the stroller. A little girl in pigtails walked in front of them. I smiled and stopped to stretch a little, watching them, and as I watched, I waited.

I waited to feel something. I waited for something to happen. I waited for something to strike me over the head, like a giant gong or a sign that said:

THAT'S IT, GRACE. THAT'S WHAT YOU WANT. THAT'S A FAMILY. GO GET ONE.

As I waited to try and feel something, a small, quiet voice spoke up.

What are you waiting for?

Shh! I'm waiting for a sign.

What do you think I am?

You're not a sign. You're the idiot who got me in trouble in the first place. You're the one that convinced me to break up with Jack.

No, love, you did that on your own.

Then what the hell are you saying? What the hell kind of sign are you?

You want a family? Who defines what a family is?

An image appeared: Holly and Nick parading into my bedroom, laughing and carrying on. Another image: Holly and me sitting on my back patio, cocktails in hand, laughing until we cried. Holly and me sitting on the floor in front of her fridge, passing the Easy Cheese. Michael and me arguing politics while others rolled their eyes. Michael and me sharing a bagel, a schmear, and the *New York Times*. Nick driving me home from the airport.

Jack.

Jack shirtless and shoeless, playing guitar for me while I

made our bed. Jack holding my boobies while I washed his hair. Jack lying next to me in bed, Chex Mix bag between us. Jack driving to Santa Barbara with his hand on my knee. Jack asleep in my lap as I played with his hair and scratched his scalp. Jack in my home, in our bed, naked, watching *Golden Girls*.

There's your family.

Who says you can't have kids someday, with Jack? People change their minds. You have time. And can you imagine two funnier parents on the face of this earth? Or no kids, and the two of you spend your lives together. Not a bad way to sail off into the sunset, eh?

One more image came to me: Jack listening to me sing to him at open-mike night.

What was the song you sang?

"Strong Enough." But it was never a question of whether *he* was strong enough.

No. But are you strong enough to be his girl?

I thought so.

Why do you doubt yourself? Who cares what the press calls you?

I do.

Get the fuck over it. That man loves you. He needs you. You walked away just when he needed you to be strong enough.

Sweet Nuts. Johnny Bite Down. George.

I inhaled so deeply, I almost choked.

Stop being afraid.

Don't worry so much about what you think you should have. Take care of what you do have. Or did have.

Oh no, what have I done?

Nothing that can't be fixed.

I'd been afraid so long, I almost didn't recognize it as fear. But it was, and it was ugly. I'd carried fear with me my entire life. Fear was what made me leave L.A. the first time. Fear was what made me give up the dreams I'd had for a lifetime—only now I'd found a way to get what I wanted. Why was I still letting fear come between me and Jack?

If I could create the perfect man for me, he would bear a striking resemblance to my George. And he was right: I *did* push happiness away. I used errant thoughts and passing fancies to distract me from what was real, what was true. Why the hell did I care that he was twenty-four? Maybe he was *supposed* to be twenty-four.

It was time to let fear go.

One last image flashed into my mind: me, at my heaviest, drowning in sadness.

No more.

No more.

I want him back.

Well, now, hold on a second there, sassafras. Who says he wants you back?

That stopped me cold. *Would* he want me back?

Last time I checked, you left his ass on his big night— walked away from him at his premiere. Embarrassed him in front of his family, then broke his heart. Who says he'll take you back?

Jesus, what a fucking mess. I was such an asshole. Everything had been about me lately—What did *I* want? What was best for *me*?—and I never stopped to think how hard all this was on Jack. I took my love from him when he needed it most. I was a weakling, totally wrapped up in my own head, when all he wanted was my heart. And all he needed was my support.

Call him. Call him now.

Right, right! Of course! Call him—where the hell is my phone?

I frantically felt myself up, trying to find my phone. Dammit, I'd left it at home. Probably sitting next to my iPod.

Well then, run your ass home, woman!

I ran like my ass was on fire. I ran out of the park and across town, my heart pounding in my ears. I must have looked like a lunatic, crying and smiling at the same time. The image of Harry running to find Sally on New Year's Eve flashed through my head. He wanted to tell her how much he loved her, and he didn't want to wait another second. I could relate.

I wanted my Jack. I wanted my family. I wanted my home. I just had to think of the right things to say to convince him I would never, ever, *ever* walk away from him again.

I made it to my building, yelled a quick hi to Lou as I sprinted past, and hit the elevator. It took what felt like ten hours, during which I tried to compose what I'd say when I called him. I also spent most of the time bent over at the waist, trying to catch my breath after running so fast and furiously.

When the door finally *pinged* open, I fell out into the hall-way. Sweaty yet exhilarated, I raced toward my door, anxious to get to my phone. I barreled through the door and ran through the apartment, searching frantically, and finally found it on the stack of mail in the kitchen. As I grabbed the phone, I slowed myself down enough to take a breath and think again about what I was going to say. I couldn't just blurt it out, could I?

Okay, you've breathed enough. Now get him on the phone and do whatever you need to do.

Yeah.

Gripping my phone for courage, I began to dial when my

gaze fell on the magazine on top of the mail stack, which featured a familiar face. It was Jack, falling out of a cab with a blonde draped on his arm. He was clearly drunk, and she was clearly victorious in the way she held on to him. He seemed to be turning his face from the camera, while she posed triumphantly. The caption?

WHERE'S THE REDHEAD?

sixteen

I stared at the magazine, unable to comprehend what I was seeing. Was he dating this blonde? Were they sleeping together? Did I even have the right to be asking these questions?

My mind whirled in a thousand directions, my eyes riveted to the picture. When I finally worked up the nerve, I read the article inside.

After the premiere in Los Angeles, Jack Hamilton went on a world tour, stopping at *Time*'s opening in his hometown of London, quickly followed by the premiere in Paris. He just recently popped back up on the scene in L.A. and was seen at local nightclubs every night last week. Our cameras caught him exiting a taxi outside the Chateau Marmont hotel in Hollywood with a stunning blonde. When asked where his redhead was—older woman and rumored girlfriend Grace Sheridan—Jack's words were mumbled and undecipherable.

He stumbled into the hotel and was not seen again until the following morning, when he beat a hasty retreat into the Hills. Does this mean Jack is back on the market?

Stunning blonde. Hmmpf. And speaking of *not* stunning, the usually beauteous Jack looked like crap. He was always such a polished pro in public. What the hell was going on?

Maybe he misses you.

More like maybe his fame is going to his head. He seems to have plenty of company.

I read the article three more times before I finally picked up the phone again. I dreaded making this call.

"Hi," Holly answered.

"Is it true?" I asked, my lower lip beginning to tremble.

"You saw the article?"

"I did. Is it true?"

I heard her sigh. "Grace, I love you, but I have a PR nightmare on my hands here, and I have to tell you, you gave up your rights to ask questions about Jack when you broke it off," she snapped.

"I know, I know. But you have to tell me!" I begged, my lower lip quivering as tears ran rampant down my face.

"I don't know, Grace. He's been so hard to get ahold of lately. After Paris, he just kind of checked out. No more press, no more interviews, and he stopped answering my calls. I don't know what's going on," she admitted, her tone softening.

"Oh, Holly. I messed up. I messed up big-time," I wailed.

"Tell me something I don't know, fruitcake," she said, and I laughed a little in spite of myself.

She put her PR nightmare on hold, and we spent a long time on the phone. I told her what had happened between me and

Michael, and she wasn't all that surprised. Despite my determination mere minutes ago, we agreed that perhaps now was not the best time to reach out to Jack. I needed to concentrate on the upcoming show. She promised to come out for the opening, and I'd be lying if I said I didn't need some girl time. I needed to focus 100 percent on the show and turn my attention back to *my career*. I'd been so focused on my personal life—and on Jack's career—that I'd neglected to realize how wonderfully my own work was going at the moment. Michael had invited a few reporters in to watch rehearsal a couple of days ago, and the early feedback was good—quite good. Particularly for the leading lady.

"Just hold on, m'dear, and Holly will be there soon," she said. "We'll toast your success, have a few cocktails, and, if necessary, I'll sleep with you," she quipped, once again making me laugh.

"Well, if there's anyone who needs to get a little, it's you. That's for sure. How long has it been anyway?" I asked.

"Hey, Grace, I need to scoot. Call me later if you need to, okay?"

"Okay. Will do, asshead."

"Things will work out exactly as they should, I promise," she said.

"I trust you," I said, then hung up.

I looked at the magazine once more, then threw it in the trash. I would figure this out, but looking at those pictures was not going to help me.

☆　☆　☆

In the final days of rehearsal, I threw myself into my work. It was my saving grace. I found strength in the connection I shared with Mabel, and I spent more time at the theater than ever. After rehearsal sometimes, I would steal onto the stage, when the crew had left and it was almost deserted. Standing center, with an empty house, I felt the energy flow through me. In this space I felt more at home than anywhere else on earth. How privileged I was to have a shot at this life, and I was taking full advantage of it. I was proud of myself and what I'd accomplished, and whether the show was picked up or not almost didn't matter.

Well, yes, of course I wanted the show to do well. Oh hell, I wanted to see my name in lights! I could own that, but I was also thrilled to be involved in this industry in any way. Even if I couldn't be on a stage, or in front of a camera, I now knew I'd need to look into a career path that kept me in this industry, as this was clearly where I was meant to be.

The days and nights of final rehearsals sped by, and soon I found myself collecting Holly and Nick from the airport. They'd flown in for my big night, and it felt wonderful to have them with me again. I focused on them and tried not to think about what Jack might be up to right now. But I did wonder if he remembered when my show was to open.

On the way into the city, they stared like complete tourists as the driver took us down Broadway. Although Nick had been a screenwriter for years and Holly by now was a grizzled old Hollywood veteran, they were just as taken aback by the lights and the built-in energy of the Great White Way as I was—each and every time I passed by Forty-Second Street. As the three of us stared at the marquees of the landmark theaters, we were mesmerized.

"Can you believe I'm here, Holls? Actually here?" I breathed, squeezing her hand.

She smiled and squeezed my hand back. "Yes, I can totally believe it."

Between rehearsals, I spent the next few days showing them my favorite haunts around the city, and in a flash it was opening night. That evening, in a tizzy of nerves and panic, my stomach once again reminded me who was in charge, and I vomited my lunch all over the floor of my dressing room. Michael, anticipating my stage fright (perhaps also fearing for his shoes), had a mop standing by.

Just before the music began, Michael found me. He was as nervous as I was, and we clung to each other for a moment before he headed out to watch from the house.

"Grace, you'll be amazing. I know it. I'm so glad you're in this show," he whispered. "Knock 'em dead." He kissed me on the cheek and went out to pace.

I gathered myself, centered myself, and when I heard my cue, I walked onstage. And I was home once more.

I floated about three feet above the floor all night. I let myself go, gave myself over completely to the character, and just . . . was. I gave it everything: my excitement over my move back to Los Angeles, the thrill of being a part of this industry again, the pain from my recent breakup with Jack, the confusion of my almost-something with Michael—all of it. Everything about this exact second of my life, and all the experiences that had brought me here, came out onto that stage with me and helped me create a performance I could do again and again and never grow tired of. I'd never stop finding something new. I felt alive, exhilarated, and scared to death, and I loved every second of it.

I felt the audience and the energy they gave me. They laughed when Mabel laughed, cried when Mabel cried, and we went through it together. That's the thing about live theater. It's different every night, and when you're truly there and truly present, it's magic. Pure and simple.

When the curtain came down and the cast assembled for bows, I finally let myself feel it. I'd made it to where I'd wanted to be since I was seven, singing along to *My Fair Lady* in front of the mirror, a Ken doll as my scene partner. Since I'd auditioned for my first play at eleven, singing "Memories" like every other damn kid in the country. Since I'd won my first leading role when I was fourteen and played Maria in *The Sound of Music.* Since I'd seen *Rent* and bawled my eyes out at the thought this was no longer within my grasp.

So to stand in the spotlight, hear the applause, and know the people I loved were onstage with me and in the audience, and that I was making a living doing something I would gladly do for free?

I lost it. I cried and laughed simultaneously as Leslie pushed me out front for my very own curtain call.

And that's when I saw him. Standing next to Holly and Nick, with a smile as big as I'd ever seen, was my Brit. He clapped harder than anyone else in the audience, with a look of such pride—and all three of them probably had bruised hands, from the way they carried on.

And if I'm being honest? I fucking killed it!

I was five different kinds of thrilled. He came! He came for me on my big night. My tears flowed as I smiled huge.

☆ ☆ ☆

After the curtain call, I paced nervously in my dressing room. The cast was in and out, offering congratulations. Michael was on cloud nine, and the early feedback from investors in the audience was good. I knew Holly and Nick would be coming backstage, but would Jack be with them? Surely he wouldn't fly all the way out here and then not come see me. Would he?

I continued to eat Tums like they were going out of style, and I heard a soft knock on my door.

"Yeah?" I said through a mouthful of chalky grit and opened the door.

"These are for you, Grace." One of the stagehands handed me the biggest bunch of peonies I'd ever seen. Where anyone found peonies in late November was beyond me, but there they were. As I peered through the blooms, I found a snack pack of Chex Mix buried inside, with a Post-it note attached. I laughed out loud as I read the "card."

> *Congratulations, Gracie.*
>
> *This celebratory Chex Mix should help settle your tummy.*
> *If you like, save the melba toasts and bring them to me tomorrow at lunch?¿¿*
>
> > *Jack*
> > *P.S. You were radiant.*

I looked out into the hallway to see if he was there, but all I saw was a flash of Holly as she barreled into me.

"Oh, girl, you were fierce!" Nick cried, taking the opportunity to look down my robe and nod approvingly at my boobies.

"Thanks, Nick. I'm glad you enjoyed it. Holly! Hey, Holly?" I tried to dislodge my best friend from her death grip on me.

Finally, she released me and attempted to clear her throat. "You were great, ya little fruitcake," she said, her voice gruff and thick.

"Thanks, dear. Wait a minute. Are you crying? Holly, no . . ." I gasped as she raised her eyes to me.

"Oh, shut up, asshead. You were amazing, okay? I'm allowed to cry once every ten years. Now piss off," she warned, smacking me lightly on the cheek. She saw me looking over her shoulder toward the hallway, and she smacked me a little harder.

"He went back to his hotel, if that's who you're looking for."

"I can't believe you didn't tell me he was coming!" I sank into my chair, beginning to remove my makeup. Nick quickly started brushing out my hair, not wanting to miss a word of what was going on. It was amazing how quickly things fell back to normal with us.

"I didn't know until the last minute. He asked me last week when your opening was, and then the next thing I knew, he had a ticket waiting at Will Call next to mine tonight. Go figure," she said, tossing her hair and looking away too quickly.

"Hmm," I said, eyeing my face in the mirror. Nick was chuckling behind me.

"And what, may I ask, is so funny, mister?"

"Holly was talking about your *opening*." He giggled, and I rolled my eyes.

"So he mentioned something about lunch?" I added, looking at her sideways to see if she would dish the dirt.

"Yes, I've been instructed to provide you with the details of where Mr. Hamilton will be dining tomorrow, precisely at noon, if you should be so inclined," she answered, her eyes dancing.

I breathed a sigh of relief. I'd finally be able to talk to my George and ask him if I could be his Gracie again. I'd have to come clean about a lot of things, but it was time. Feeling immensely relieved—and thrilled to have Holly and Nick at my side—I set off for a celebratory dinner with the cast. My two-drink rule was back in full enforcement, and I went to bed that night feeling proud, confident my eyes would be cabbage-free in the morning, and a teeny bit hopeful.

The next day, a few minutes before noon, I walked into the Four Seasons. I let the concierge know I was a guest of Jack Hamilton, as I'd been instructed to do, and he immediately said, "Ah, yes. Ms. Sheridan? Yes, Mr. Hamilton is expecting you in one of our private dining rooms. Allow me?" he asked, taking my coat and gesturing toward a semi-hidden elevator.

We went up a few floors, then he took me to an ornate door at the end of a darkly paneled hallway. As he prepared to open the door, I smoothed my skirt. I had nixed several outfits before settling finally on this one: a trim black skirt with a soft pink angora sweater. Fabulous tits (my strong point in this scenario) and black boots completed the look, and the nervous smile on my face hopefully didn't show everything. I took a breath, and he opened the door.

Jack sat at a table for two, facing the door. He rose when

I came in, and I was struck stupid once again at how beautiful he was. The face, the curls, the eyes were the same, but the smile was sad. I was the cause of that sadness, and shame gripped me once more.

Suck it up, lady. It's time to sing for your supper.

As much as I wanted to run to him and throw my arms around him—and my legs for that matter—protocol and our last encounter precluded this. So I waited for him to make the first move. We both stood, staring, and finally the concierge broke the tension by asking us to let him know when we were ready for lunch. Jack nodded, and we were left alone.

"Hi."

"Hi, yourself," he said, and just hearing his voice brought tears to my eyes.

"Thank you for the flowers. They were beautiful."

"You're welcome."

"And the Chex Mix—that was a nice touch," I added.

He grinned. "I thought so."

We were silent for a few seconds, then we both spoke at the same time.

"The show was great—"

"Thank you for coming last night—"

We laughed, and the tension eased a bit. I stepped a little closer to him, and he moved toward me as well. I set my bag down and admired the room. Wood paneling, gilded mirrors—it was beautiful. When I turned back toward him, he was right behind me. Having him so close affected me as it always did, and before I could stop myself, I reached for him.

We fell into each other's arms, instantly molding into what was once so familiar, and was now so desperately missed. My skin remembered his. His touch and his scent filled my head.

Once again, tears sprang to my eyes as I clutched him to me. I felt his lips graze the top of my head, and I absolutely melted. I lifted my face up, my lips seeking his.

But then his arms straightened, and I found myself back where I was when I'd first walked in: alone.

"I can't do this, Grace. I can't just see you and hold you and have everything go back to the way it was," he said, his eyes roaming over me.

When they finally came back to my eyes I saw such hurt there, and . . . anger?

"I've been trying to decide what I wanted to say to you for weeks now. I was so angry with you, Gracie. I *am* so angry with you." He sighed and turned from me, running his hands through his hair.

"I know. You have every reason to be angry with me, but if I can just—"

And he snapped.

"Dammit, Grace. I don't want to hear it! If I have to listen to you say again that we aren't right for each other, I'll seriously lose my shit. Do you have any idea what it was like to hear that from you? Now you'll sit there, and you'll listen to what I have to say," he instructed, pointing to the chair across from his.

Surprised by his vehemence, I sat and waited for what I surely had coming to me. I owed him that. I owed him more.

He began to pace, and I was struck again by how hurt he was. I had truly broken his heart.

"What you did that night . . . was thoughtless and so cruel. And I don't mean choosing the worst possible night for your little flip-out, I mean ending this relationship without even discussing it with me. What we've gone through, what we've shared— Jesus, Grace, if that meant so little to you that you couldn't even try to explain your feelings to me, well, that makes me question everything I thought you felt for me. Maybe you never really loved me."

He choked out that last bit, and with that I was out of the chair and in front of him.

"No! That's not true, I—"

He looked at me fiercely. "Grace, seriously. I really need you to shut up right now and let me get this out," he warned.

I fell silent again, returned to my chair, and nodded for him to continue.

"But then I realized that was too easy. That was bullshit. Because I know you, Grace, and I know you loved me. I know you *still* love me. Whatever you think is too much to get around, or push through, or work past, I know it isn't—because you love me. And, fuck me, but I love you too," he said, and abruptly stopped pacing. He looked me square in the eye, his green eyes blazing.

"So if you think for a second I'm going to let you end this without giving me a legitimate reason, you are truly crazier than I thought. I'm in this thing *with* you, a willing participant, and you can't decide for both of us," he finished, and we stared at each other.

I watched as his face darkened with tension, waiting for me to argue with him.

"Can I say something? Please?" I asked, and his eyes grew dark as well. I hated myself for hurting the person in the world I loved more than anyone else. The one who was made for me.

"I think you damn well better," he huffed, slouching into the chair across from me.

I took a deep breath, knowing I needed to come clean on everything.

"You're absolutely right that I can't make decisions like that for both of us. You're also right that I was cruel. I'm sick over what I put you through. I was and am so proud of you, and I hate to think I ruined your big night. It was childish and reactive and wholly inappropriate," I said. "And most important, I am very, very sorry."

He nodded in agreement, and I continued.

"I need to try to explain why I said the things I said, why I decided the things I did. Maybe that will help you understand the true level of crazy you're dealing with here," I said, and he smiled briefly at the word *crazy*. I allowed myself one tiny swell of excitement at the thought he might let me be *his* Crazy again, then I launched in.

"See, Jack, the thing is, when I came to L.A. the first time, well, things didn't go exactly according to plan," I began, and as I told my story, I lived it again. I saw it all happen and went through the emotions of realizing I wasn't nearly as special and unique as I'd thought I was. I remembered how I came to the difficult decision to leave L.A.

"Holly nearly throttled me, she was so mad," I said, feeling the waves of self-loathing all over again. "She called me a quitter and told me she couldn't believe I was giving up so easily. Part of me knew she was right, but part of me also believed that show business wasn't the right place for me. So I went home. And I went back to school."

I told him all about the work I discovered for myself. How I enjoyed the writing and the educational details I worked on with clients. I told him how that was good enough for a while, but then I started to change.

"I worked all day and all night, but from home. I could go days without actually seeing anyone, and while the relationships I had with my clients were good, I kept myself very isolated," I said. "I, well, I put on some weight. And then some more weight, and, well, eventually—you saw my picture. I stopped dating. I didn't allow myself to meet anyone or take a chance on anything. Holly came home to see me once, and even though she never said anything, I knew she was disappointed in me," I said, thinking back to the sad look she had when she saw me for the first time in years.

She'd caught herself and recovered quickly, and we went on to have a wonderful girls' weekend. But I could still feel the awkward pain of knowing that when she thought I wasn't looking, she was looking. She was watching, and she was worried. But I made myself forget it. I pushed it down and away and continued on with my life, such as it was.

"Jack, I was so introverted at that point— All the stuff you say you love about me? The crazy? You wouldn't even have recognized me back then, and I don't just mean physically." I sniffed, the tears beginning to collect and spill over. But I wiped my nose on my sleeve and pushed on.

"Eventually, I realized leaving L.A. had been harder for me to deal with than I thought. It represented all the things I grew up wanting, but when they didn't come easy, I quit. Holly was right: I was a quitter. And to ignore that, to push that down, I coped the only way I knew how. I just withdrew. And as the layers of protection added up, I shut down. I don't know what I would have done or what I would have become, if it wasn't for one totally random night when my few friends dragged me out." I sniffed again, feeling my emotions threaten to overwhelm me. But I welcomed them, as it meant I was feeling something again.

I told him about going to see *Rent* and how it had reawakened something inside me. How it changed me, altered my course, reminded me of who I was, and revealed who I'd let myself become. As I talked about the power I felt, sitting in that theater, Jack's face came alive and he nodded. He seemed to know exactly the feeling I was talking about. I explained how that night had become the catalyst for everything in my life to change. In the following weeks and months I started counseling, began working with a trainer, and began to allow myself to dream about the life I'd always wanted again.

"And even though you might not want to hear this part, at that point, I hadn't been on a date in years—*years*! When I started to feel better about myself, and I began to *look* more like myself, I found I enjoyed being in the company of men again . . . I might have gone a little crazy," I added with a shy smile.

He just grinned back, and I felt lighter and lighter as I continued, explaining how I'd battled my way all the way back to L.A. and letting go of the black fear I was still cloaked in— even after all this time.

I told him our relationship had taken me by surprise, and I was unprepared for how completely he'd captured my heart and loved me, crazy and all. I told him I loved him so intensely it scared the shit out of me.

"But, Jack, as much as I've fixed things on the outside, there's still a lot of work to do on the inside. That's still very much a work in progress, and my baggage, sadly, has become your baggage. The meltdown at your premiere? That's evidence right there. Do you know how hard it is for me to even conceptualize that you want to be with me? With everyone in the world wanting you, you want to be with *me*." I shook my head in wonder.

"That's a heady thing for any woman—especially one with such big issues."

He started to speak and reached for me, but I took his hands and asked him to bear with me just a bit longer.

Then I told him the truth about the relationship Michael and I had in college. I told him how Michael and I had been closer since I'd moved to New York, and that this had made me question what was "right" and "appropriate" and "good" for me. I told him how Keili had put me on the baby train, making me question things I thought had been decided years ago. I'd had some major tunnel vision.

On the morning of the premiere—fueled by nerves and paranoia—I saw myself, in my mind's eye, with children I didn't even know I wanted. And rather than discuss it, or let the idea marinate a bit, I immediately dove for the opposite end of the spectrum, where the idea of Jack and me, and the idea of children, could never coexist.

"You were totally right when you said I push happiness away. You knew it before I knew it. There's a part of me that doesn't really believe I deserve good things," I said. "That's going to take some time to change. I clearly have a lot more work to do.

"But I never wanted anyone but you. You have to believe that. For weeks I've been searching for the right time to call you and beg you to take me back, to apologize for being so shortsighted and not realizing that every single solitary thing I've ever wanted in a man is in you."

I'd left my seat by this point and was on my knees in front of him. The tears had begun at *Rent* and hadn't stopped since.

He was perfectly silent, just taking it all in. When he started to speak again, I stopped him.

I still had one more confession to make—one that could break him. This was where he'd either stay in this with me or decide it was too much.

"There's something else I need to tell you. I know in my heart if we're ever going to get past this, I need to be totally honest with you. About everything." I took a deep breath.

Say it. Be strong. You have to tell him.

"A few weeks ago, I went out with Michael," I said.

The color had drained from his face. His eyes were almost gray.

"We went out for dinner, and then he came back to my place," I continued, my throat beginning to close.

I couldn't finish. I couldn't *not* finish.

You can do this. Tell him. Come clean.

"What did you do, Grace?" he asked, his voice gruff and almost inaudible.

I breathed deep.

"Did you fuck him, Grace? Did you? Oh, God, you fucked him, didn't you?" he snarled suddenly, standing and leaving me on the floor. I scrambled after him.

"No, no, it didn't get that far, I swear!"

He whirled toward me. "Did he kiss you?" he hissed, his face stormy.

"Yes," I whispered.

"Did he touch you?" he asked, his voice a low growl.

"Yes."

He put his hands on me.

"Did he you touch you here?" he asked, placing his hands on my breasts.

I started to sob.

"Did he?"

I nodded. I nodded in horror at what I had done, what I'd allowed to happen.

He stared at me, and I saw the tears. *He* had tears.

He sat back down, head in hands.

"This is so fucked-up," I heard him murmur, and I went to him. I was going to fight for this.

"Jack, I'm telling you because I don't want to keep anything from you, not anymore. When I was with Michael—" I started.

His eyes closed as he winced. Without another thought, I clasped his hand. I needed to feel him, and instinctively I knew he needed my touch as well. He calmed a bit, and I continued.

"You may not want to hear this, but I need you to know. I need you to know how close I came to throwing this away, but I stopped! I stopped because I realized I don't ever want to feel another man's hands on me. Not ever."

I lifted our hands between us and looked at them. I felt his hands grasp mine more tightly.

"These are the hands I want to hold, that I want on me, and around my waist, and in my hair, and holding my boobies when I go to sleep at night," I said fiercely, no tears anymore.

Jack seemed captivated. He held one of my hands in both of his, and I raised my free hand to his face, brushing his hair from his forehead, then letting my fingertips graze his lips.

"This is the mouth I love—the only mouth I want on me," I said.

He sighed heavily, tension either beginning to leave his body, or starting to build again.

I dropped my hand to his chest and worked my way inside his jacket. I rested my palm flat against him, and I could feel the warmth through his shirt.

"This wonderful heart right here?" I said, tapping his chest. The side of his mouth quirked up a little. "This is the heart I need. And if I have this—and a little schmaltz—I don't need anything else in the world," I said. He finally smiled, the smile that had changed my life months ago.

But then his face changed. "But what about everything that you said? What about the nine-years age difference?"

"I don't care. Clearly you are more emotionally mature than me, so we balance out."

"What about the fame, the cameras, the photographers? What about people finding out about us? What about the next time someone posts a picture of us and says something nasty about you?"

"I'll deal with it like an adult."

"What about Michael? What if you decide you want to be more than friends with him again?"

"That's a fair question. And he will likely be around—we're working together. But know that there *could not* be anything other than friendship between us. I thought he was back in my life for a reason, but I know now that reason is nothing other than being a friend and the creator of the show I'm in. That's all there is, and that's all there ever will be. I know this, he knows this, and now you know this. I belong to you, if you'll have me."

After what seemed like an eternity, he smiled again.

"So screw lunch. Let's go fix this," I said, tugging on his hand. He finally stood, but once again, he pushed me away.

My heart sank. What if everything I'd said wasn't enough?

I was still determined. It didn't matter what I had to do. I was never letting this man go again.

"I need to tell you something too, Grace," he said, sinking back into his chair. He took a deep breath.

"Tell me what?" My heart began to pound a funny beat, as though it knew something my brain hadn't quite caught on to yet.

"Back in L.A, well, something happened with me too," he said, and I knew without question what he was going to tell me. The pictures in the magazine with the blonde. He'd done what I'd done. I don't know how I knew, but I knew.

"After the movie came out and I got back in town, well, I went on a bit of a bender," he said, digging the heels of his hands into his eyes. I took my seat once more, waiting to hear what he needed to tell me.

Breathe . . .

"I was so mad at you, Grace. So mad, and I was drinking so much and . . . other things were happening, and I just was out of my mind, totally out of my mind. One night, one thing led to another, and, well, I went home with someone. Totally random. It meant nothing, but . . . oh, God, Grace, it was awful."

He looked at me with tears in his eyes, and I saw once more what I'd done to him.

"I tried, Grace. I was so damn mad at you, but, Christ, I missed you, and this girl, she was so beautiful, and she smelled like coconuts, you know? She smelled like coconuts, and that reminded me of you, but they were awful coconuts—synthetic, and syrupy sweet, and not at all like my girl, and I just—I didn't, I mean, I did things, but I didn't . . ." he rambled, so torn up inside.

I couldn't take it anymore. I'd heard enough.

I came around the table and knelt in front of him again, then I lifted his head so he'd look at me. He looked so very sad and so very young in that moment. I pressed my fingers to his lips to stop his words and leaned in. My heart was thumping wildly.

"I don't care. I don't want to know. Do you love me?" I asked.

"What?" he asked, his voice muffled by my fingers, looking at me with wide eyes.

I chuckled lightly and removed my hand, cupping his cheek with my fingers. "Do you love me?" I asked again.

He was quiet for a moment, and I couldn't breathe. My world stopped in that instant.

"I do love you, Grace, of course I do. But—"

I was on my feet and in his lap in a nanosecond. I pressed myself into his arms and kissed him square on the lips. This was my man, and I needed his mouth on mine—right now.

"Then I don't care what you did," I told him. "They can cancel each other out. I don't want to know the details. Please don't ever tell me." Then I kissed him again. This time he kissed me back hungrily. His hands found my hips and pulled me against him, pulling me home.

We kissed eagerly, passionately, and I forgot everything except his lips, the scratch of his stubble, and the feel of his hands on me. My fingers found his hair and dug in. I scratched his scalp, and he sighed into my mouth at the sensation.

I heard a scuffle, then a muffled giggle. I turned to see a few ladies from the hotel restaurant peeking in, then all but one immediately scrambled out the door. The one remaining blushed deeply.

"We just came to see if you were ready for your lunch, Mr. Hamilton," she said, clearly feeling his star power.

I looked back at Jack, and he nodded slightly to say it was my choice.

"I think we've decided on a little room service instead, right, George?" I asked, grinning cheekily at him.

"Whatever the lady wants." He grinned back at me as I led him past the still-stunned hotel employee and out the door. He then led me to the bank of elevators next to the banquet center. As we waited for the elevator to arrive, we began to kiss. At first slowly, tiny little pecks, but they quickly grew into wonderfully sloppy kisses.

An elevator arrived just as the doors to the adjacent banquet room opened, and dozens of women from the Greater New York Area Quilting Society poured out after their buffet lunch. And there they found their Super Sexy Scientist Guy groping an older redhead. Shocked whispers turned to swooning frenzy in less time than it took to blink. Phone cameras appeared instantly.

"Grace, we need to get out of here," Jack whispered in my ear, trying to shield me from the cameras as we hurriedly stepped into the elevator.

I laughed out loud. Nothing was gonna kill my buzz. "Ah, fuck it, George. C'mere." I giggled and jumped up into his arms. I wrapped my legs around him and kissed him. *Like it was my job.*

He responded without hesitation, kissing me back with equal force as the doors closed. The quilting bee took plenty of pictures, and I didn't care for a second.

This was my life, his life, *our* life, and we might as well get used to it.

seventeen

*J*ack held me the whole way up in the elevator, refusing to put me down. We kissed slowly and leisurely, exploring each other's mouths again, with serious attention to detail. When we got to his floor, he swung me up onto his back and carried me piggyback down the hall.

"Wow, swanky digs, Hamilton," I said as I took in his suite from my perch on his back.

"Nothing but the best for this guy," he said, closing the door and locking it behind us.

"I'll say," I responded softly, laying my cheek against his shoulder and squeezing his waist with my legs.

He walked me over to a big chair in the corner and dumped me unceremoniously.

"Hey!" I exclaimed.

He settled himself on the floor in front of me on his knees, his hands holding on to my legs. His fingertips made little patterns on my thighs.

"We need to finish talking," I said gently, tracing his cheek-bones and jawline with my fingertips. We seemed to need the physical contact.

"I know." He sighed and laid his head in my lap.

I scratched his head.

He made Jack's Happy Sound.

We sat like this for a while. Just being.

"Grace, I want to ask you something," he said, his voice a little muffled by my thigh.

"Ask me anything." And I meant it. No more secrets, no more half-truths, no more keeping anything from him.

"Did you mean it when you said you thought we were in a little sex bubble? Is that really all you think we are?" he asked, his voice barely above a whisper.

I sighed. "I was out of my mind when I said that. I do think we were in a bubble when we first were together in L.A., but only because everything was so fast and concentrated—and it was fantastic. Then I left. And we never got to see each other. There was never a normal progression to our relationship. Amazing, but not normal."

It was his turn to sigh. But I put my hand under his chin and turned him back toward me.

"Here's what I realized, Jack. What's normal? That's one of the things I was concerned about—this need to be normal, to be defined. Is it normal for two people so far apart in age to fall in love? Nope, but we did. Now think about everything else. Neither one of us is living a normal existence. Everything about us—our lives, our careers—is the opposite of normal. And how amazing is that?"

He grinned. "Fuck normal."

"Yeah. I don't want normal. All I want is you, George."

He rose to his knees, bringing himself within kissing distance. "We still need to talk about some things," he said, his green eyes beginning to darken.

"Yep," I said, sliding down a little in the chair to get closer to my Brit.

"I want to hear more about this—what did you call it? Baby train? I want to hear about this baby train you may or may not be on," he said, his hands slipping below me and hitching my legs up around his waist.

"Mm-hmm . . ." I snaked my arms around his neck as he lifted me out of the chair. He began to walk me toward the bedroom.

"And we need to have a very long talk about what we're going to do if you get freaked out again," he said, his eyes the color of the sky before a big, fat, Midwestern summer thunderstorm. In other words, really fucking dark.

I shivered a little. "I'm not gonna freak again. What if *you* get freaked?" I asked as we moved into his room.

He rolled his eyes as he held me above the bed, then dropped me. His eyes raked me up and down, and I scooted to the edge of the bed, wrapping my arms around his waist and resting my head against his tummy. I inhaled deeply, breathing in that inherent Hamilton scent, and I felt warm and toasty instantly. I inhaled again and he chuckled, bringing his hands to me, brushing my hair back from my face as I looked up at him. I rested my chin on his belt buckle and gazed at him as he traced his fingertips across my forehead, my eyelids, my cheeks, and finally my lips.

I parted them and took his thumb into my mouth, sucking gently. I pressed down slightly with my teeth and delighted in the lust that tore through his eyes at the sensation. I brought his thumb deeper into my mouth, tasting the salt of his skin, and I knew I wanted to take care of this man for the rest of my life.

I reached up and grasped his shoulders, pulling myself up, dragging my body against his along the way. Then I turned him so he was against the bed, and in one swift move, I removed his shirt and tossed it to the floor. He smiled, and I grinned back as I began to work at his jeans. I quickly pulled them down and helped him step out of them, along with his shoes.

I stepped back, tearing my sweater over my head and disposing of my bra. I stood before him, watching his eyes grow even darker as he took me in. Finally, I nudged my skirt down, stepping out of my panties so he could see all of me.

"Brilliant," he breathed, and I pressed myself into his arms, kissing him deeply with everything I had. I trailed my hands to his boxers and pushed them down as well, again helping him step out of them.

We stood, gazing at each other, our eyes taking in all that we'd almost let get away—all I had very nearly thrown away. I reached behind him, grabbed a pillow, and dropped it at his feet. I pushed him backward to sit on the bed and placed his arms around me, pressing his head against my belly, hugging him close. His hands held my body, face nuzzling at my skin as I ran my hands through his hair. He began to kiss my tummy, dancing soft, wet kisses left to right, his nose dragging deliciously across my skin.

But this was about him.

I dropped to my knees and looked up at him. He cradled my face in his hands as I perched on the pillow, totally bare and full of love. "I could not love you more," I whispered, and took him in hand. I stroked the length of him, fluttering my fingertips along his smooth skin, feeling the softness over the hard, silk over steel.

He closed his eyes and grinned that crooked grin as he felt me tending to him.

I kissed him sweetly and tenderly, then gently took him inside my mouth. His hands continued to hold my face, with just as much tenderness. I took him in slowly, exquisitely, and as he hit the back of my throat, he moaned. I withdrew slowly, following with my hand, squeezing gently and taking a quick look up at the perfection that was my Jack.

His head was thrown back, strong jaw clenched as he let me take care of him. I took him in again, swallowing and sucking and making my mouth tight around him. I swirled my tongue around his head, and then underneath, tickling gently while my nails dragged up and down the inside of his thighs and across his abdomen, eliciting a truly magnificent groan.

I let my teeth graze his length as I withdrew again, and as my hands took over for my mouth, I watched him. "Look at me, love," I prompted, and he opened his lust-filled eyes. There was my green. His hands dug into my hair as I took him in my mouth again, and he groaned as he watched me pump him in and out of my mouth, faster now and with conviction. I sucked, swirled, teased, tantalized, and loved him as only I could—and only I would, from now on.

As his hips began to buck faster and his hands became more urgent, I could feel myself becoming aroused by his arousal and the sweet sounds he made before he came. I moved with him, taking him in deeper and deeper and letting my hands take over what my mouth could not.

His hands were constantly in my hair, guiding me, moving me with him, and I knew he was seconds away from his release. Selfishly, I wanted to watch him—there's nothing in the world more beautiful than the sight of my Jack coming. But this was about him, and making him feel this as intensely as possible, so I kept my mouth around him while I felt him begin to shake.

His breath came fast and loud, his groans grew guttural, and just before I brought him to where he needed to be, he moaned my name.

"Grace," he said, the word falling from his lips as he came brilliantly.

I stayed with him the entire time, caring for him while he moaned above me, his hands lazy in my hair as his breath slowed. Then I kissed up one thigh and down the other, smiling into his skin.

He was shaking, and as I stood to climb into bed with him, his hands shot out and cuddled me to him. He hugged me close, clutching as his breathing became steady again. I wrapped my arms around him as tightly as I could, sweeping kisses across his forehead, pressing my fingertips to his temples and cheeks.

"Come here, please?" I asked, and moved to lie on the bed. I pulled him down to me, draping the comforter over us as we tried to get as close to each other as we could. His head nestled between my chest and shoulder, and his hands came up to my breasts. I trailed my fingers up and down his back, drawing circles as I wrapped my legs around his thighs, hugging him with my entire body.

He was still shivering a little, still coming down. I held him close and whispered "I love you" over and over again as I kissed his head.

He finally stopped shaking and sighed greatly. "I love you

too, Gracie, more than you could possibly know," he whispered and nuzzled into my neck farther.

"Thank you, George. Thank you," I whispered as I clung to him.

"You smell like coconuts and clean laundry," he breathed, and promptly fell asleep.

I was home.

☆　☆　☆

We woke from our nap a few hours later, hunger finally drawing us to the room-service menu. Our long-forgotten lunch, coupled with our coupling, made for a famished George and Gracie. I padded about in his shirt and he lounged in his jeans, and we ordered PB&Js and chicken noodle soup, Four Seasons style.

After our feast arrived, we returned to the bedroom, sandwiches and bowls of soup along for the ride, and crawled back into bed. We ate sitting cross-legged next to each other, and I admitted that I'd seen *Time*.

"Was the theater crowded?" he asked through a mouthful of jelly.

"Don't talk with your mouth full, Sweet Nuts, and yes, it was very crowded. There was a fair amount of squealing when you first appeared on-screen."

He blushed and rolled his eyes.

"And the love scenes? Hot, love, very hot. The women loved it. Of course I was miserable," I told him, sipping my soup.

He choked a little on his own soup, dribbling noodles onto his chin.

I laughed and handed him a napkin.

"Thanks, but why were you miserable?"

"Because I didn't know if I'd ever get to be with you again, and it made me really sad," I said, looking down into my soup, chasing the noodles with my spoon. "I'd also eaten an entire bucket of popcorn, so I felt a little sick to my tummy," I added, which made him smile.

He rubbed my tummy absently as he took another bite of his PB&J, chewing thoughtfully. I set my bowl on the night-stand and brushed the crumbs off my lap.

"I wondered that myself, Grace—whether I'd kissed you for the last time, and if we'd ever be here again, like this," he said, swallowing hard and setting his plate down on his side of the bed.

Different city, different bed, and yet we each gravitated to our own side. Comforting. But now we were in the middle.

I leaned against his shoulder, and he brought his arm up around me, letting me snuggle into his side.

"It's a damn good thing we're back together, Nuts Girl," he said.

"Mmm, yes it is," I said, snuggling closer and draping my leg over his, angling me toward him.

"Especially since the last time we had sex, you had a T-shirt on your head for most of it. That's hardly the way to go out." He laughed.

"As I recall, you weren't complaining for long." I giggled as I let my hand wander across his tummy, my fingers grasping here and there at the little hairs on his happy trail.

"Oh, God, no, it was amazing as always. But hardly the way you'd want to do it, if that was gonna be our last fuck," he said seriously, his eyes betraying his tone.

"That's crass, George," I sassed, letting my fingers dip below the top of his halfway-unbuttoned jeans.

His long fingers began to work the buttons on my shirt, and my pulse raced instantly.

"Did I tell you, by the way, how much I enjoyed that earlier?" he whispered, his tongue grazing the skin my opening shirt revealed.

I shivered and felt my skin tighten. "I had a feeling," I said, pulling open the last few buttons on his jeans.

He knelt in front of me, finishing with the shirt and parting it before him. He left kisses on my skin as he moved down my body, stopping to look back up at me with a devilish grin. As soon as he was able, he was between my legs.

Yes.

He kissed up and down each thigh, making me shake as he pressed his lips to my skin. "The thought that I'd never taste you again, Crazy? Almost more than I could stand," he whispered, as he kissed my sex softly.

I moaned thickly and let my head drop back to the pillow.

"The thought that I'd never get to watch you come again? Impossible." He groaned and swept me open with his magic fingers. His tongue found me instantly, perfectly, and my entire body tensed, then relaxed under his mouth.

There truly was no man better suited for me in the world. He was mine, I was his, and that was the truth.

I let myself go, let myself feel everything he was giving me. His hands, his lips, his fingers, his mouth, his tongue all flowed together into one insane moment, and as I felt my body contract, tighten, and then unleash, I was filled with the most sublime sense of awe. I was blessed.

When he marked me with his brand, my breath left me. I

belonged to him completely. I would never belong to anyone else. He called me his Nuts Girl, and I knew this was the man I was put on this earth to love. And I finally knew I was strong enough to be his girl.

When he entered my body and filled me up, there were tears—my own and maybe even a few of his. But we smiled as we came together, in every sense of the word. We both said, "I love you," and it meant everything.

And when the lovin' was through, and he was behind me, arms around me and hands on boobies, I was blissfully content.

We were silly, we were unique, we were thankfully not normal, and we were perfectly matched. George and Gracie were back.

Jack could only stay one more day. He was booked so solidly with interviews, it was amazing he'd managed to come out at all, but the man was determined. Thank God. He accompanied me to the theater that night and watched the show a second time, cheering loud and proud all over again.

After the show I futzed in my dressing room and had just finished scrubbing off my makeup when I saw him walking down the hall. I started to open the door wider for him when I saw Michael 'round the opposite corner. They almost collided, and when each realized who the other was, they both tensed. I considered going out to referee but stepped back to listen instead.

"Hey," Michael said, determined to be nonchalant.

"Hey," Jack said, intentionally nonchalant as well.

"It's great you could be here. I know Grace is thrilled."

"Of course I'm here. Where else would I be?" Jack responded, a pronounced edge to his voice.

"Hey, man, you should know. Grace and I? Friends. That's it. I thought there was something there, but I was wrong."

"Yep."

"So I guess I'll see you around?"

"Yep," Jack said, continuing down the hall toward where I was hiding behind the door. He stopped a few feet away and turned back around.

"Hey, O'Connell," he called.

"Yeah?"

"It's a good show, man. It's really good." Jack smiled a little.

"Thanks. Grace makes it better," Michael called back, smiling as he walked away.

"Grace makes it better," I heard Jack repeat slightly snarkily under his breath. Then he walked into my dressing room with a genuine smile on his face.

"Hi," he said, closing the door.

"Hi, yourself," I answered, primly tightening my robe around me. He took my hands and kissed them before kissing my lips once, twice, then a third time, sweetly and succinctly.

"Beautiful," he whispered, and pulled me into a bear hug. He lifted me off the floor, and I laughed at the tightness of his arms. He let me go finally, and his eyes were shining as he looked at me. "Are you gonna go all Broadway on me now, sweet girl?" he asked, chucking me under the chin.

"Not unless you go all Hollywood on me," I answered, messing his hair.

We spent another not so quiet night at his hotel, and the next morning I rode with him to LaGuardia. I sat on his lap in the cab, holding him tightly. This time it was going to be even harder to let him go.

We'd spent the night catching quick cat naps between love and talk. I told him I'd like the chance to apologize to Marcia, and perhaps we could all get together for dinner the next time I was in L.A. Who knew when that was going to be, but I was hoping for Christmas.

We were never going to have the kind of relationship that allowed us to see each other every day, at least not for the foreseeable future. And Jack would probably never come home from work with a briefcase after a hard day. He'd probably never cut the lawn on the weekend. And while I do own several aprons and make a kick-ass meat loaf, I'd likely never be the "little woman," marinating in a traditional house in the suburbs.

Neither of us really wanted that, but I did divulge a little fantasy I had about role-playing: me in only an apron and him with a briefcase. He agreed wholeheartedly, providing that I wear high heels like Donna Reed. And we both dissolved into laughter when I mentioned I'd also wear my pearl necklace. We watched as the Manhattan night gave way to a gray morning, then showered quickly and headed out.

We knew there were still things we had to talk about and work through, but we were both optimistic now. We were a team. And when we pulled up to the airport and I had to let him go again, I felt a newfound strength of spirit. I kissed him fiercely in the cab, wrapping my arms around him and telling him I loved him over and over again. Our antics in the Four Seasons elevator the day before, while romantic and sweet, were not smart, and we'd agreed to go back to being as discreet as possible. We weren't hiding, but we wouldn't flaunt it either. It just made more sense to use discretion.

And besides, there was something wonderfully wicked about knowing he and I could have something private, just us. The entire world was clamoring to know about him, but we could have our personal life be just for us, for as long as we could keep it that way.

"Call me when you land in L.A.?" I asked, sweeping kisses across his face as he held me tight.

"Of course," he answered, kissing me breathless.

"And you behave out there, hear me? No more benders?" I teased, but I did have a legitimate twinge of concern over his coping method of choice when left on his own.

"No more benders." He smiled back.

"Thank you, George." I sighed into his neck, feeling the tears begin.

"For what, Gracie?" He raised my chin to look at me.

"For not giving up on me," I answered, and he smiled my favorite smile.

"That's my schmaltzy girl," he said, his eyes full of love.

A horn blaring shocked us out of our reverie, and we laughed as our cabbie swore in three languages at the other driver.

Jack kissed me once more, told me he loved me, and was gone. He disappeared into a sea of people inside the terminal, hoodie up and shades on.

I was sad, but not as sad as I thought I'd be. I knew now we could get through just about anything, including the sort of terror I alone could produce. I knew now what it felt like to be without him, and that would never happen again.

As the cab headed back into the city, my phone blipped. I had a text.

Thanks for leaving me with a little schmaltz.

eighteen

$\mathcal{A}$fter Jack left New York, our relationship changed for the better. We were more open and honest with each other. I held back nothing. I told him my thoughts and fears, and bolstered by my admissions, he shared with me as well. We talked every night long past my bedtime, and though I didn't think it possible, we fell more in love.

He'd been all over the place and hardly in L.A. since he came to see me, and he was still busy with additional *Time* obligations. Box office sales from the first two weeks alone had ensured that the film was now a franchise, and the studio had already green-lighted the second installment. The script was being written, and they'd told him shooting could start as early as February. He'd also been in negotiations for several other studio films, all of which Holly was overseeing like a hawk. They were both exhausted, but very happy with the way his career was shaping up.

Over time, the fallout from the pictures of him with the

blonde died down, and shockingly, there *was* no fallout from our elevator groping at the Four Seasons. Whether those quilting ladies just hadn't gotten the money shot, or they decided out of the kindness of their hearts to keep the pictures for their own private collections, they never made the papers. Or TMZ. Or *Access Hollywood*, or anywhere.

I stretched out leisurely in my airplane seat, removed my earbuds, and put them back in my bag. It was December seventeenth, and I was almost home. It was time to return all belongings and make sure my tray table was in its upright and locked position. I looked out the window at the familiar landscape and thought about the last time I'd been on a plane bound for California. What a disaster.

I finished the last of the warm chocolate chip cookies so thoughtfully provided to first-class passengers and sipped the last of my complimentary wine. Why I always felt the need to indulge in free alcohol I'll never know, but I was pleasantly sauced. And happy.

As the plane banked left, I saw the ocean for the first time. I thought about the last month and what had now led me back to L.A.

The show? Well, it went . . . well.

When the reviews came out, I was thrilled to see it had been well received. They thought I killed it too! We still didn't know if the show would be picked up or not, but this was encouraging. We sold out every night for all three weeks, and the show was beginning to generate quite a bit of buzz. The *Village Voice* even wrote a little piece, which highlighted Michael as a talented writer and yours truly as a new voice in the world of musical theater. We were flying high.

So when we got word that the show wouldn't be picked up for a full production—at least not right away—we were all a little surprised. Michael explained patiently during a teary cast meeting that sometimes even the best shows never see the light of day outside a workshop, but it was a tough pill to swallow. We'd worked so hard, and I'd put everything I had—and some things I didn't know I had—into making Mabel real.

Nevertheless, the cast bid each other tear-soaked good-byes, and Michael and I parted ways in a much better place than when we'd parted years ago. He had another project lined up, and he was headed to Connecticut to spend the holidays with his family, including Keili's new baby. We promised to keep each other in the loop, and he said he'd let me know if he heard anything. I knew this time we'd keep in touch.

Which led me to here and now, back on a plane to L.A. I had some freelance writing projects I could pick back up, and Holly was already beginning to line up auditions for me in the new year. The life of the actor—always so close and yet so far away.

But I was quite pleased to be heading back to L.A. My New York adventure had been grand and exciting, but I missed my home, I missed my friends, and I missed my Brit. He'd soon be back in L.A. after another quick UK press tour for *Time* (evidently London missed their Brit too). I couldn't wait to be alone with him, in my home, in our bed.

I knew it would be hard to find another role as perfect as Mabel had been, but I'd adapt. And although it was a little scary not knowing what would happen next, after so many years of knowing *exactly* what the next day would bring, I kind of liked not knowing. Plus, since I'd killed it with Mabel, I felt pretty sure I could do just about anything.

The plane began its final descent, and as I yawned to keep my ears clear, I indulged in a little daydreaming about my George.

Since I'd opened the floodgates, we'd talked a lot over the past weeks about some of my, and therefore some of *our*, issues. I finally had the nerve to bring up having kids again on the phone late one night. Being the emotionally mature one, turns out he'd been waiting for me.

"I wondered how long it would take you to bring this up again, Crazy. Come on, out with it."

"Christ on a crutch, you know me well." I laughed, feeling my face burn a little at the knowledge that he was always—and apparently always would be—one step ahead of me.

"I know you better than anybody, but I can't read your mind," he said. "So tell me what you're thinking. What you're *really* thinking, Grace."

"Hmm. Well, the thing is, it's not that I suddenly want kids or anything—I'm still pretty convinced that I don't . . ." I trailed off, trying to consolidate my thoughts before throwing them out all over him.

"But," he prompted.

"Don't but me, mister. I guess I've just realized that while I'm still pretty sure I don't want kids, my chances of having them are also getting considerably smaller."

"Right, well, being forty-eight doesn't help matters," he said, the smile evident in his voice.

"No, forty-eight is rather old to begin a family. And it's not that my clock is tick-tick-ticking, but when you realize the baby-making years are beginning to wind down, it's a little scary. Just because I know the options are somewhat limited, I suppose. But seriously, what if you decide ten years from now that you want kids? At that point, for me, it's not so possible. You could be giving up a lot being with me, ya know?"

I'd twisted down lower in the bed. He was in San Francisco doing press, and I was still in New York, trying to seek comfort from a duvet as we talked about this very sensitive topic.

"Well, first, I'm flattered that you think you'd still have me ten years from now, so thanks for that." He laughed, and I smiled underneath the covers.

"And sure, it's possible that I might change my mind. Who knows? At my very young age, there could be a lot of things I'm undecided about. There's one thing, though, that I am fairly certain about."

"What's that?"

"You. I'm fairly certain about my redhead."

"Well, that's good to know. I'm fairly certain about my Brit."

We'd finally gotten to a place where we were totally honest with each other, even if we didn't have all the answers. This is what I meant about falling more and more in love.

The plane touched the ground, and I felt my heart swell. Christmas in L.A. was unlike Christmas anywhere else, and I couldn't wait.

☆   ☆   ☆

Holly had some open time in her schedule that afternoon (amazing!), so she was the one who got to fetch me from the airport. As I walked through baggage claim after collecting my stuff, I texted her to let her know I was ready.

She texted back almost immediately.

Thank God you're home.
No one has cooked for me in ages!
I'll be there in 5.
Your favorite bitch

I smiled to myself. I'd shipped most of my things back, so they'd be arriving within a day or so. I was so happy to get back to life in L.A. and finally make my house a home that I exited the airport with the biggest shit-eating grin on my face.

Outside in the California sunshine, I breathed deep: smog and oranges and excitement. Yummy. I felt the breeze and sunbeams on my face, and I was home. Holly waited at the curb, flipping off several people honking at her. I almost didn't recognize her. She leaned against the hood of a brand-new car, looking fierce. She was on the phone as I approached.

"No, dear, you're not hearing me," she said. "He cannot take a meeting tomorrow . . . No. He's not meeting with anyone until after the holidays . . . Nope. Not gonna happen . . . Okay, we'll speak again after the New Year. Great. Kisses," she said, rolling her eyes and clicking her phone shut.

She finally spied me and grinned. "Asshead!"

"Dillweed!" I answered. I dropped my bags, and we hugged it out.

"Fuck, I'm glad you're home." She giggled as we embraced.

"Me too." I laughed, then jumped as we heard another round of honking start.

"Oh, settle down! We're moving, we're moving!" she yelled as we piled my bags into the back of her new wheels.

As I settled into the plush leather seat of her Mercedes, I

sniffed. I loved new-car smell. "So what's up, Hollywood?" I asked, running my hands along the wood grain on the dashboard, admiring the lines of her newly chic ride.

"Shut it. It was time to upgrade, and I totally deserve it," she said, swerving out into traffic and heading for the freeway.

"Yes, you do. I'm amazed you lasted as long as you did, frankly. You've wanted one of these since college." I dug out my phone and began texting the Brit to let him know I'd landed.

"Are you texting Jack?"

"Yep, I told him I would when I got in. Why?"

"He has some interviews this afternoon. He's so glad to be almost done with this press tour. I got him on an early flight from Madrid, and he should be here sometime tomorrow afternoon."

"That's what I heard. I'm so glad we have these few days here together before he goes to London," I said as I sent the text.

Sweet Nuts,

Just landed and headed HOME!

What the hell time is it where you are?

I don't care—call me before you go to sleep.

Love you and miss your body more.

Dorothy Zbornak

He loves it when I talk *Golden Girls* to him.

You sure about that?

"He's leaving on the twenty-third, right?" she asked, weaving in and out of traffic with the reflexes of Danica Patrick. L.A. driving could prepare anyone for that circuit.

"Yep." I sighed. I was glad he was going home for some

time with his family. He needed it. When I saw him in recent interviews, my Brit just looked totally exhausted. But still pretty . . . oh, still pretty.

"But you have all this week with him. Any plans?" she asked, missing a Bentley by mere inches on the 405.

"Nope, just the Christmas dinner on the twenty-first."

Since most of our friends were staying in L.A. for the holidays, I'd volunteered my house as Holiday Central. We were having a dinner party to celebrate together, and everyone was in charge of something. Jack and I were cooking, and Holly was bringing wine. Nick was providing the entertainment (which terrified me a little), and there might be a few more dropping by.

We chatted and laughed and giggled as we made our way through the Hills of Beverly and on up to my house. As we turned on to Laurel Canyon and the trees closed in around us, I was reminded why I loved this street so much. Growing up in the Midwest, it was easy to think of L.A. as a very cheesy, very plastic, very shiny place. And there was definitely some cheese in this town.

But I truly believe you see what you want to see. And if you looked past that, L.A. was beautiful. The pocket neighborhoods, the architectural mishmash, the palm-lined streets. And then there were the canyons: Coldwater, Topanga, Benedict, and finally Laurel. There was something mystical about Laurel Canyon: the way it wound around the mountain, the houses dug into the landscape, the ancient trees, the stillness at night.

And there was my bungalow. Cozy and warm. When we pulled in, I sighed contentedly.

"Happy?" Holly asked as she shut off the engine.

I heard birds chirping. I inhaled and smelled . . . lemons.

"Hell yes," I answered.

She helped me get everything inside, then paused when she saw the Post-it on my fridge next to the picture of Jack and me in Santa Barbara.

"You wrote yourself a welcome-home note?" she asked, laughing.

"I sure did. I knew I'd be coming back," I said, gazing at the picture of me and my Johnny Bite Down.

"Okay, fruitcake. I gotta head back to the office. There's a war going on about who's gonna play the lead in some remake. Can you believe this town? Adios, asshead!" she fired over her shoulder as she walked to the front door.

"Adios, dillweed," I shot back, and began to plan which bag to unpack first.

"Hey, Grace?" she said.

I looked up at her. "Yeah?"

"Glad you're back."

"Me too, dear."

I smiled, and she showed me her middle finger as she left. I looked around, and my eyes settled once more on the Post-it.

"Welcome home, Grace," I said out loud with a smile.

First I just walked around my house for a while, over-whelmed by everything I had to do. But then I sprang into action. Thankfully, the housekeeping service I'd hired before I left had kept ahead of the dust, and the house was basically clean. But having never been lived in, it was missing some essential items. I put my clothes away and made a list. The list to end all lists.

After list-guided trips to Target, the Container Store,

and Ralphs, I spent the rest of the day and most of the evening putting stuff away and arranging. My things from storage were arriving the next day, and I was anxious to start hanging pictures and personalizing. But even now, my home was beginning to look lived in. Clothes hung in the closets. There was soap in the soap dish and peanut butter in the pantry.

At ten thirty that night, I stood in the shower with my eyes closed and my hands braced against the wall. I was beat. The work of the day had taken its toll, and my brain was still partially on East Coast time. I stood under the water, letting it beat down on some of the knots in my neck. I mentally planned everything I still had to do, everything I wanted to accomplish before Jack came home tomorrow.

As I packed my tired ass into bed, I started another list. Included in the boxes coming from storage were all my Christmas decorations, which would need to be put up. I'd done some of my Christmas shopping in New York, but I still had a lot to do. Before I turned out the light, I reviewed my list from earlier today, crossing out what had been completed, and adding to it a bit. I still needed to get my Christmas tree and get my boughs decked with holly.

As I settled under the covers, I heard my phone beep. A text!

Dorothy,
Just waking up. No clue what time it is or where I am.
France, I think? I'm connecting thru Chicago
and should be there sometime late afternoon.
I'll call when I land. Can I come straight to your house?

Love you, and I miss your body as well.
Please say you will let me be on top of it soon . . .
Stanley Zbornak

Okay, I'd officially made him watch too much *Golden Girls* if he knew Stanley's name. I couldn't wait for tomorrow.

nineteen

The next morning I was up and out before eight. I zipped through Starbucks to grab a venti Caramel Macchiato with three sugars (a drink Leslie had started me on—I would really miss that little shit) and ran errands all morning. I got them all finished and even managed to pick out a fantastic Christmas tree. If you shopped for a tree on the right side of Doheny (which I did), they'd deliver it to you! I also picked up a new iPod for Nick. He'd left his at the gym a month ago, and every e-mail I'd gotten from him since lamented the loss. I even got him a Hello Kitty case, because I was a bitch like that. And I knew he would secretly love it.

I got home just in time to sign for all the boxes delivered from storage, and I set to work immediately. By early afternoon, it was really starting to look like my house. Pictures were placed, although not hung yet. Books were back on the bookshelves, dishes were in the cupboards, and I was a mess. When I got the text from Jack saying he was getting ready to leave Chicago, I knew I had only a few hours left, so I kicked it up a notch.

I got all my Christmas decorations out and arranged them around the house. I probably owned more Christmas decorations than anything else—more than half the boxes from storage were marked XMAS. I raced around like a madwoman with my ass on fire, and I finally placed the last Santa mug on the kitchen counter and hung the last of the stockings by the chimney with care. I had added a new stocking this year, for the Brit.

I glanced at the clock and realized Jack's plane was due to land any minute. I quickly prepped the dinner I'd planned by dicing vegetables for the salad and setting the table. I wanted to test out my new gas grill and make Jack play barbecue man for me. Then I set out the steaks to take the chill off and was frantically chopping shallots for the salad dressing when the phone rang. It was the Brit.

"Hey," I said, running around the kitchen like an insane person. I still had potatoes to peel and asparagus to clean. I was panting.

"Hey, yourself. Are you out for a run?" he asked.

"No, just finishing up a few things. Where are you?" I asked, trying to slow my breathing.

"Just got in a car and I'm headed your way. I can't wait to see you, Gracie," he said, his voice full of intent.

My heart flipped—both at his voice and the realization that he was so close and I still hadn't had a shower. Why the hell had I decided to cook tonight? I should have just ordered from Chin Chin.

"Mmm, I can't wait to see you either. I'm just getting ready to run through the shower."

"Hmm, I could use a shower too. Sure you don't want to wait for me?"

Jesus Lord, that was tempting. I quickly sniffed my armpit. "Um, no, I'm going to go ahead, but there will be fresh, clean towels for you when you get home." I smiled as I thought of him naked in my shower. Where he belonged.

"Okay, I'll see you soon. And Grace?"

"Uh-huh?" I said, struggling to take off my shoes and stay upright as I headed straight for that shower.

"I'm hungry," he growled, then hung up.

Once again, Jack Hamilton had made me lose all power of speech.

☆ ☆ ☆

Twenty minutes later, I stood in the bathroom with wet hair and a bloody armpit. What was it about razors and my pits that seemed to argue every time? I dabbed Neosporin on it, contemplating whether I had time to dry my hair, when I caught a look at the clock in the bedroom. Nope, wet hair it is. I ran a comb through it and made sure to put on some lotion. Which burned the shit out of my freshly shaved legs. I hobbled into the bedroom and threw on my white polo sleep shirt while I decided what to wear.

I went into the kitchen to pour myself a glass of wine to steady my nerves. But as I poured, I missed, spilling wine all over the counter. Cursing, I grabbed a dish towel to wipe it up. Finally sipping my wine, I looked around at the room and noticed I hadn't lit the candles on the table yet. I quickly did so, wanting everything to be perfect. As I glanced around the kitchen and dining room, everything seemed to be in place.

Table set? Check.

Salad made? Check.

Potatoes prepped? Check.

What was I forgetting?

Fucking put some clothes on, Grace.

Right!

I threw the dish towel back toward the counter and started for the bedroom. However, I miscalculated and the dish towel fell short—right on top of one of the candles. With a whoosh, it ignited. I squealed and turned to run to the sink for some water but tripped over a footstool and went down with a splat.

"Ooof!" I grunted as all my breath left me. I was struggling to stand when I saw a blur run past me and dump a bottle of water on the dining room table. As I lay on the floor in my white polo, legs twisted and naked bum showing, I parted my hair so I could see.

There stood Sweet Nuts, dumping the rest of his bottle of water on the now smoking dish towel and appraising the situation. He turned to look down at me, dropping his duffel on the floor.

He cocked his head and smiled curiously. "What the hell are you doing on the floor when your house is on fire, Crazy?"

"Oh, shut it, Hamilton," I sighed, banging my head against the tile floor. Ouch.

"You know I can see your business, right?" he asked, bending down to offer me a hand.

"I'm aware of that. Maybe this is the homecoming I had planned," I said, mortified.

He swiftly pulled me to my feet and slapped me on the bum.

"That's how to keep your lady: barefoot and half-naked in the kitchen." He laughed.

"Ass," I said, wrapping my arms around him. He smelled like airport and gorgeous.

We hugged for a moment, swaying gently while the scent of wet, burnt cotton bloomed around us.

"I'm so glad you're here," I whispered into his chest.

"Me too. Otherwise it would have gotten a little crispy in the kitchen." He kissed the top of my head.

"Hey, I need a real kiss, please," I pouted, sticking out my lower lip.

"Oh, I haven't begun to get to the real kissing yet," he said softly, bringing my face closer to his and brushing his lips against mine. I sighed into his mouth and his hands tightened on my waist. As things became more intense, I heard a knock at the door.

"Dammit, if that's a carload of Joshua-seeking women, I'm not here." He groaned, then lifted his eyebrow as I flashed him my naked buns on the way to the door. "Don't you think you should put some clothes on before you open the door?"

"Hmm, you could be right. If it's the Christmas tree man, tell him I'll be right there. If it's a carload of women, you're on your own, dear." I laughed and skipped off to the bedroom to find some shorts.

Turns out it *was* the Christmas tree man. As I supervised the placement of the tree, I encouraged Jack to go take his shower and get comfortable. I was going to do all I could do to get him in the holiday spirit. Including a little stocking stuffer . . .

Once the tree was in the corner, beautiful and smelling

piney, I tipped the guy and closed the door. With a smile on
my face, I headed to the bedroom. I'd heard the shower turn
off moments before, so I was hoping to catch him before he
had a chance to cover up that fantastic body. I crept into the
bedroom, and there he was. Sprawled out on the bed in his
boxers. Hair standing on end, legs akimbo.

Sound asleep.

I smiled as I watched him, his chest rising and falling
with his breathing. He looked so sweet, so vulnerable. I sank
down on the bed next to him, and he rolled over toward me
in his slumber. His arms reached out and he mumbled, "Tits,
please . . ."

I sighed and slipped into his arms. Snuggled in, with his
ever-present hands on my ever-constant boobies, I let my Brit
sleep.

☆ ☆ ☆

I must have fallen asleep as well, because when I opened
my eyes, it was fully dark. I forgot where I was for a second,
and my body tensed as I became aware of someone in the bed
with me. As I struggled to sit up I heard, "Shhh, sweet girl. It's
me."

I felt his warm breath in my ear, and I remembered where
I was—and who was with me. I sank back into his arms, his lips
still near my ear.

"Mmm," I moaned, then sighed as I stretched out against
him. My legs tangled with his, and I clutched his hands against
my breasts. His mouth kissed my neck and slowly worked
down toward my shoulder. He nudged my shirt down a little
so he could kiss my shoulder, and I felt my toes curl.

"That feels nice." I sighed again with contentment, my tummy flipping at his touch.

"That's good to know," he whispered in my ear, his tongue darting out to lick my neck.

"Jesus, that feels nice too." I chuckled and arched my back, pressing my breasts into his hands in a very pronounced way. His fingers swept across me, unbuttoning my shirt slowly. He moaned in my ever-loving ear as his hands, warm and soothing, touched my bare skin. As I arched again, I pressed my bottom into him, and he hissed as I made contact with a very specific part of him.

"Now that? That feels nice," he said, pressing into me farther, his boxers barely concealing his—ahem—intent.

His hands found my now-naked breasts again, and he slowly began to tease me, ghosting his fingers across my heated skin, dragging up and down the sides, sneaking underneath, finally capturing my nipples in his hands as he groaned in my ear again.

Sweet Jesus, the man was talented.

I snuck my arm behind me, clutching his hip and pulling him closer. His right hand left my breast and his fingers walked down my side to *my* hip, Yellow Pages style. I giggled as they slipped beneath the waistband of my shorts and grabbed my curves. He pulled me back against him suddenly, and we both moaned at the contact.

"Gracie . . ." he said, in that accent, in my ear, and I felt every molecule in my body reach out and call to him.

He quickly removed my shorts and pressed his hand between my legs. I cried out at the feel of his fingers as they moved into me. I struggled to drag his boxers down as well, needing to feel him flush against me, with nothing in between.

His hands left me for mere seconds, and when he returned, I could feel his warm skin press against mine in the most heavenly way. We both made quick work of my shirt, tossing it to the floor. He remained behind me, and as he worked me with his fingers I rocked my hips against him.

"Inside, please. I need you inside," I cried.

And he obliged. He slid into me, invading me completely. He anchored my hips with his hands, and as I pushed back against him, he stopped his motions, then pushed in again, making us both crazy.

"God, I missed this," he said softly, and I nodded in response.

I couldn't speak. The feeling of him back inside my body was overwhelming, and I was stunned silent.

We kept a slow pace, our hips moving together, our hands entwined as he kissed my neck, my shoulders, my back, my cheek. I turned my head so I could take his sweet tongue in my mouth, gazing into his eyes as he worshipped my body with his own. Making me his once more. We moved and slipped and slid and rocked, and what was mine was his.

His hands clutched my breasts once more, circling fingers and pinching and teasing and tantalizing me with his love.

My hands were lost in his hair. I kept my body flush against his as I lost myself in the waves of pure, intense pleasure that worked their way from the tips of my toes to the center of my being.

"I love you, I love you, I love you," I whispered, and I began to shiver and shake in his arms, in his embrace, with him inside me. He drove into me, chanting my name in my ear as he felt me coming around him. I was silent as my own tiny universe cracked open and left me floating. I was aware only of his love, his touch, and the feeling of him as he stayed in my body, in my mind, in my heart.

He collapsed against me, cradling me to him as tightly as our bodies would allow. He told me he loved me again and again, and I smiled into my pillow as I felt him kiss me. Bliss.

Moments later, he rolled away and sat up. He stretched and messed his hair with his fingers. As he scratched his head, I could see how long his curls had gotten. He gazed around the room, then glanced down at me.

"Hey."

"Hey, yourself," I answered, smiling up at him.

"Did I totally ruin dinner?" he asked sheepishly, looking at the clock on his side of the bed. His side.

"Yep. You owe me thirty bucks for the steaks, moneybags." I laughed, poking him with my toe.

"Grace, what's this on the nightstand?" he asked.

I grinned and didn't need to look. I knew what it was. I'd put it there. "What does it look like?"

"It looks like a bowl of candy."

"You're a genius. That's exactly what it is." I laughed, sitting up against him and peeking over his shoulder. There, on his nightstand, was a crystal dish with individually foil-wrapped candy.

"You're *sharing* candy, Nuts Girl?" he asked incredulously.

"Yes. I'm tired of being the emotionally stunted one in this relationship. I'm an adult, and I can share. Besides, I have my own. On my side," I said, pointing to the identical dish on my nightstand.

"Wow, that's progress." He whistled, laughing at me.

"I know!" I said, launching myself at him and stealing a candy from his dish.

"Hey!" he said as I unwrapped it.

"Shhh," I answered, placing the chocolate between his lips. "Don't say I never gave you anything." I smiled.

He grinned that sexy half grin and kissed me sweetly. He tasted like s'mores.

☆　☆　☆

The next morning in the shower, we discussed our plans for the coming days.

"So, I've got interviews this afternoon, and then I'm supposed to go to this party thing at some restaurant, but I can get out of it if you want me to—the party, not the interview. Spin 'round," he said.

I turned so he could rinse my hair. As soon as it was clean, I grabbed some shampoo and began to wash his hair.

"No, it's cool. I'm having dinner with Holly tonight, so I'll just see you back here afterward. At some point we need to pick a menu for this holiday shindig. Anything particular you want? Okay, rinse, please," I instructed, trying not to notice the way he was rubbing my nipples persistently.

"I want a traditional American Christmas dinner, so make what you'd normally make," he replied, releasing me so he could stand under the water.

I began to lather up with shower gel and offered him some. "Okay, then I need to head to the store today and start getting shit together. We only have two days."

"Let me know what you need help with; I can always pick up some things on my way home tonight."

"What the hell are you going to drive, by the way? Your car is toast, and I need my car today."

He grinned sheepishly and stood under the water again. He didn't answer.

"What's going on?" I nudged him out of the way so I could rinse off. He smirked. "What did you do, George?"

"Well, I might have bought a new car. It's being delivered today. I hope you don't mind, but they're bringing it here," he said, shutting off the water and getting out. He grabbed two towels and handed me one as he started to dry off.

"What did you buy?" I asked, wrapping my robe around me and putting my hair up in a turban.

"Just something sporty." He looked sheepish again, and also a little guilty.

"How cute are you?" I asked, setting my lotion bottle down so I could admire him fully. His towel hung low on his hips, and he ran his hands through his damp hair, making the curls jump and twist the way I loved.

"Why cute?" he asked, looking at me in the mirror.

"You feel guilty for wanting to drive something new, don't you?"

He looked down again. "Yeah, a little," he admitted, and his cheeks turned pink.

I turned him around to face me and wrapped my arms around his waist. His hands found the small of my back and settled there.

"You deserve everything you have, and everything that's coming to you. Enjoy it, love. If you want a fun car, then get a fun car. It's okay to have fun with this, ya know." I kissed his chest and then rested my head against him.

His chin settled on the top of my turban. "I *am* having fun," he said.

"Good," I answered, and hugged him more firmly.

Soon after we stood in my driveway, admiring a bright, shiny, new silver Porsche convertible. He was grinning.

"Wow, this *is* fun," I said, walking around and admiring it.

"Mmm-hmm," he said, sliding in and twirling the key ring around his finger. "Wanna go for a spin?"

"Hell yes!" I cried and jumped in. He slid on his Ray Bans, and we were off. We drove Mulholland for a while, then made our way back down the canyons. We were close to his apartment.

"When's the last time you were at your apartment?" I asked as we pulled into a gas station. We needed to put the top up, now that we were back in town. A redhead in the front seat was just asking for a TMZ headline.

"Hmm, what month is this?" He smiled as we finally figured out how to operate the top. "Actually, right after the movie came out, some fans posted my address on the Internet, so now there are always a few girls outside waiting for me—when I'm there," he said. "They're usually pretty cool. They just want to say hi when I come out in the morning to get the paper. Sometimes I talk for a bit. It hasn't gotten too out of hand, and I've been traveling most of the time anyway."

"Ugh, that's so weird." I shivered in dramatic disgust.

Top in place, he returned to the driver's seat and his hand made its way back onto my knee. I smiled, and we were off.

"They're not really pushy—other than the fact that they're stalking me outside my apartment—but it would be nice to go home and not have to deal with that," he said, his voice dropping just a bit.

I knew better than anyone how grateful he was for his fan support, but he needed some anonymity as well.

"No worries, love. I can handle it," he said, kissing my hand firmly as we drove through the streets of Beverly Hills.

Once home, I started to make a list of the things I needed at the grocery store, and he settled onto the couch. Within seconds I heard the TV click on. I smiled at how at home we both seemed here. I went in to see if he wanted to come to the store and got pulled onto his lap. I kissed him soundly and told him I was heading out.

"Do you want to come with me?" I asked, nuzzling his ear until he cried uncle. "We could dress you up in a hat and glasses. I might even have a wig around here somewhere."

"No, I think I'll stay here. I can help you when you get back." He smiled and ruffled my hair.

"I'm going to be making piecrust," I said, snuggling into his arms.

"Okay, sounds good," he replied.

"You want to help me make piecrust?" I asked in disbelief.

"Sure. Why not?"

"Is there somewhere you want to go, friends you want to see? Aren't you going to be bored? Making piecrust?"

"Are you kidding me? For the first time in weeks, the phone isn't ringing, no one's telling me I have to go somewhere, no one's knocking on my door asking me for an autograph, and I can pick my nose if I want and not worry about it ending up on *Perez*. Making piecrust sounds about fucking perfect if you ask me." He laughed and lay back on the couch.

"Okay, then. Piecrust it is. Want me to pick you up some Fatburger while I'm out?" I asked, extracting myself to grab my purse. I heard a moan behind me. I turned, and he was smiling hugely.

"Grace, I knew I was right to keep you around," he said, winking.

"Yeah, yeah, I know." I winked back as he threw a couch

pillow at me. I paused when I got to the door and looked back at him. "Is it me, or did we just say the words *pie* and *crust* like seventy times?"

"We said piecrust a lot. Piecrust, piecrust . . ." he answered, saying it differently every time.

I left him mumbling to himself. With a giant grin I walked out to my car, which now looked a little paltry next to his Porsche, and slid in. I turned on the tunes and realized life really didn't get much better than this.

twenty

$\mathcal{F}$our hours, five piecrusts, and six orgasms later, I packed the Brit into his new car and sent him to his interview. Then I headed to Holly's to pick her up. We were going to our favorite little sushi restaurant, tucked away up in the hills on Beverly Glen, for a girls' night. When we arrived, we ordered dirty martinis and spicy tuna rolls, and told our waiter to keep them both coming.

We toasted each other, sipped, and sighed at the same time. Nothing was as good as a dirty martini, extra dirty.

"So all is well with the Brit, I take it?" she asked, sucking on an edamame.

"Things are fantastic with the Brit. So glad we worked our shit out," I said, matching her suck for suck.

"You mean you worked *your* shit out." She snorted into her cocktail.

"Yes, exactly." I smiled at her. "I mean, I still have plenty of shit to work on . . ."

"Ya think, Little Miss Meltdown?" she interrupted, which I stopped by tossing a soybean at her head.

"I do have plenty of shit to work on. Thank you. But I feel better about it than I have in a long time. Even though my way of coping was a little too dramatic even for my taste, I think coming clean with Jack about it all was the best thing that could have happened to us. We talk a lot more now, about all kinds of things. It's good for us."

"Imagine, talking in a relationship. We are so evolved." She rolled her eyes, and I reared back to throw another bean when she kicked me under table.

"Look at who's evolved now!" I laughed. "So now that I have *my* shit worked out, when are we gonna see about getting you a man, huh?" I kicked her back.

"I'm fine. Don't play matchmaker with me," she warned, gulping down her cocktail and waving at the waiter, indicating we were ready for a second round.

"I just think it's a shame that such a fine-looking piece of ass is going to waste. You need to get some, girl!" I sipped my drink, trying to tease out the olive.

She blushed a little, then tried to distract me by pointing out Randy Quaid over in the corner.

"Don't go all Quaid on me. What's up with the blush, please, Ms. Holly?" I prodded, setting my drink down with a flourish.

"What? I'm not blushing. It's the spicy tuna roll," she said, looking at the table.

"Idiot, they haven't brought the tuna roll yet. Are you— wait, are you seeing someone?"

The blush deepened. She was now trying to get Randy Quaid's attention.

"Don't you dare try to bring Cousin Eddie over here while I'm interrogating you. Are you seeing someone? Fuck me, you *are*! Who are you seeing?" I asked, pointing a soybean at her.

"Ya know, you point food at people a lot. Just sayin'. And I'm not *seeing* anyone, okay?"

I sat back and looked at her. "You've been with a man, haven't you?" I asked, dissolving into laughter.

She glared at me and sucked her soybean, hard.

"Oh man, who are you fucking?" I laughed harder, almost choking on a pimento.

"Okay, look, I'm not fucking anyone. There's someone I've . . . well . . . who I've fucked a few times, but it's nothing. I have needs from time to time, by God, so shut it!" she huffed, and sat back in her seat.

"Hey, girl, I get it. I'm glad for you. I just can't believe you didn't tell me. Why wouldn't you tell me? Unless . . . wait a minute . . . do I know him?" I asked, eyes wide.

She slunk down in her chair and hid her face behind her hands.

"Does this man happen to have killer blue eyes and a very sweet disposition?" I asked, arching my eyebrow.

She nodded, still covering her face with her hands.

"And does he happen to have abs you could grate cheese on?"

She nodded again.

"I knew it! I knew it when I saw you two at the premiere. You've been schtupping Lane, haven't you?" I screeched, and she finally lowered her hands.

"Grace, shut up," she hissed.

The waiter brought over our second round.

"Lane, Lane, Lane. Well, I'm impressed. Well done, sister." I nodded and raised my new glass.

"You think it's okay?" she asked, looking guilty.

"Do *you* think it's okay?" I asked right back.

"It's more than okay. It's amazing," she said, smiling big.

I clinked my glass to hers. "Here's to the hottest thirty-four-year-olds in this city, getting it on with two of the hottest young actors! Hell yes!"

She grinned back at me. "Actually, Grace, you're thirty-three. I'm thirty-four," she corrected.

"Oh, I know. I just wanted to make you say it." She threw her napkin at me.

Over the next few hours she brought me up to speed on what had transpired between her and Lane. Apparently when she first met with him (right after I left for New York), there were definite sparks flying. However, she'd been concerned about representing two actors in the same film, particularly one who was branded so heavily. But she enjoyed their meeting so much that when he asked her if she wanted to grab a drink later, she said yes. She would never date a client, but since they'd agreed that her representing him wasn't a viable option, she felt okay about it.

Later that evening, she felt more than okay about it. She confided that it was the most powerfully raunchy, explosive night of amazing sex she'd ever had. But she quickly concluded that was *all* it was, and she'd tried to pretend nothing had happened. Poor Lane was lost in the signals and tried for weeks to get her to go out with him again. She continually refused, which explained the tension I'd noticed at the premiere. Finally, he cornered her after an event and she came clean.

That night, they struck a sort of sex-only accord—it wasn't

as if Lane was looking for a soul mate—and they'd been getting it on every so often ever since. I was happy for Holly, as she'd needed to get laid for such a long time, and by someone who knew what he was doing. And since neither was interested in pursuing anything beyond the physical, it seemed to work for them.

She was concerned about anything being leaked to the press about this arrangement, so she was reluctant to tell even me. I, of course, assured her I wouldn't tell a soul—especially since I was one of the few who could empathize with her predicament.

☆　☆　☆

We stayed at the restaurant long enough so I was okay to drive, then I dropped off the slut and headed back down the mountain toward my canyon.

The Porsche wasn't there when I got home, so as I pulled in I made sure to leave him enough room in the driveway. I let myself in and headed toward the kitchen. I wasn't quite ready for bed, so I poured myself a glass of red and slipped out to the patio. I sank into one of the comfy deck chairs and turned on the stereo. I'd taken a page from Holly's house when I remodeled and had speakers installed throughout. I selected my "quiet sexy times" playlist on my iPod and settled in. The canyon was so still at night, even though mine was a well-traveled street.

I smelled the honeysuckle and lemons and relaxed into the solitude. Did I miss the hustle and bustle of New York? Eh, a little. But not enough to ever give this up. I sat quietly in the dark, in the quiet, in the wonderful. I soaked in the moon and the few strong stars that punctured through despite the city lights close by. I absently wondered why my cheeks hurt until I realized I'd been smiling for hours. And when I heard Jack's new car purr softly into the driveway, the smile grew bigger.

I tracked him through the house, hearing the jingle of his keys on the table inside the front door, the lock clicking closed for the night, the slip of the leather jacket as it left his shoulders, and the soft slap of his shoes on the floor.

Comfort.

He spied the open door and came to stand in the doorway, squinting into the darkness. "Gracie?" he asked quietly.

"Hey," I answered, stretching in the chair as he walked toward me.

"Hey, yourself," he said, settling on the ottoman in front of me. I placed my feet in his lap, and he took off my flip-flops without thought. He began to rub my feet, and my toes curled.

"How was the interview?" I asked.

He smiled a knowing grin. "It was good. Holly's going to kill me, though."

"No filter?" I asked, arching my eyebrow.

"No filter," he confirmed, winking at me like the devil himself.

"Good party?" I asked, leaning up a little, but keeping my feet in his lap.

"Eh, it was fine. These L.A. parties are just not my thing, but it was pretty cool, I guess. How was dinner with Holly?"

"It was fun. I know a secret . . ." I said in a teasing voice, offering my glass of wine to him.

He took a large swallow and handed it back. "About Holly? A secret? Is it that she and Lane are having the sex?"

"You knew? And you didn't tell me?" I cried, slapping him lightly. He increased the pressure on my feet and began to work his way up my calves. His long fingers slipped underneath my legs, rubbing circles and kneading my muscles.

"I knew, but it wasn't my secret to tell," he replied, lowering his gaze and looking at me from beneath his lashes. I could feel my heartbeat speed up.

"Well, she seems to be enjoying herself," I said, rubbing my legs together slightly as he continued his massage, working his hands now to the backs of my knees. My skin tingled and warmed under his fingers.

"I should think so. Lane says they're having *quite* a good time. He wonders why we didn't start dating older women years ago."

His hands slipped higher on my legs. His palms rubbed in between my knees, parting them slightly. He wrapped his hands under my thighs and suddenly pulled me closer to him, bringing me to the edge of the chair.

"We love taking young pups and training them. You're so much more moldable when you're young, ripe for the picking. And the recovery time is reason alone . . ." I teased back, trying not to moan as he pushed my legs open farther.

"Recovery time, you say?" He laughed, his eyes staying on mine as he pushed my skirt up higher, his hands now inches away from my panties. He continued to watch me as he scooped underneath me and pulled me into full recline in the chair. With precision, he flipped my skirt up and removed my panties slowly. His breath quickened as he brushed against me and felt how he had already affected me, how he always affected me. My body never, *ever* failed to respond to him.

"Jack," I breathed, opening my legs to him and arching

my back in invitation. He grinned that half grin that was mine alone and, without another word, stood and unzipped his jeans. The sight of him bringing himself forward from his boxers was insanely stimulating. I leaned forward and pushed him back down on the ottoman. I imagined he'd been mentally fucking me since I heard his car pull into the driveway. He sighed heavily at the sight of me, and I peeled off my shirt and straddled him, skirt still on, but now bare beneath.

There was no sound except the crickets, the occasional car, the music, and our breathing as I sank down onto him, taking him inside me. No matter how many times this happened, it never failed to stop my breath as I felt him within me, perfectly. We both exhaled as I rose up, my feet flat against the flagstone, controlling this completely. I lifted, then lowered again, increasing the sweet friction between us. His hips drove into me, uniquely positioning him to hit that spot, both inside and out, every time I brought myself down onto him. His mouth found mine, our kisses frantic as I tasted the wine on his tongue. He unclasped my bra, his hands and mouth each finding one breast and addressing them equally. He rained kisses on my skin as my hands clung tightly to his shoulders.

"You feel amazing . . . how can you feel this good . . . every . . . single . . . time . . . God . . ." I struggled to speak, continuing to maneuver myself above him, legs shaking in exertion as I gave him everything I had.

He watched me move above him, teeth biting his lower lip as he groaned and closed his eyes at my words. I breathed in his ear, nibbling on his earlobe and kissing the space just below, the way I knew drove him crazy.

"I love feeling you around me, Grace. So warm . . . so

fucking warm . . ." He moaned, his hips increasing speed and pressure, and I could feel myself tightening, my stomach clenching, toes curling, hands fisting, then fingers turning into little daggers as I dug into his back.

"So good . . . please . . . please . . . please . . ." I cried, and I screamed his name as I shook and shivered on top of him. He drove into me, holding me tightly against him, grabbing my legs to push deeper into me. I let him have me. He made me come a second time, the first rolling right into the next as he burst into me, sinking against my chest and calling my name.

"Jesus, Grace." He sighed, and I cradled his head, running my fingers through his hair and scratching his scalp. We stayed like this for a few moments, and then I laughed. Laughing in this position was a little uncomfortable, and so he lifted me easily, and as we replaced our clothing, he looked at me curiously.

"Why are you laughing, Crazy?"

"I was just thinking that if any paparazzi followed you home, this would be all over the world tomorrow."

"Not funny," he said, slapping me on the ass as I tried to put my panties back on.

"And that right there? With that shot they'd say you're into rough sex, you deviant, you!" I laughed, dodging his next swat.

I ran toward the house and turned to see him pulling up his pants. "Now you look like you had a little solo love out there all alone. Poor lonely Brit," I sang out, still laughing.

He turned to me, eyes twinkling. "What was it you said about recovery time, love?" he asked, striding toward me.

I laughed and ran into the house, with Jack right on my heels.

☆ ☆ ☆

The next morning we had to get up and move. Jack had a photo shoot, and I still had quite a bit to get done for our dinner party the following night. Jack had invited Rebecca and Lane, and I was very interested to see how things would go down between Lane and Holly—although I wasn't so sure about Rebecca.

Apparently she was still upset with me about what I did to Jack at the premiere. And frankly, I couldn't blame her. I knew how close they were, and I knew how Holly would feel if someone did that to me, especially on such an important night. But if Jack and I could move past it, she was going to have to as well. I was glad she was coming to the house, and I was happy to have her to dinner. I hoped this could be the impetus for a new start for us. I was in Jack's life to stay, as was she, so we needed to get past this.

Jack left early for his shoot, and I spent the day prepping for the party and wrapping all my presents. We'd be exchanging gifts as part of the festivities. I baked pies, peeled veggies, and made as much as I could in advance so I could enjoy the time with my friends and not be stuck in the kitchen all night. Before I knew it, it was almost 4:00 p.m., and I still hadn't had a shower. I made my way to the bathroom, stripped down, and stood under the spray for almost a solid hour, pruning. I had something I wanted to ask the Brit, but I wasn't sure how to present it . . .

Later that night, starved, we drove to Pink's. I craved a hot dog for some reason, and nothing would satisfy like a Pink's.

There was no way Jack could get out of the car and stand in line without being recognized, so he pulled into a parking lot half a block away, and I gladly hopped out and stood in line. This was one of the first places I'd frequented when I moved to L.A. the first time, and I'd seen a celebrity on each and every visit. Everyone loved Pink's.

After waiting for almost an hour and having a tiny fangirl moment when I saw Jim Carrey getting a dog, I took our treats (Mulholland Dog for him and Martha Stewart Dog for me) back to the car and we devoured them—top up, as we didn't want to risk pictures. Paparazzi tended to circle Pink's at night since one never knew who was going to show up. In between bites of the best hot dogs ever (they snap when you bite them), we laughed and joked and talked. He told me about the day's photo shoot and then about the fans at his apartment when he'd gone by that afternoon.

"Even though that's been my place for more than a year now, I'm ready to let it go," he said. "Enough with the constant fangirls."

I swallowed hard, thinking of what I'd been wanting to ask him.

"I mean, I'm headed back to London, and who knows where I'm going to be in January. Then I'm on location for the next film. I'll never be here," he continued, his voice trailing off.

I wiped the pickle juice off my fingers and turned to face him in the car. His eyes were serious. We each took a breath, then spoke at the same time.

"So, I was thinking—" we both said, then laughed.

"You first," I said.

"No, you go."

"Uh-uh, you," I insisted.

"Ladies first."

"There ain't no ladies in this car," I said, accenting my statement with a loud burp.

He wrinkled his nose and shook his head in mock disgust. "Age before beauty, Grace," he chided.

"Did you just call yourself beautiful and me old?"

"Yes, yes, I did."

"Well, hell, I really can't argue with that logic. Okay, I'll have the balls to say it first. Why don't you just move in with me?" I said quickly, not giving myself a chance to puss out.

He stared at me, then started to speak.

I shook a finger at him and pressed on, "Wait, let me say this. You travel so much, and who the hell knows what I'm going to be doing? When we're in the same town, when's the last time we spent a night apart?"

He thought for a second. "I can't remember. Not since we started . . . well . . ."

"Fucking?" I asked, laughing.

"Yes, exactly. You're so crude, love," he said, smiling.

I knew how much he loved it when I was crude.

"So, it just makes sense, yes? Do you even like your place?" I asked.

"Not anymore. I mean, it was only ever just a place to sleep, never a home. And now with the paparazzi knowing where I live and all the fans surrounding the place, I suppose it *does* make sense . . . You sure about this, Crazy?" he asked, brushing my hair back with his fingertips.

"Yes, I'm sure," I answered, kissing his fingers as they got closer to my lips.

"I can't guarantee the press won't figure this out. You ready for them to be camped outside your house?"

"What's the difference? You're there anyway. Who cares if you bring your shit over?" I smiled.

He sat back in his seat and ran his hands through his hair. He stared out the window, then looked back at me. His gaze was piercing.

"What are you thinking, George?"

"I was going to ask you the same thing—if I could move in with you."

"Are we insane?" I asked him.

"Totally and completely," he answered, leaning in to capture my lips with his own. His mouth was warm and sweet, tasting of relish and mustard, and I couldn't get enough. We kissed slowly and romantically, the glow of Pink's neon sign in the distance.

And when we went home and walked inside, it felt good. We slept wrapped around each other in our bed.

twenty-one

*T*he day of our Christmas dinner party was warm and sunny, but with enough of a nip in the air to remind you it was the holidays. And if you still weren't sure what time of year it was, there were always the reindeer strung across Rodeo Drive to remind you.

Jack slept in while I busied myself around the house. When he finally got up, he helped me as best he could. I assigned him to help me trim the brussels sprouts, but instead he kept trying to throw them away when he thought I wasn't looking. "Brussels sprouts, Grace, really? These are our friends. Why are you doing this to them?"

But I made brussels sprouts so well that even people who never liked them asked me how I made them taste so good. I had mad brussels skills. The Brit was not convinced. Finally, I sat him at the counter and put him in charge of dicing celery for the stuffing. He paid great attention to detail, making sure each dice was the same size as the sample I sliced for him. With him doing busywork, I had time to finish every-thing else.

Once I got enough stuff done that we could relax a little, we burritoed ourselves in a blanket on the couch and watched retro specials, starting with Charlie Brown and ending with Rudolph. The rich scent of turkey wafted through the air, and it was incredibly cozy.

When it was T-minus two hours, I finally got up to take my shower. I repeatedly refused his attempts to get into the shower with me, as I knew we'd never make it out in time. I needed a utility shower today; showers with Jack always turned recreational.

Sixty minutes later I was in the kitchen, beginning the gravy and letting the turkey rest. Veggies and stuffing were in, whipped cream was made, and we were in good shape. I bent over to grab the turkey platter and heard a low whistle behind me. I straightened up and turned. Jack leaned on the counter, taking in my dress. It was a deep green with a full skirt. I'd paired it with little gold heels and a string of pearls. Over the dress? A retro-style apron.

It was going to drive him mad all evening.

"Fucking hell, Grace. What are you wearing?" he asked, as his eyes took in everything.

"I wanted to get dressed up a little, that's all," I answered primly, twirling so my dress flared out.

He clenched his fists and bit down on his lower lip as he watched me. He came closer, and I pointed my hot pad at him.

"No, no, Sweet Nuts, after dinner. I still have too much to do. Self-control, please," I instructed, and he finally backed away. As I futzed with a few last-minute things, he set the iPod on shuffle and got us some drinks. Heineken for him, dirty martini for me. He'd been practicing the last few months, and he could now mix me one mean cocktail. I sang a little as I finished up, and soon the doorbell rang. Jack went to get it, and I heard Holly's and Nick's voices from the entryway.

"Get in here, dillweed. I need help!" I yelled.

"What the fuck do you think I can do?" she asked as she entered. "I'm kitchen disabled." She headed for the martini shaker.

"Yes, I know this. But you can open cans. I've seen you do it. There are olives over there, and cranberry sauce, and they need to be on the table. Hop to it, missy. Jack will make you a drink," I instructed.

She rolled her eyes, but she went for the cans. Jack walked back into the kitchen with Nick stuck next to him. His arms were looped through Jack's, and he gazed at him adoringly. I laughed when I saw them, and Jack smiled down at Nick.

"Would you quit molesting my boyfriend and get your ass over here, so I can hug you properly!" I squealed. He reluctantly let go of the Brit, then launched himself at me.

"Girl, I've missed you so much!" he said, and he picked me up, twirling me around the kitchen. Then he stepped back to admire my dress as I giggled. "This is nice. Very fifties-house-wife-meets-porn-star. It works for you," he said, sneaking an olive from the dish Holly wrestled with.

"Yes, it does," Jack whispered in my ear as he snuck up behind me and put his arms around my waist. I sighed as he kissed the back of my neck and released me with a squeeze, off to make drinks for our guests.

I heard my phone ring, and as I was up to my elbows in gravy, I asked Holly to answer it. I heard her voice rise in excitement, and I looked curiously at her. She gave my address, and Jack and I shared a glance over Nick's shoulder. Nick was now eating olives with no regard for whether anyone else wanted any. Jack finally took them away from him like you'd take something from a child.

Holly hung up the phone and turned to me. "Is it cool if we have one more for dinner?" she asked.

"I guess so, since it would seem you've already invited someone. Who's coming?"

"Um . . . Michael," she answered, and glanced at Jack. He stiffened for a moment, but then relaxed. I looked at Holly, then back at Jack.

"Michael? Why is he in town?" I asked as Jack handed Holly her martini. He rubbed my shoulders reassuringly. I looked at him, and he nodded. He was okay with this.

"I'm not sure. He didn't say," she answered, sipping her cocktail. "Jesus, Jack, this is great. Is there anything you're not good at?"

"Nope," I answered, winking devilishly at him.

He waggled his eyebrows back, and Nick sighed happily.

By the time I finished my gravy, Rebecca, followed quickly by Lane, had arrived. Rebecca greeted me coolly, but seemed to soften as she walked around the house, complimenting me on the festive decorations. Lane swept me into a fierce hug and kissed me on the cheek.

"Glad you're back. I missed this sweet rack," he said, openly staring down my dress.

I saw him wink at Holly, then saw a blush creep into Holly's face. She busied herself with the sweet potatoes, but Jack caught it too. I smiled when Lane pulled out his cigarettes and Jack immediately dragged him out back. Jack knew the rules: no smoking inside. He was already asserting himself as the man of the house—charming.

I began to carry the dishes out to the table, and Rebecca joined me.

"So, you back for good now?" she asked, setting down the brussels sprouts, which had turned out great. She eyed me carefully as I smoothed my skirt and looked back at her.

"Yep, back for good. I know you're still upset with me, Rebecca, but I'm glad you're here tonight," I said.

"He loves you so much, Grace. I'm glad you realized that. But if you ever hurt him again—"

"Then you have my permission to kick my ass," I finished.

She looked at me hard, then broke. "Shit, girl, like I need your permission." She laughed, then went to grab the last few dishes.

I saw Jack smiling through the doorway to the patio, and I jiggled my boobies at him. He closed his eyes and dropped his head back. I giggled and was still laughing when I heard the doorbell. I answered it, and there was my friend. Michael. With flowers.

"Hey!" I yelled, and hugged him.

"Hey, Grace," he answered, hugging me back. He let me go quickly and handed me the bouquet.

"Thanks for the invitation. I didn't know I was going to be here until the last minute, and I'm headed back tomorrow. Wow, great house!" he exclaimed as we walked inside.

"Thanks. Why are you in L.A., anyway?" I asked as I set the flowers down and led him to the dining room.

"Actually, it's an interesting story. Tell you about it tomorrow?" he said, shrugging out of his coat.

"Well, you're Mr. Mysterious, aren't you? Yes, tell me tomorrow. We're about to eat," I said, going to the back door.

"Hey, Sweet Nuts, time to eat," I called, and Jack and Lane filed in.

"I might have to share that nickname with the rest of the cast, don't you think, Bec?" Lane asked, elbowing Jack in the ribs as everyone found a place at the table.

"No way. No one calls him Sweet Nuts but me." I glared at Lane, who took a seat across from Holly. I sat at one end of the table, and Jack sat at the other.

Introductions were quickly made for Michael, and soon everyone had a glass of wine.

"Before we start, I would like to say a little something," I said, standing.

Everyone looked at me expectantly. I cleared my throat, which was suddenly thick.

"This has been an amazing year for me, personally and professionally. Every one of you has played a part in this," I said, looking from face to face, concentrating on each of them. "I've made new friends, and renewed old friendships I thought I'd never have again. I fulfilled a dream I've had since I was very young. And I was lucky enough to fall crazy in love. This has been a fantastic year. I hope I'm fortunate enough to spend next year with such incredible people." I felt my eyes sting as my gaze settled on Jack's sweet face. "You're my family. Merry Christmas," I whispered, and sat down quickly before I made an ass of myself.

We were all quiet, looking at one another.

"And Happy Fucking Hanukkah!" Nick yelled through his own misty eyes, producing a dreidel from his pocket and spinning it in his hand.

We laughed, and Holly leaned over to kiss Nick on the mouth. The mood was festive as we passed the plates and dishes and loaded up. Everyone told tales of their childhood holidays, and as we laughed and talked, I looked around again at all their faces. Each represented something different that I cherished: Lane for pure comedy and his good heart; Rebecca for her power and loyalty; Nick for his passion and energy; Michael for his support and comfort; Holly for her strength and love; and Jack for everything. He was everything I'd ever wanted, and everything I hadn't even known I needed.

I truly had my family.

☆　☆　☆

After dinner was over and the dishes were done, we went into the living room, gathered around the tree, and passed out presents. Holly and I gave each other the same thing, two days at a spa in Palm Springs, and Nick received iPods from both Holly and from me. He loved them equally.

We drank more, ate dessert, and played games. The music got steadily louder, and as we consumed endless bottles of wine, we got crazier. Michael and Jack somehow ended up on the same team for Pictionary, and they did surprisingly well. I was so happy they were getting along.

Finally, Rebecca was the first to get up to leave. With hugs from Jack and me and a Merry Christmas, she took off. Nick was soon to follow, hugging me tightly at the door.

"So glad you're back, my dear," he said. "It was getting dreadfully boring without you." He kissed me on the cheek.

"Oh, please. You just wanted me back so you could stare at the pretty close up," I teased.

He looked over my shoulder at Jack, who was talking to Lane and Holly by the fireplace. "It's true; he really is quite pretty." Then his eyes became serious. "Grace, let him take care of you, okay?"

"I will, Nick. Thanks." I kissed him again.

He squeezed my ass, shouted to Lane and Jack that he was ready for the three-way whenever they were, and was gone.

Michael was next to leave.

"So you're gonna tell me tomorrow why you're out here, right?" I asked as I walked him outside.

"Yep, I'll call you in the morning," he said.

We stood quietly, taking in the darkness around us, and the peacefulness. There was a howl nearby, and he jumped.

"What the hell was that?" he asked nervously.

I laughed. "Coyote." I listened for another one.

"You have coyotes around here?" he whispered.

"Sometimes you can hear them. I even see them every so often when I'm driving the canyons at night."

"Coyotes in the middle of Los Angeles. What a great place to live," he said in wonder.

"I know. You see now why I love it here?"

He looked again at the night sky and lemon trees. A soft breeze blew through his hair, and he nodded. "I definitely see the appeal."

We were quiet another moment, and then I said, "Thanks for coming tonight. It was nice to have us all together."

"Thanks for having me. Call you tomorrow."

"Yep. 'Night, Michael." I hugged him. This time the wool and sage and lemons—from him and the nearby trees—was perfect and sweet.

"'Night, Grace," he said, and he was gone.

Holly and Lane left together after taking a little ribbing from me and Jack.

Lane swept me into a bear hug, once again lifting me off

the ground. "Killer party, Sheridan. I told you we'd break this house in right."

"Hell yes! Glad you could make it. We'll see you soon?"

"You got it." He winked, taking one last peek down my dress.

"Knock it off," Jack admonished as he and Holly walked over.

"Can't. They're fantastic," Lane replied with that huge smile.

I swear, I could live in those dimples.

"I'll show you something fantastic," Holly said, pulling her dress down a little in front and flashing Lane and Jack the top of her lacy black bra.

I laughed as their eyes bugged out. You wave a boob in front of a guy, and he's perpetually thirteen.

Tucking her girls away, Holly turned to me. "Great party, asshead. Lunch tomorrow?"

"Yep, call me in the morning. Not too early, though."

"Deal," she said, and gave me a hug.

Jack slipped his arm around my waist and tucked me into his side as she and Lane walked to their cars and he opened her door for her.

"Olive juice, Holly!" I called as she started her car.

She leaned out the window. "Olive juice too, ya little fruit-cake!"

The two cars left the driveway, and I noticed they both went the same direction, even though I knew for a fact Lane lived the other way . . .

Jack and I walked back into the house and surveyed the damage: board games all over the room, wineglasses and half-eaten pie covering the coffee table. I yawned as he started turning out lights.

"You want to do this now or tomorrow morning, Crazy?" he asked, returning to my side and slipping his arms around my waist.

"We should do it now, but I don't want to," I admitted, leaning into him and relaxing my head against his chest.

We looked at the tree. The twinkle of the lights and the patterns they made bouncing off the ornaments made the room very cozy. Lane and Jack (with a lot of surreptitious help from Michael) had managed to worry a fire together, and it crackled merrily in the background.

I'd switched the music a little while ago, and my favorite Christmas carols now played.

"Hey, we still need to do *our* presents!" I exclaimed, sliding out of his embrace and starting for the coat closet in the hallway where I'd hidden his.

"You want to do those now? Christmas isn't for a few days, Gracie."

"Yes, but the spirit is moving me now. Come on, George. Didn't you get me anything?" I teased.

"Oh, I did. And when you see it, you're going to let me do that thing to you you said I could never, ever do." He disappeared into the bedroom.

"Get over it, George. Never means never. I don't care what you get me. Not going to happen." I laughed.

He came back to the living room. If he'd retrieved anything, I couldn't see it.

My present for him was big, so I made him sit on the couch and close his eyes. I removed it from the closet and set it in front of him.

"Okay, open," I said. He complied, and then his eyes widened in surprise. It took him a few moments to realize what it was.

"Grace, you really shouldn't have done this," he breathed.

Sitting in front of him was a brand-new Breedlove Revival OM-M acoustic guitar. He picked it up like a father with a new baby: gently and with reverence. His hands explored the smooth lines, the curved planes, and with exquisite dexterity, he strummed. A beautiful tone came forth from the wood, and a wondrous smile broke across his face.

"Oh, love. This is too much." He smiled and made no move to set it down.

I sat quietly next to him on the couch and listened to him play for a few minutes, losing himself in the music.

"This is extraordinary. Thank you so much," he whispered, setting the guitar carefully beside him and turning to me. He placed his hands on either side of my face, with the same care he'd used to hold my present to him, and stared into my eyes for what seemed like hours. He leaned in and kissed me softly, barely pressing his lips to mine.

We kissed gently and sweetly, my hands coming up to cover his as he held my face.

He leaned his forehead in to rest on mine. "I love you so much," he whispered.

I smiled at him. "I love you too."

He pulled away and put both hands behind his back. "Okay, your presents. Pick a hand," he instructed.

"Presents? You got me two things? Not fair," I said, wrinkling my nose.

"Gracie, shut the fuck up and enjoy this. Now pick a hand, please," he said, his eyes dancing.

I sat back and looked at the beautiful man in front of me. I pointed to his left hand, then looked at him expectantly.

"Okay, close your eyes," he said.

I raised an eyebrow, but did as I was told.

"Put out your hand, love."

I stuck my hand out, and into it was placed what felt like a small velvet box.

What?

My eyes fluttered open and stared at the box from Harry Winston.

*What? And I say again—*what?

"George, what did you do?" I asked, my heart beating against my chest.

"Just open it, Nuts Girl," he said, nudging me with his knee.

Carefully, I opened the box and stared. It took me about thirty seconds to comprehend what was inside, and then I threw myself into his lap. The tears began immediately. "Jesus, George, I love you so much!" I choked through my tears and maniacal laughing. I was having a full-on breakdown.

He laughed with me, both of us falling backward on the couch. I kissed him repeatedly, my kisses mixing with tears as I kissed his eyes, his temples, his cheeks, and his chin. I tried to kiss his mouth, but he was grinning too wide so I ended up kissing his teeth.

"You know we are totally crazy, right?" he asked me, brushing my hair back so he could look at me.

"Well, you don't call me Nuts Girl for nothing. You wanted a crazy girl, and you sure got one."

"And how lucky am I?" he said, still smiling.

"No one will understand this. You know that, right?" I said, still trying to kiss him.

"They don't have to. This is about you and me." He kissed

me deeply, and I melted. I actually melted into his arms as I started to cry again.

"I didn't mean to make you cry." He chuckled.

"What the hell did you think was gonna happen, Hamilton?"

We looked at the gift together, both smiling hugely.

"Well, I guess it's a good thing I asked you to move in, huh?" I teased, then I remembered—"Hey, where's my other present?"

He rolled his eyes. "See, now to most girls, that would be enough," he answered, sitting us back up.

"I am not most girls," I explained, sitting primly on the edge of the couch, admiring my first present.

"You are ruddy well right about that," he scoffed, and told me to close my eyes again.

"Jesus, George, just give it to me."

"That's what she said," he said, laughing the high-pitched laugh he reserved for when he cracked himself up. Which was often.

I closed my eyes once more.

"Put your hand out," he instructed.

This time, I felt something paper.

"What is it?" I asked.

"Open, please," he said.

I looked down at my hand.

It was a plane ticket. A plane ticket!

"What? Am I going on a trip? Where am I going?" I squealed, my voice climbing so high that he clapped his hands over his ears in defense.

"Jesus, Sheridan, just look at the bloody ticket." He sighed, but he was smiling.

I looked at the bloody ticket. "Shut up," I breathed, and looked at him incredulously.

He smiled.

"I'm going here? *Here*? Are you kidding me?" I asked, the tears starting again.

"Yep, you and me. Fancy a trip?" he asked.

I stood up and set everything down on the coffee table. Then I straddled his lap and wrapped my arms around him. His hands went to the small of my back and held me to him.

"George, you're going to get so lucky tonight," I said, laying my head on his shoulder.

"I'm already lucky, sweet girl," he whispered in my ear.

We clung to each other in the light from the Christmas tree and the fireplace, with the music enveloping us, in my home. In *our* home.

Later that night, when he slipped into me, we were wrapped around each other as tightly as two people could be. I could feel his heart beating against mine, and it was perfect.

We'd gone through hell and back, and he'd stuck with me. Everything I'd been through, everything I'd done, had brought me to this place with Jack.

We were solid. We were strong. And we were moving forward together.

☆　☆　☆

He stirred in his sleep, holding me closer. I scratched his scalp, feeling the silky strands of hair slip between my fingers. I felt the weight of his body press against mine. I rubbed my present back and forth between my fingers again, feeling it against my skin.

He came awake momentarily and rolled me onto my side, snuggling in behind me.

"Love you, Grace," he mumbled, and slipped back to sleep.

"Love you too," I whispered.

And his hands?

Please. Where else would they be?

twenty-two

I closed my eyes and let the sun wash over me. It was so strong that even with my eyes shut, the world was bright.

I felt the sand between my toes, warm through the thin bamboo mat I was curled on. I smelled the tang of the ocean, rolling in only a few feet away. I tasted the salt in the air, and the afternoon heat was thick and lazy on my tongue. I heard the waves knocking against the sand, and the call of a seagull overhead—careful there, bird.

Then I heard the door swing shut, and I turned and saw the most beautiful man in the world. He trotted down the porch steps holding two beers and headed my way. He wore a pair of loose jeans rolled up at the bottom, no shoes, and, God, no shirt.

"Hey," he called, shuffling through the sand.

I leaned up on my elbows, exposing myself to him. What was the point of a private beach if you couldn't sunbathe topless?

"Hey yourself," I answered, rolling a handful of sugar sand between my fingers. His eyes widened when he saw I was topless, and his mouth stretched into that grin I loved so damn much.

He sank down on the mat next to me and handed me my beer.

"You weren't checking your voice mail in there, were you?" I asked, arching my eyebrow at him as I sipped. Cold and delicious.

"Nope. I promised. No e-mail, no cell phone, no messages. Holly has the house phone, but she knows it's only for emergencies."

I sighed happily and sat up. I scooted over and tucked myself into his side so we could both stare out at the ocean. I pretended not to notice that he was sneaking peeks at my boobies. We smiled and sipped and watched.

When I'd opened the plane ticket at Christmas, I couldn't believe what I read. I had to look on a map to make sure I knew where I was going. The Seychelles were a tiny chain of islands in the middle of the Indian Ocean. We were about two hundred miles off the coast of Africa, and two hundred million miles away from anything Hollywood. When I realized what he'd planned and how we were going to ring in the New Year, you could have knocked me over with a feather. And the hits just kept on rolling.

The day after our Christmas party, I'd met Michael for coffee as planned, and he told me why he was in L.A.

"So, interesting story," he said, sipping his latte. "When the show was running in New York, a producer friend of mine saw it, and he really enjoyed it. When he heard it hadn't been picked up, he gave me a call. He said he thought it was a great concept for TV and wondered if I was interested in adapting it for the small screen."

"Are you kidding me? That's fantastic news, Michael!" I shouted, throwing my arms around his neck.

He laughed and hugged me back. "So I flew out here, met with some of the other producers, and worked up some different ideas. They want to shoot a pilot and position it for cable."

"Like TNT? USA?" I asked.

"Like HBO." He grinned widely.

"Holy shit," I breathed.

"And, of course, the kicker is . . . they want you too, Grace."

So, my life was about to become unreal.

I spent Christmas in L.A. with Holly, while Jack flew home to London. He needed to spend some time with his family, and after the Premiere Implosion, it wasn't really the best time for me to come along. There would be plenty of time for that, and I wanted him to have some time with them by himself.

So after Christmas, I flew across the Atlantic and met up with him in Paris. We spent almost an entire twenty-four hours flying in progressively smaller planes—not to mention watching three movies, rehashing the holidays, and talking about all kinds of things—until we were finally over the Indian Ocean.

As the archipelago began to appear, and tiny islands and atolls began to dot the water, I clutched Jack's hand in excitement, startling him out of his novel. He was interested in producing one day and was cramming in a last little bit of work by reading books he was considering optioning. He promised to be in full relaxation mode by the time we landed at our destination, though. We were both exhausted but ready for a vacation.

We changed planes one last time, picking up a puddle jumper for our last island hop. When we landed at the tiny airport, Jack had arranged for a car to pick us up. Even though we were excited, we were positively dragging by this point. The early-evening sun was just beginning to dip as we drove along the quiet roads. The island Jack had chosen was almost uninhabited—just a few vacation homes, one small store, and miles and miles of peace.

When we pulled up to the house, we both gasped. He'd seen pictures but apparently they didn't do it justice, because we both stood there, mouths agape.

It was huge and secluded and private and gorgeous.

As we explored, we found the caretaker had already brought in a supply of food, wine, beer, and everything we would need. As we walked through the house, the ocean breeze billowed through the gauzy white curtains at every window. The back of the house opened completely onto a huge deck, and there was the ocean. In our backyard.

Too exhausted to do anything, we'd snuggled into the giant bed, pulled up the covers, turned out the lights, and let the ocean lull us to sleep.

Jack nudged me now, and I snapped out of my reverie. We'd been here for three days, with almost another two weeks to go. I was turning a pleasant shade of tan. Jack had burned a little, but was now bronzing and becoming even more beautiful.

So while I sunned my buns in the middle of the ocean, Michael was hard at work in L.A., writing the pilot. We were due to begin shooting in March.

How the hell was *this* my life?

New Year's Eve we sat on our deck, sipping wine and

watching the fireworks someone was setting off on the other side of the island. It really doesn't get better than that.

And my other present? I smiled as I sipped my beer, feeling Jack's hand gently rubbing my back. I'd been wearing nothing but a sarong and bikini top (sometimes not even that much) for the last few days, plus my new piece of jewelry.

Before I opened the box from Harry Winston, the thought naturally flitted through my mind that it was . . . well . . . a ring. But he was twenty-four, and neither of us was in any position to get married. We'd barely been together six months, and it was way too early to be thinking marriage. We hadn't even managed to move all his stuff into my house yet. Would I like to get married someday? Yep, absolutely. And hopefully to this man. But we both had some growing up to do, and things were pretty freaking awesome the way they were.

So a ring? Nope.

His gift was so much better.

In the box was proof not only that Jack loved me but that he got me. He *got* me and understood everything I needed.

On a platinum chain was a thin circular platinum charm a little bigger than a dime. Engraved on the side that faced my heart were the words *George Loves Gracie*. And on the side that faced the world?

Schmaltz.

No one would understand it, which was what made it perfect. It was just about him and me—our own little private joke.

I felt the weight of it against my skin, and my fingers slipped up toward my collarbone, coming to rest against the charm. I could feel the engraving, and I rubbed it constantly. Each time Jack saw me do it, he grinned.

As we sat and watched the end of another day, I snuggled

deeper into his side. Here we were just another couple relaxing on the beach.

"You getting hungry, Nuts Girl?" he asked, kissing the top of my head.

"Yeah, a little. We still have some of the shrimp from last night. You okay with that?"

"Sounds good to me," he replied, standing and draining the last of his beer. He shuffled around in the sand a little, not really walking away, just dragging his feet.

I watched the last of the sun as it dropped below the horizon, making everything glow yellow and red and orange. The lights from the house cast an inviting warmth behind me, and I stood slowly, tying my bikini top back on.

He frowned as I covered up the girls, but took my hand when I extended it to him. As we walked back to the house, he tugged my arm, turning me back around. His eyes were twinkling mischievously.

"What's up, George?" I asked, smiling back at him.

He nodded back toward the beach.

There, in the sand, he had written me a little message with his feet:

GRAND GESTURE

"What the hell?" I asked, laughing.

"I know you don't like *big* grand gestures, but I thought that one was perfectly sized." He chuckled as he kissed on my neck.

"You know me way too well, Hamilton. It's a little frightening sometimes." I squealed as his kisses became more and more persistent, managed to get out of his grasp, and dashed toward the steps. I got halfway up before I felt his hands grab my waist and begin to undo the knot in my sarong.

☆ ☆ ☆

From *People* magazine, press date December thirty-first:

Rumors continue to swirl regarding the whereabouts of popular *Time* actor Jack Hamilton. Last seen in London's Heathrow Airport just before the holidays, he has since fallen completely off the radar. Fans want to know where he is—and they're getting desperate.

Stories have been percolating since late summer about the possibility of Jack being involved with an older woman—a redhead he was spotted with in L.A. on numerous occasions. This woman, eventually revealed to be stage actress Grace Sheridan, 33, shares Jack's manager, Holly Newman. Although the entire management team has denied claims that Jack is romantically linked to her, the Internet has been flooded with pictures of them together. After Sheridan attended the *Time* premiere in Los Angeles, the rumor resurfaced, along with pictures of the pair in New York City, where the two looked cozy as they walked in Central Park.

When asked for comment, Newman said, "They're great friends. They met at a party I hosted for several of my clients months ago. They're thrown together a lot. They're not a couple."

Nevertheless, for many fans, whether he's disappeared with Grace or not, the question still remains: Where have you gone, Jack Hamilton?